The Virin Project

In search of a never-ending source of
pleasure and social control

Oscar D'Agnone

This is a work of fiction. Names, characters, businesses, places, events and incidents are either the products of the author's imagination or used in a fictitious manner. Any resemblance to actual persons, living or dead, or actual events is purely coincidental.

For those who struggle to break free from any kind of self imposed dependencies and social engineers.

To my dear friend and colleague John Stewart for all the ideas and ideals we share.

Oscar

04-01-17

London

The Virin Project

In search of a never-ending source
of pleasure and social control

PART I

God's new medicine

I

THE TWO BODIES were lying motionless, not more than two metres apart.

People fell silent as they stepped past them, gazing with a morbid curiosity. The silence passed unnoticed in the hurly-burly of the vast mass of ravers. There were thousands of them, laughing and shouting, moving in unison, losing themselves in the monotonous rhythm of the heavy, throbbing, deafening sound, driving into the brains of the crowds that gave themselves up to it that night on the beach at La Fontanilla in Marbella.

The lives of the two boys ebbed swiftly away, vanishing like the spray from the waves breaking close by, taking with them all the dreams, hopes and desires that would never now be realized.

The three hard-faced, fair haired men looked at each other and shook their heads in a gesture of anxiety and annoyance.

"Let's get out of here," said the one who seemed to be in charge. "We already know what's going to happen next." They left the scene just as the paramedics began to arrive and the circle of curious onlookers grew larger.

A Spanish gypsy looked on in silence, with suspicion. He seemed to say something to himself, as if swallowing his words, perhaps an oath or a curse. His gaze followed the blond men closely until he saw them leave in an inconspicuous car. Then he turned on his heel and walked decisively away, in the opposite direction.

The party went on.

Hardly anyone had noticed what had happened. Just two more to boost the statistics of deaths from overdose. Two futile deaths, two young lives cut off in their prime, nothing more.

Perhaps this year's figures will be higher than last years, perhaps not. In any case it is hard to imagine that anything will change. Surely time and oblivion will sweep everything away, like the unending seas that devastate the coast from time to time.

What was it that killed these young men? Was it drugs, carelessness, ignorance on their part, traffickers, a stupid fashion and a hedonistic culture that overwhelmed them and in which they were willing victims?

All these abstractions held no meaning for someone like Steve Dariet. He had spent his life unravelling mysteries that invariably led either to a large amount of money in a bank vault or a small amount of lead in the cranial cavity.

However, behind these deaths lay something else, something new, unlike anything Steve had come across before.

The twenty-first century alchemists who turn lead into gold don't need a philosopher's stone. They use complex technologies, promising a never-ending source of pleasure, and facilitate the social control of the masses, indispensable elements so that others can carry on, getting the gilded metal.

And so a small amount of lead may still be necessary... eventually.

II

Five Years Earlier

THEY DIDN'T LEAVE ANY ASHES or rubble in Tottenham, where it had all started, or in Hackney, Brixton or Croydon, where the disturbances had reached their climax.

Everything had been tidied up for the next big event, at which London – and, by extension, the United Kingdom – at a cost of thirty-six billion dollars, would show a different face to the world. The London Olympics of 2012 was the starting point.

But the memory of the mob, out of control in the city centre, setting fire to businesses and private properties, pillaging, robbing and almost killing those who stood in their way, still lived in the minds of many people.

The public was distracted with other trivialities that the media had taken it upon themselves to present as major news items. The mass media was the preferred weapon of strategists and politicians when it came to waging war on the home front. A war...but who was the enemy?

――――

The headwaiter and his small army of uniformed underlings served coffees, cognacs, whiskies and Cuban cigars while others cleared the main table, still littered with the remains of the banquet.

The sweet scent of the *Partagas* wafted in the air, the pleasant spiciness flooding the atmosphere. Dr Kurt Render and his VIP guests had been enjoying a dinner party he had thrown in their honour.

Most of them were international experts in investing in moderately risky new technologies. Each one represented investment funds that were highly reputable and worth a great deal. His clients mostly consisted of companies, banks and a few private investors, the origins of whose wealth were as finely woven as their suits of fine alpaca. The combined value of all of his guests probably came to well over one hundred billion dollars.

At a very discreet gesture from Render – a slight, almost imperceptible movement of approval, followed by a penetrating look from his unfathomable blue eyes – the headwaiter immediately led his band out of the dining room, closing the door behind them without making a sound.

He was very well aware of Render's strict etiquette for these proceedings, and also of the generous tips that would be handed out after a successful evening. This was not the first banquet, and it would not be the last, at which Render entertained his friends, colleagues and business contacts.

The Burlington House Club, or 'the Club,' as it was affectionately known among its members, was his chosen spot for affairs of both business and pleasure.

The Club was housed in a building boasting splendid Edwardian architecture, designed by Sir James Pennethorne in 1867 at the heart of Bloomsbury in London; it provided an environment that was warm, comfortable and welcoming, but above all, very exclusive.

Candidates for membership had to be proposed by two current members. Only after a strict vetting process, both formal and informal, during which the integrity, discretion and social contacts of the potential member were fully investigated, would the appointing committee approve the admission. Even then it only became effective after the handing over of a non-recoverable deposit of thirty thousand pounds, the equivalent of three years' membership fees in advance.

The building offered its members a unique refuge, its Victorian atmosphere providing a deceptive feeling of lasting stability even in the uncertain times in which we live. That same uncertainty and instability their business deals created every day. But the club members were indifferent to something they have decided to ignore.

From his place at the head of the solid mahogany table, Render picked up the little silver spoon that accompanied the coffee and gently tapped three times on a crystal glass.

He got to his feet to reinforce the feeling of solemnity and to ensure the undivided attention of his guests. He looked all round him, smiling warmly, establishing a convivial atmosphere and making sure everyone felt at home.

What he was about to say was extremely important; this was the real reason for the gathering. Render needed his audience to be relaxed but still attentive.

Gradually the laughter and cheerful voices died away, giving way to an expectant hush. Everyone knew the reason why they were there. The guests hadn't flown in from New York, Los Angeles, Zurich, Tokyo, Dubai and London itself just to enjoy the meal, but rather to hear what Render was about to say.

"Gentlemen – my friends, I should say. We've been partners in different projects and business deals for a long time now, and there's no doubt that the outcomes we've achieved have, almost without exception, turned out very favourably for all of you, in spite of the constant element of risk and some sacrifices on that account. This is what the spirit of enterprise in business and science is all about. This is the force that drives the world towards progress and the reason for the privileged positions that we enjoy.

"I am fully convinced that this same spirit of innovation and enterprise will lead us to even greater heights, if we continue our commitment to investing our financial resources in the research and development of new scientific and technological products that respond to our present-day challenges."

Render paused and, with a calculated gesture, sipped some water to clear his throat, but also to reassure himself that he had captured the total attention of his audience. What he was about to say was most important.

"Twenty-five million people used opiates last year, three quarters of whom were heroin addicts. Europe and America are still the principal world markets, mainly supplied by opium produced in Afghanistan. As you know, from the start of the war against the Taliban, production has tripled, and prices have dropped by at least fifty per cent. But you can be sure I'm not here to talk to you about illegal products, but to focus on the nature of the demand for them!

"The constant increase in medical prescriptions containing opiates has become a problem in many countries, especially in the United States. Last year they prescribed enough to sedate every adult American all day for an entire month. This is one of the reasons the death toll from prescription drug overdose has now overtaken deaths from road traffic accidents for the first time, making it the chief cause of accidental death.

"These bare statistics may seem boring to you, but nevertheless, they reflect an actual volume of trade currently valued at seventy-seven billion dollars, corresponding to the massive global demand for powerful sedatives."

Some of the guests started to shift in their seats, possibly because they felt uncomfortable with the word *heroin*, but they all continued to give him their undivided attention, thanks to the irresistible magnetism that the word *billions* held for them.

Render went on with his speech. "Not without reason did Sir William Osler, the father of modern medicine, call opiates *God's own medicine*. They leave us without the slightest trouble or pain; they produce a calming effect; and at the same time, they give us a sense of wellbeing not easily understood by those who have never tried them. Taken in the right quantities, opiates can facilitate a deep, healing sleep that is like nothing else.

"However, as we all know, there is a downside.

"First of all, if you take too much, and especially if you inject, it can lead to death from respiratory arrest. Second, opiates lead to dependency and addiction. Regular users constantly need to up their dose to get the same effect, thus increasing the risk of overdose. On the other hand, if they stop using, within a few hours they develop very unpleasant withdrawal symptoms known as 'cold turkey.' The skin becomes pale and sweaty, like chicken skin. The addict is overcome by a frenzy of anxiety accompanied by muscle pains (especially in the shoulder), nausea, vomiting and diarrhoea. As if this was not enough, a state of constant sleeplessness prevents the subject from freeing himself from this torment, even for a few seconds. It's a total living nightmare. Like a jealous, vindictive lover, opiates won't leave you without causing grief."

Newton Crowe, the well-known banker from California, glanced to his right with a smile, cigar still between his lips. Crowe's silver-grey hair, sleeked down and combed back, gleamed with elegance. Smiling, he almost applauded the last calculated, witty remark from Render, who at this level was all friendliness. Newton didn't know much about opiates but he was well experienced with vindictive lovers.

After his little joke, Render allowed a further slight pause to take another sip of water and let his audience digest his introduction. Then he continued, "During the last few years, the global consumption of heroin has increased, while the price has dropped." He spoke with great emphasis followed by a rather uncomfortable silence that reflected the irony of this last sentence. They all remained quiet, without passing any sarcastic comment and with no hint of a smile. The subject was too serious for that, and everyone wanted to know where Render wanted to go with this topic that was so unexpected, almost in bad taste.

"So, let's take a few moments to consider the facts and figures that I have just given you, but think about them in the context of a deep, prolonged global economic crisis. A crisis that threatens to destabilize the social and political structures of the West. You, as well as I, will have read hundreds of technical reports that predict the end of the Euro, the weakening of the American and Chinese economies and their global consequences.

"According to many of these reports, the future holds in store for us high rates of unemployment and social unrest. Some countries, such as Spain, Ireland, Italy and Greece, already have more than fifty per cent of their young people out of work."

Render did not seem unduly put out in describing this depressing scenario, but his voice became rather more serious. He spoke in level tones, his voice calm and serious; technical, as if describing the symptoms of a very serious illness that he was considering treating.

"There can be no doubt that alcohol and drug consumption will go up in such difficult times. Some people will carry on drinking at home or in some pub or other; many others will resort to drugs, if they fail in their attempts to find a job or remain outside a social network. These are the usual remedies for depression and despair. However, there are many others who will try something else. This group of the unemployed non-conformists and malcontents, who have nothing more to lose and no more hope, will take to the streets, demanding political changes that can't be carried out, because there won't be the wherewithal to do so. These groups will be joined by others, who will aim not for peaceful demonstrations but violent protests.

"Let us remind ourselves of what happened a few years back, when several districts of Paris were set on fire, and again recently in London. Throwing money frantically at the problem led to a relative stabilization of the issues, but it has not solved them. We still don't know what the economic consequences will be, and nobody wants to talk about it, but we all know that at some point we will have to face up to the underlying inflation.

"Many experts in sociology, economics and politics on both sides of the Atlantic think that this is only the beginning. It looks like the tip of an iceberg but it really is a volcano about to erupt. Everyone is working to gain time to find a solution that, if it can't eliminate the spectre of social revolution, can at least help to contain and deflect this popular discontent.

"Recently I found out from well-informed sources that some of our governments in America, Europe and Asia are preparing a joint strategy that can be applied in a more or less coordinated way to contain the social outbursts, before it is too late and they spread like wildfire across all borders. They have agreed on a raft of preventive measures, involving a series of political and social interventions to extinguish the violence at source, at its point of origin.

"The first and most controversial of these means is the repeal of the laws that penalize drug possession and use.

"In the coming months, we will see and hear well-known, reputable experts calling for drug legalization and the payment of taxes and duties on certain drugs and substances. Many leading figures from society and the media will join in a chorus of demands that the money coming in from these taxes should be invested in making treatment more readily available to all users. A very praiseworthy objective, but one that is hard to carry out for authorities that have to run countries on empty coffers.

"The police will also praise the advantages of legalization, which will bring an end to dealing with traffickers, and the decriminalization of everyday use. It will reduce their day-to-day workload and allow them to concentrate on the big fish – a doubtful result for this simple, naive plan. What can stop the police from getting them now?

"Businessmen, political radicals and libertarians from both left and right will campaign for the rights of the individual, the repeal of repressive legislation in favour of the resulting benefits for the free market, which will now include drugs. According to these groups, the invisible hand of capitalism is the cure for everything, including addictions. Of course, everyone will have their own agenda, but their common interests will unite them in exerting pressure.

"The media will also play their part in this game; and once the climate reaches its peak, and a social consensus emerges, the governments will agree on measures for what they have opposed up to now in the name of freedom and democracy.

"It's the politicians who most need this consensus and social pressure to legislate for legalizing drug use without paying a higher price in case something goes wrong."

Render went on to describe the gradual, progressive increase in drug and alcohol consumption, especially legal highs and other designer drugs, to be expected over the next ten years. The same studies thought that prescriptions for synthetic opiates for pain relief – such a difficult condition to define – will also be on the increase, as will the medicines to treat the various addictions arising from their excessive consumption.

The actual figures for these markets would be known only to a few people, as funds for statistical studies would also be cut in line with the general reduction in health budgets. Because of this, the true volume of consumption could only be precisely estimated in relation to the sales of specific products, leaving a wide margin of error in relation to substances traded illegally, which could only be calculated in relation to seizures of drugs and illegal substances.

Continuing with his detailed analysis, Render assured his guests that once these measures had been adopted, the floodgates would be opened to a market with almost limitless possibilities. The rapid development of a variety of products and the volume of sales, together with the changes in habits and social perceptions of the new consumers, would make it very difficult, if not impossible, to reverse the permissive legislation or the open legalization of consumption.

"The second series of executive measures will be based on the strategic use of high technology to implement what we have called *Operation Viral Triviality*. Both strategies, for drugs and for infective triviality, will run in conjunction, as they are both intimately connected, although the public will not see it that way."

"Viral Triviality, what's that?" asked Newton, with a mixture of interest and bewilderment. This was the first he had heard of any such thing.

With the same interest and passion with which he had related his version of the social situations and their future consequences, Render went on to describe something of which he lacked detailed knowledge, but which he found conceptually fascinating.

"Viral Triviality is a strategy developed by American, British and Indian scientists to contain violence in society by means of the communication systems that work through particular social networks, directed at specific targets. The general idea is to occupy the leisure time of those individuals identified as potentially dangerous. It would be about controlling them through a barrage of trivial content in the social networks relevant to them. Their virtual world would be riddled with sporting and pornographic content, video games, music that can be downloaded for nothing, television programmes as well as many other group activities that could be organized and managed across the Internet.

"To this end the governments will distribute a large number of intelligent mobile phones, tablets, games consoles and high-definition TVs among high-risk social groups whose members have been identified as priority targets. This will start in the districts most heavily involved in the rioting and burning, as well as in areas of high racial tension.

"The UK government have already ordered the purchase of a thousand digital devices for distribution in southeast London, Birmingham and Manchester, where pilot studies have already been carried out.

"Very few people really know what these programmes are really about, as they are announced as being for social integration."

"Dr Render, are you actually saying that our governments are planning to keep the unemployed drugged and stupefied?" asked Werner Jurgen, a reputed fund manager from Switzerland.

"Not all of them, just some, starting with the most conflictive ones. My dear friend, at this moment there are more than a hundred and seventy thousand people to whom the government regularly prescribes large amounts of the opiates methadone and buprenorphine. Some of these people have been on medication for more than twenty years, during which they have received every kind of social benefit, just to keep them peaceful and not committing robberies or other serious crimes. This is known as *maintenance* treatment.

"Many others regularly drink large quantities of alcohol, eat junk food and/or take part in promiscuous activities fostered by the TV programmes and video games that you and I never watch but to which they have been addicted from an early age. Imagine what might happen if all these substances and trivialities didn't exist!

"The problem facing our governments is that these solutions are not sustainable in the long term, for various reasons. One is that their physical consequences entail chronic conditions such as obesity, liver problems, cirrhosis and viral diseases such as hepatitis and AIDS, which are already almost causing the collapse of the health services. Also, mixing alcohol and drugs greatly compounds the risk of overdose and death, not only for those who consume them but also for the victims of road accidents caused by those who drive under the influence. Furthermore, the promiscuity promoted in the media on one hand lowers social tension but on the other hand very much increases the number of unwanted pregnancies among the unemployed. This alters the balance between tax contributions and social benefits and will end up destroying any sort of benefit system. The few who pay their taxes will be massively outnumbered by those who only exist on benefits and lack the motivation or capacity to join the workforce.

"Our governments must get better control of these social groups before it is too late. All the politicians facing these problems have been able to agree on implementing both strategies. The alternative would lead to shooting people down like the South African miners. This would look very bad on the late night news bulletins. It would be political suicide!"

"I'm not entirely sure about this," put in a veteran operator from the City of London. "The metropolitan police only had seven hundred rubber bullets before the disturbances of 2011, but five months later, they increased their stocks to ten thousand twenty-four. As you know, our police forces have never had recourse to these means to disperse the crowds here in this country. Perhaps the climate is changing."

"As always, Sir George is very well informed," replied Kurt. "Down to the last bullet...." They all smiled in unison. "But as you will understand, this isn't an option. The consequences of firing on an angry mob would be very serious. Our governments have opted to *prevent* disturbances. It is more effective. They can control lots of small groups of alcoholics or drug addicts through the police, but if numbers grow and people get organized, we shall need military force. That will be the end."

"I agree," said Hachirou Mikita, the experienced investor from Tokyo. "But all the same, your version of events seems to me to be alarmist and dramatic."

"My dear Hachi, I don't think so. My impression is that we are advancing towards a series of crises, one after the other, that are creating the conditions for a detailed study of these government strategies.

"Triviality is already with us. Almost seventy per cent of all text message traffic is taken up by young people communicating with each other. This major communications infrastructure and technology is, for the most part, being used by adolescents or by adults with an adolescent mentality.

"This triviality is not as banal as it seems. When it signs up to a suitable market, triviality could turn into big business. Triviality sells because it is in great demand. Triviality is infectious and is disguised as technology by marketing experts. But triviality alone will not be enough to maintain a harmonious society. Digital triviality is not available to everyone yet.

"Soon we shall see presidents, prime ministers and other politicians announcing the free distribution of these electronic gadgets under the banner of democratic access to social networks for the poorest and most vulnerable. But the valuable information that will circulate in these gadgets will give detailed insights into the users' habits and tastes, in a way that reacts to specific content. These gadgets can already follow the user's gaze and predict his reactions, while body temperature and also electrical resistance from the skin adds to the information gathered. All of these elements will help to generate highly specific content that will be distributed on the social networks."

"Very interesting, Dr Render, and that will also be reflected in the opinion polls. The voting intentions for the politicians who implement these strategies will go up, even though the people don't really know what is going on.

"You're right Newton, we live in the age of the image. Today it doesn't matter much what is inside the parcel, so long as the wrappings are bright and shiny.'"

"This is all very well, Kurt," Hachirou interrupted again, feeling uncomfortable at the unexpected direction things were taking. "All that, although it's not very pleasant to listen to, can't fail to be interesting. But the word 'heroin' doesn't fit in with the profile of any of my clients. As you can understand, they won't want to be associated with anything that sounds illegal or criminal."

"I imagine," Newton broke in, almost interrupting Hachirou, "they are bound to prefer to invest in nuclear projects by the sea, whaling factory ships, industrial plants in China or new technology bubbles."

Everyone turned to look at Crowe, with a supportive look in their eyes. Some were struggling to suppress their laughter after such an interjection, ironic to the point of rudeness.

Hachirou continued to fix his gaze on Newt, tight-lipped and frowning darkly, then burst suddenly into noisy laughter. Hachirou interjection had been as sincere as his initial reaction, but he didn't want to give an impression of timidity or uncertainty among his colleagues. At the end of the day, these were bankers and businessmen who thrived on opportunities and risk.

Render, still on his feet, cast an affectionate look at Hachirou, friendly and almost paternal, before he continued, all smiles, with his speech. "At this point I have two questions for all of you. The first is, how much do you think the patent is worth for a product that supplies all the effects of opiates, pain relief, sedation and pleasure while blocking out the negative side, preventing deaths from overdose? A product with which governments could replace existing tranquillizers for something safer. A drug that could be marketed for its sedative and antidepressant effects but without the neurological, cardiac and metabolic risks that traditional medication involves. A drug that could also be combined with contraceptives. A drug that could be used alongside alcohol without risk of respiratory failure. A safe drug that everyone will want because we ourselves will teach them to want it!

"What value would you put on a substance that could give temporary access to a paradise of serenity, shielding the consumer from the harsh realities that he must face with his slender resources? A product that would be the ideal complement for Viral Triviality, making out of that virtual experience a phenomenon that is almost real! "A product that *guarantees* the person under its influence will be passive and calm.

"How much do you think this product would be worth, a substitute for all the legal and illegal substances that, at the moment, make up a world market of eighty billion dollars a year?"

A sudden swelling murmur of conversation filled the room. Everyone was talking excitedly at the same time and not listening to anyone else.

The word *billions* had once again worked its old magic, casting its spell over those who made their living selling promises of future unimaginable gains.

Although on the surface their financial activities seemed very different from the world of science in which Render moved, they could completely understand what Render was talking about, because for many of their clients, as well as themselves, money was also a kind of drug. The thought of an enormous profit achieved in a short time and without too much effort gave rise to a feeling of ecstasy not unlike taking cocaine, heroin or both together.

But these men would never be marked out as addicts, just ambitious businessmen. The poor get blind drunk, the rich just have a good time!

Silent and impassive, Render watched them attentively as he played with the cigar between his fingers, rolling it back and forth between his thumb and his index finger. He held his enthralled guests in the palm of his hand.

"Remember, gentlemen, that an illusion, a safe illusion, is one of the most precious products," he added finally. It was the phrase that best described sellers of financial products, futures and derivatives, fantasies of astronomical short term gains. Yes, the product that Render was talking about was something they understood very well. They were experts at selling the dreams and grandiose fantasies for which many had lost their fortunes – and their lives.

"Millions," someone was saying from the other end of the table. "Billions," replied others, waving their hands or wiping the perspiration from their brows. Kurt Render had achieved his first objective: he had roused them with the scent of money, millions, billions of it....

"Thank you, thank you. I can see already that you've answered my first question. Now, allow me, please, to put the second one. How much are you prepared to put up to get a share in this project?"

It was then that the excited murmur first gave way to an animated discussion that, in turn, degenerated into a disorderly hubbub, seemingly chaotic but filled with the strange logic that dominated the trading floor.

That was the natural surroundings in which they had all grown up; it was the heart of the markets in which their passions turned into dollars, euros or pounds sterling, and the resulting joy in the bank balance.

The dinner guests felt passionately about the deals to which they had dedicated their lives, for which they had paid prices that could be reckoned in divorces, dysfunctional families and the occasional suicide.

And just as the addict can't love his drug of choice, despite needing it desperately every day, they were unable to love the deals for which they had given up their lives. One could perhaps say that they felt a great passion for their work but never affection, fondness or love.

Such feelings were too complex and contradictory for taking the instant, serious decisions needed in their workplaces.

Like an experienced chef waiting for the meat to reach the exact point when it needed to come out of the oven and not a moment later, Render remained silent, expectant and attentive. When the right moment came, he finally spoke. "Gentlemen, please, you don't have to answer this question right now. No, take your time over it. Take another look at your portfolios and talk it over with your clients and business partners."

"But Kurt," asked Newton Crowe, "does this drug really exist, or is this just a clever ploy to revive us after this gargantuan supper and your excellent wines?"

"As many of you know, I have always had a lively sense of humour," replied Kurt, "but I would never make fun of my friends and colleagues. Everything I have said to you is absolutely true and in good faith. For the last few years, I've been working on the project and am halfway through, but I need financial support to get the necessary technical means to complete it."

Such was his pride and confidence in his new project that Render seemed to swell as he spoke. He stood taller, his eyes widening under raised eyebrows and his cheeks flushed by the intensity of his feelings and the French burgundy. He was drawing them in like a proud father with his sons.

He moved his arms in harmony to add just the right emphasis to his speech; his voice was firm and his tone convincing. His cadences and the brief pauses between sentences added even more emphasis to the emotion and logic of his reasoning.

The project was a reality and held out the possibility of rich pickings, though this was not yet guaranteed. His potential investors craned their necks and raised their heads without taking their eyes off Render as they privately pondered their mental calculations. Like hunting dogs before the chase, their natural instincts led them to the scent of money.

"Gentlemen, I invite you to be partners in this new enterprise, to deliver a product that will play a key role in the coming era. Remember..." he said, with a hint of a smile that emphasized the dimple in his right cheek, giving him an air of cunning and boldness "Remember that crisis brings opportunity, and this is a big crisis that is going to last a long time." With these final words, he raised his right hand and pointed his index finger. He wasn't pointing to Heaven as a mark of religious belief – nothing could be further from the truth; rather, he was pointing out his vision of the future. "In the next twenty years, new industries and businesses devoted to keeping the mind busy and entertained will continue to flourish.

"This isn't a new idea, but our modern idea of paradise is more concrete and down to earth. The IT, entertainment and pharmaceutical industries are the ones that are ranked highest on the stock exchange. They operate in these areas and have more influence on actual lifestyle than any of the political and philosophical ideas of the past.

"Leading people from these fields – artists, business people and entrepreneurs – are the role models for millions. They don't impose their ideas or products by force but by persuasion and the magic of marketing operations. Stories about fairies, wizards, star warriors, superheroes, vampires and other such creatures fill the heads of young and old both East and West.

"In the near future, we will be able to incorporate a certain type of substance that will bring these fantasies to life, although they are unreal, almost obliterating the difference between fantasy and reality. It will keep them busy for even longer. Infectious triviality will be able to grow to unbelievable levels, and social harmony will be secured with firing a single rubber bullet."

Render was reaching the finale of his dramatic and gripping speech. His eyes were restless, as were his hands. His voice alternated between ringing tones and moments when he seemed to be whispering a close secret. His passion and enthusiasm for the project had captivated his willing audience.

"Within the next three years, I'm going to need fifty million dollars to complete the Virin project. That's what the drug is called." he threw at them, taking his potential investors by surprise. "That will be around fifteen million a year. That is the projected time it will take to start applying for a provisional licence from a sympathetic European regulatory body."

"Is that all it needs?" asked Francoise Lussard, who had hardly said a word until that moment.

"I need fifty million to complete the project, but that will only cover the cost of acquiring a twenty-five per cent stake in the company that will get the licence for Virin. Once we have acquired the first licence, the value of Virin will go up at least four or five times. My team estimates that the investor will be able to get a return of about three hundred per cent at the end of three years. We know that this is a very high reward, though not entirely risk free."

"Kurt, what will happen if the product doesn't work, or if something goes wrong with the Virin project? Is there a plan B?" asked Newton Crowe, this time as serious as he was interested.

"It is going to work; however, I understand your question, and I know very well what you mean. Risk control. In that case, the answer to your question is yes, I do have a plan B and even a plan C," Render said with a smile. "However, I'm not going to tell you what it is, as it won't be needed. Everything is going to turn out fine.

"My dear friends, forgive me for taking up so much of your time talking business. Those of you who are interested in getting involved with the Virin project can call me next week to talk about offers. Now I would like to enjoy your company for the rest of the evening."

After this last remark, Render gently rang a little silver bell placed under the table to his right, and straight away the small army of waiters, led by their chief, returned to the room.

Resplendent in smart uniforms of black trousers, white jacket and blue bow tie, they set about offering fresh rounds of Conjure cognac, Cuban cigars, freshly made Java coffee, *petits fours* and other exquisite delicacies.

Render lit his cigar almost absentmindedly as he talked, laughed and played the perfect host, regaling his guests with an unending series of anecdotes, jokes and stories as interesting as they were original.

He had achieved his ultimate objective.

They had all happily taken the bait.

III

IT WAS ANOTHER SUNNY summer morning in Marbella.

From the café on the promenade, where Steve was enjoying his breakfast, he could make out the pallid foreigners newly arrived from the north. By evening their pallor would turn to that particular shade of lobster pink that was peculiar to them alone. Covered with creams and sunburn lotions, by nightfall they would devote rigorously to their second summer ritual, drinking until they were completely plastered.

Every day he strolled from the spacious apartment he rented only a few streets away from the beach to the Las Brisas café, where the obliging Manolo, after a formal "Good Morning," would ask "Your usual?"

His usual was a glass of fresh orange juice, half a slice of toast with tomato and a dash of olive oil, white coffee and the morning paper. A breakfast that was almost fat free, very different from the bacon and eggs that he used to eat in the past.

Steve drank his coffee with long, leisurely sips, closing his eyes now and again, trying to forget, taking his time. He revelled in the light breeze that started off warm in North Africa, becoming fresh and moist as it crossed the Mediterranean to brush his cheeks with a gentle white and blue caress that tasted of orange blossom and ancient empires.

The restless waters of the sea seemed to stir as he celebrated his decision to take a break, as much needed as it was well deserved, in his professional career. After several years of being *on Her Majesty's Service*, this was his new life.

Now he only had to pay his respects to the sun, the sea and some pretty woman or other.

Steve could not help almost breaking into a smile at the thought of what his former boss and fellow workers would be doing at this precise moment in London.

It was several years since he had seen them, but he still thought of them, without affection, without regret, without knowing why.

Several years back Steve had requested a transfer abroad. At that time he was a young official with no greater emotional attachments than to his father, who professed himself happy with his son's decision.

"You run along and enjoy yourself. Find something different if you feel stuck in a rut. If you're having fun, you're bound to meet someone to fall in love with, and you'll be happy. I'm quite happy." Steve smiled with respect at the simple, homely wisdom contained in his father's words and the dignified way in which he had told his lie.

He wasn't happy at all. Since the death of his wife many years earlier, he had only pretended to be. However, like much of the advice he gave that was filled with the wisdom of experience, it was designed for others rather than himself. Like nearly everyone else, when it came to giving advice, he felt exempt from practising what he preached. His father had not graduated from University College London, as Steve had done, but from the school of life, a place far more difficult and demanding and where only the tough and intelligent survived.

Steve's first years of working for the Agency, if they hadn't exactly been enjoyable, had at least produced interesting results. However, after ten years in the service and two well-deserved promotions, they were starting to become routine and bureaucratic.

As his colleagues' conversation turned more and more towards benefits and pension plans and the latest budget cuts, and as the paperwork continued to mount up on his desk, Steve decided it was time to leave.

Although he was still quite young, when he looked in his mirror each morning, he became aware of a grey paleness creeping over him. Or rather, not so much a grey pallor as a deep, progressive colourlessness, arising from boring routine and emotional deprivation.

One starts to live on automatic pilot and end up by turning into a machine. Steve found the calm monotony of his everyday life irritating. This was not what he had expected from his job.

In spite of a few passionate love affairs, up to now, his only real love had been his work. But that, too, was beginning to pall.

Steve hated the endless paperwork that took up most of his time. To him it was the price he had to pay for the new responsibilities of his promotion.

He was interested in *getting* results, not filling in forms that were often altered to *show* results. But he was a civil servant, and as such he had to prioritise system and process over results. Systems and data were less concrete, because they could be manipulated, modified or changed to give the most convenient results. The way the data were gathered and presented was crucial. For example, by slightly changing the definition of a crime or offence, or fractionally altering the field he had to report on, he could get very different results from the same set of figures. Facts alone mattered to the victim, but to the bureaucrat, the system was what mattered; and the more thorough the system, the more adaptable the results.

The day he handed in his application for a transfer to international operations, Steve felt as if he was escaping from that featureless world of grey men, fleeing an epidemic of mediocrity that threatened to engulf him.

Because of his fluency in French, Italian and Spanish, as well as his native English, after a series of exams and interviews, he was posted to the Balkans. Although that wasn't an ideal assignment, he was at least in the Mediterranean region that he loved so much.

Steve's origins were a mixture of Anglo-Saxon and South European. A slightly unusual combination in these multicultural days, though not as much so as when his parents got to know each other in the seventies.

His hair was dark, with a slight wave, and his green eyes changed colour slightly according to the weather. He was tall and slim, with an upright, elegant bearing. A sharp-eyed observer might have discerned in Steve a distant aristocratic past now lost in the mists of time, a lineage so ancient that it had passed into family mythologySteve was an equable person with a slight tendency to melancholy, though capable of occasional explosive outbursts of anger or joy, not unlike the Mediterranean waters themselves.

His first mission was in Serbia. In his new role as liaison officer assigned to OCA1 (Organized Crime Agency, section 1) Serbian branch, his role was to monitor and collect intelligence and report on the activities of the former Serbian militias, now linked to the criminal gangs operating in the region. These groups had established a very lucrative arrangement with the Calabrian mafia from southern Italy, the notorious Ndrangheta.

What had begun as a straightforward cigarette smuggling operation had, within a few years, escalated into a business that now included arms and dugs, ferried in speedboats across the thirty miles that separated the ports of Bar in Montenegro and Bari in Puglia.

The reports he sent to London played a crucial role in enabling the European Union and the United States to exert enough pressure on the Montenegrin government to put an end to an illegal activity from which it gained fiscal revenues that allowed them to finance the public administration of this small emerging state.

The operation he was involved with was labelled a political success.

Steve had had a flying start to this new stage of his career, and promotion with a transfer to Marseilles followed a year later. During his three-year stay there he perfected his French and gained first-hand knowledge of the intricate connections that existed between the various criminal gangs operating on both sides of the Italian peninsula and the south of France.

Six years after Steve left England, he had been promoted again to the post of senior liaison officer for the Costa del Sol region, a position that he held until he decided to take a sabbatical.

During the last eight ears in Andalusia, he had come to know the area very well. Malaga, Marbella and Cadiz were the main centres from which he had coordinated many intelligence operations between OCA1, Interpol, Europol and some American agencies.

As a consequence of his knowledge of the area and the intelligence operations he coordinated, Steve had created a network of important local contacts and understood, as few others did, the complex ties that bound together the interests of the different criminal gangs operating in the Costa del Sol, Costa Blanca and the French and Italian Riviera, as well as the central zone of the Adriatic. Owing to the fact that crime knows no frontiers, but countries and their jurisdictions do, intelligence operations and direct interventions are always highly complex and delicate. Nobody liked having foreign agents operating on their soil, even to catch criminals.

Steve had gained experience beyond his fourteen years in the southern European region, and this was a signal to move into the minefield of international relations. He was already an important asset to the OCA1 headquarters based in the region. His experience was valued by his colleagues, some of whom asked him for advice. Although he didn't know it yet, he would be making his living from this in the not too distant future.

Like a skilful surgeon, Steve knew exactly how and when to make an effective incision without harming the vital organs dangerously close to the tumour that had to be removed.

Steve knew how to negotiate with the most influential people in the region. Long-established families, large landowners, industrialists, developers, politicians, business men, well-known artists, bullfighters, flamenco singers and footballers, as well as every sort of parasite and bloodsucker that filled the pages of numerous rags, tabloid newspapers and fashion magazines. Steve was able to distinguish clearly between these and the criminals who had arrived recently or were already established on Andalusian soil.

Before starting on an operation, Steve would send out discreet signals, so that innocent parties could keep out of the way. Ignoring his hints or warnings could mean a serious security risk for those who found themselves in his path, both to their persons and in their legal affairs.

This earned him the trust and the confidence of the local elites and other influential groups that were crucial to achieving his ultimate objective: defending British interests. His London bosses appreciated the unusual mixture of diplomatic skill and flair for police work that made Steve both captivating and relentless at the same time.

Among his numerous local contacts was Chief Inspector Don Romero Fernandez, whom he thought of as a colleague and could almost call a friend. This particular link was forged during the complex operation to catch Ismael Profirio Santos a Mexican drug trafficker who had infiltrated the Marbella social scene, setting up personal and business relationships designed to allow him potentially to transfer his operations to the town.

Steve played a key role in providing intelligence that came both from the countries the trade passed through and its final destination. His department also helped with sophisticated communications intercept equipment for Romero's operational group to use. Both had a common interest in getting Santos out of the game, but it wasn't easy. Some money had changed hands, and several doors had been opened that Santos was quick to take advantage of. Steve and Romero embarked on the delicate task of issuing discreet warnings to those who, given the benefit of the doubt, had simply acted naively. Among them was the mayor, who had had meetings with Santos above and beyond the call of duty in the hope of ensuring the construction of a lucrative real estate enterprise that some of his commercial contacts wanted to build.

At the end of two weeks, Steve and Romero closed in. Those who were indiscreet and ambitious, reluctantly at first and then in a headlong rush, left Santos isolated and ready to be arrested.

Romero Fernandez was at the forefront of the operation, taking all the credit that would later lead to his promotion, a medal from the mayor himself and perhaps something more…. But least said, soonest mended.

Steve stayed in the background, in the shadows, where he belonged. It was enough for him to have achieved his objective. The part he had played had not passed unnoticed by his superiors in London. The success of the operation cemented the professional and personal bond between Steve and Romero, even though the latter thought Steve charming but rather odd.

All this added up to Steve finding Marbella a perfect place in which to take his career break and enjoy life. Although it sounded like a contradiction, for Steve Marbella was a place where he felt he was safe and he knew what was going on.

Halfway through his breakfast, Manolo brought over the *Andalusian Times*, the favourite paper of the expats community. Steve glanced at the main UK headlines with detached interest as he continued to drink his coffee with long, slow sips.

The United Kingdom was on the point of embarking on another armed intervention on a country that was poor in economic terms but rich in natural resources. Once more as part of a coalition of nations led by the United States. The Prime Minister had adopted an attitude almost of defiance against the majority who opposed entering into something that would mean more deaths and higher taxes.

This isn't the first time I've seen that danger, he thought, barely taking any notice of it.

Manchester United and Manchester City were playing each other in the English League Cup Final. Steve wasn't interested in these events, which he thought were more about business than sport. *Popular naivety, boring Sunday afternoons and television. I couldn't care less.*

Inflation continued at a high level, but the governor of the Bank of England gave assurances that the index would go down in the next quarter. *The best way to lie is to tell people what they want to believe. I couldn't care less.*

With a disinterest verging on apathy, Steve turned the first page, then the second. At the bottom of page four, a headline caught his attention straight away. "Two British dead at a rave in Marbella."

He had just started to read the article when an irritating intermittent buzzing noise broke his concentration. Steve tried to ignore it and carry on reading, but his mobile went on ringing insistently.

"Ughh." He tried to read the caller's number but couldn't. Whoever wanted to get in touch with him was careful about privacy.

Steve tried to keep focus, but he couldn't. His eyes were on the paper, but his mind wasn't. Slowly, almost angrily, he reached for the phone. "Hullo."

"Hi, Steve, it's Chris."

"Chris, oh yes, hi Chris," he answered, trying to hide his astonishment.

"How are you?" Chris asked. Steve could sense an unusual tension in his old friend's voice.

"Fine. What a surprise. How are you?"

"So you don't know anything, then." Ignoring the polite greeting was unusual for Chris.

"Anything about what? What am I supposed to know about?" By now Steve was no longer staring at the paper or the breakfast table or the beach; he had fixed his gaze on some vague point in the distance.

"Well, I was hoping you might be able to tell me something, some detail or other, but obviously you don't know anything."

"All right, Chris, cut the crap. What's all this about?" Steve's impatience convinced Chris that he had no idea what he was talking about and in a strange way this calmed him down. Perhaps because he realized that his friend was acting in good faith.

"Somebody just called me from Spain. Neither her English nor my Spanish were the best and I couldn't understand everything she said. But the fact is that Johnny is in hospital. I'm not sure if he is dead or alive. Apparently he overdosed last night during a rave held in the beach in Marbella."

"What? What the hell are you talking about?" Steve spat the words out as if fending off an attack. "I was with him yesterday afternoon. Johnny was in good spirits, he had plans –"

"Well, he doesn't have them anymore," Chris interrupted him. "We've got to find out what's going on. I can't believe it… he was making such a good recovery."

Steve recognized in those words the hint of a reproach as bitter as it was hard to control. "You've really thrown me, Chris. I can hardly believe it. Why, how?"

"That's what we want to know as well, on our side," Chris replied.

With a bitter taste in his dry mouth and a lost look in his eyes, Steve tried to make sense of what he was hearing.

"I understand how you must be feeling, and I'm sorry if I sounded rough or abrupt. I'm also deeply grieved. It's such an unexpected shock. I'd pinned so many hopes on him, and I know you did, too," Chris went on. "Please find out what you can. You have the contacts, and you can soon find out what happened. I'll call you back this afternoon. I'm flying out tomorrow with Moira, Johnny's mother."

"Damn it, Chris, you can be sure I'll put out some feelers right away. What time are you arriving? I'll come and pick you up at the airport."

"I think it's the earliest flight. The ten o'clock one…. Shit…."

"I'll be there, Chris. I'm so sorry…I don't know…I…."

"All right, all right. I've got to stop now," Chris interrupted him, unable to keep the grief and irritation from his voice.

"OK. We'll talk later. Bye for now."

There was no reply, just silence as Chris hung up.

Steve sat there in shock, still staring into the distance and holding his mobile phone to his ear, although there was no one left at the other end.

Marbella was still bathed in brilliant sunshine. The sun was high in the sky, and the shadows were growing shorter by the minute. The sky was clear and cloudless, but Steve was no longer there. Dark thoughts were rapidly crossing his mind, driven by the hurricane of anger that was rapidly overcoming him. He didn't know who he was most angry with – himself, Johnny, Chris, the person who had supplied the drugs…. Doubt and the lack of answers made it even worse.

His pulse quickened, and his blood pressure rose. Adrenalin surged quickly through his veins. He needed to bring himself out of the initial shock that was paralysing him. "Damn it," he said to himself, bringing his fist down hard onto the table.

He got up and drank the last dregs of his coffee, by now cold and tasteless. He tossed ten euros onto the table and left hastily.

When Manolo came back, he guessed that something serious had happened when he didn't find his client at the table.

Don Dariet never goes without saying good-bye, he thought, shrugging his shoulders as he cleared the table.

From instinct, almost a reflex, or perhaps driven by a feeling of guilt mixed with rage, Steve Dariet was returning to the fray.

IV

IT COULD HAVE BEEN the outskirts of Detroit, the *banlieues* of Saint Denis to the north of Paris, maybe Frankfurt Oder in northern Germany or any other town in the throes of deindustrialization with more than 20 per cent of its workforce unemployed. But Chris had met Johnny on a cold, grey, damp afternoon at one of the youth social services in Lancashire, England.

Johnny was fifteen years old, but his childish looks set him apart from the other local boys of his age from the area. They seemed older and tougher because of the regular abuse they had been subjected to.

Long-term unemployment, alcohol dependency and violence were three persistent, related conditions that seemed to have a genetic origin in some families. But so far, no one had found a gene for poverty and lack of opportunity. The causes were a lot more complex than that.

Johnny's forebears had worked for generations in the *rag trade*, but the steady decline of this industry had left them searching for fresh opportunities in Stoke-on-Trent, where the pottery workshops still needed manpower. When Johnny was born, he seemed destined to become the third generation of an unemployed family existing on social security. They had lost touch with the labour market quite a long time before. His mother and grandmother spent their lives in a parallel universe, occupying the same physical space but living in another dimension, invisible to the eyes and hearts of many who had risen from the same background but now resolutely refused to look back.

Mr Joseph Smith, Johnny's grandfather, would never have imagined that, along with his own future, the future of the next generations of his family would be lost when the textile factory in which he had worked all his life closed its gates.

He was well known for being the most experienced textile worker there and also because his job was a family tradition. Both his father and his father before him had worked in the same factory for decades.

For men of his generation, work meant something hard and physical, where skill and honesty, along with a bit of brain power, guaranteed a job for life.

Joseph had started work at eleven years old, and it had never occurred to him to do anything else or look further afield. He would get up before dawn to be at his post promptly by six o'clock, and after ten gruelling hours, he was still deafened by the noise made by the weaving machines all around him. He was in this state every day when he returned home. Yet, he thought himself a lucky man to hold down a job that was secure and paid well enough for him to bring up his family.

By the time his bosses found they had no choice but to close down the factory, he had spent twenty years of his life there, during which time he had risen from apprentice to master weaver.

To make matters worse, everyone around him had lost their jobs, too. The closure didn't just mean economic problems but the disintegration of the social fabric that he used to be part of, that used to give him an identity, a sense of belonging, a position in life in which he felt respected and valued.

When the gates closed for the last time, a part of him was left behind in there forever. Now there would be no one to talk about his father, or his father's father, and no one to defer to his skill and experience in the job. Joseph was thirty-one years old.

That was the time when the traditional English cotton industry went not just into decline but free fall. In Lancashire, the cradle and centre of the international textile industry, factories were being closed at the rate of one a week. There was plenty of talk about it being the end of an era, but to Mr Smith, it was simply the end.

Few would have imagined that the decline and fall of the English textile industry through competition from the United States, India and soon China was just the slow prelude to the global twilight of Western industry and the rise of a new world order whose centre had shifted east from the Greenwich meridian.

Several generations would pass before the social, political and economic consequences of this could be fully understood.

After many months of fruitless job searches in Burnley, Oldham and other towns where a few textile factories were still struggling to survive, Joseph realised that the industry was finished, and his skills were now useless.

He had little in the way of savings, and that meant that he would have to take anything he could get, the first decent job to come along. Now his skills as a weaver were no longer of any use to him; all he had to offer was his brute strength, his willingness to take whatever he could get, his honesty and his poor hearing. Years in the factory had left him almost deaf to everything except for an incessant sharp whistling noise that often became unbearable at night.

These qualities were not in great demand, but even so, he managed to get work in a pottery factory in Stoke-on-Trent. With his wife and his little daughter, Moira, he moved into a little cottage not far from his workplace on the Caldon canal.

He wasn't happy, but at least it was something to keep him going. That job gave him a break, and on top of that, there was something to keep his mind active, so he wasn't continually harking back to the good years that were now past – his former friends and neighbours and a world that he used to feel a part of.

Joseph worked in Stoke for sixteen years before the factory closed, throwing four hundred fifty-three men and women onto the scrapheap. Their faces showed tears, fear, rage and incredulity. After working there for more than forty years, some of them had received redundancy pay equivalent to six months' earnings. What hope could there be for someone who had only worked there for sixteen years and was already forty-eight years old?

There was no way Joseph could understand the complex causes that, from the other side of this now-globalised world, were destroying everything he knew and clung to. It was a world in which neighbours and friends had turned into markets, and the value of personal dedication had been replaced by mechanized processes. A world where consumption had priority over production, expenditure over savings, and finance over labour.

He put it down to bad luck, incompetent governments, capitalism or the banks, but none of these reasons was enough to explain the collapse of his environment or to relieve his suffering. He was overcome by a deep bitterness that overcame his physical strength and determination, which by now were ebbing away. He was a broken man, having lost the even the hope that a man clings to until the very end.

From then on Joseph became withdrawn and bad-tempered. He had fits of rage that only beer or whisky could soothe. Joseph had been a social drinker all his life, like everyone around him, but he had never had problems at home or at work to make him get drunk.

He'd always been a man of few words and an open smile, but now he felt different. He couldn't pin down that strange sensation that he could only recognise from the reactions of his wife and daughter, from some risqué argument or other in the pub, from his neglected appearance and the hours he spent lying in bed without being able to sleep a wink, from the memories…they went round and round in his head like a waking nightmare. A man like him could never have known that this was depression. He wouldn't even have recognised the word.

Joseph had become an elderly, unemployed drunkard. Who could have any more use for him? Now, in spite of all that he had been through, which most people had no idea about, many of them thought it was his own fault and put it down to the drink.

"If he would just stop drinking," commented a social worker, when his wife applied for benefits for the first time.

Joseph felt like an old dog that had lost its teeth and had to be looked after to survive.

In his final, embittered years, Joseph turned into a caricature of his former self. He was drunk most of the time, blaming all his troubles on his wife. Alcohol, the only thing that could bring warmth and colour back into his life, had turned into a newly destructive force, this time of those who were close to him.

Not one of the doctors who treated him or the social workers who visited was able to understand his attachment to drink or his blindness to the chaos he was creating around him. How could they possibly know that alcohol was the only thing that kept him going, if only as a shadow of the man he used to be. That drink was the only thing that allowed him to have memories without pain and afterwards forget them, to sleep without dreaming….

"It's the drink, it's the drink. Joseph is a good man at heart, but drinking is killing him," his wife said, again and again, trying to excuse the blows and ill treatment.

Moira would bite her lip, swear under her breath and shake her head, unable to believe what her mother was saying. From time to time, she would think, *It's her own fault*, only to regret it immediately.

During the day she prayed for her father to go and drink at the pub. These were the only moments when there seemed to be any peace at home. Admittedly, it was a tense and anxious peace, but peace nonetheless, free from shouting or abuse, free from violence.

However, all this changed to darkness when the shadow that hung over them would come back home.

Moira would go to bed early, but she couldn't sleep. She waited…waited anxiously, aware that she was utterly defenceless. She hid her head under the yellow, threadbare blanket that covered her bed. She waited with eyes tightly closed and teeth clenched whenever she heard the street door open. The monster was coming home, and who knew what he would do….

The monster was fifty-one years old at the time, but he looked like "a wretched old man of at least sixty-five," she once commented to Chris.

Every night, at the very same time her friends were watching television, Moira was preparing herself for the next instalment of the on-going real-life soap opera that her parents regularly played out each night.

With time and the repetition that arose from his deterioration and her own naivety, Moira had learnt to recognise the tiny details that enabled her to anticipate and predict what was going to happen. The anguish and anticipation somehow allowed her to keep control of herself and not to give way to despair.

First she heard the small irregular tapping sounds. Then there was a sharp metallic sound, amplified by the wooden door and the echoing atmosphere inside the silent, almost empty house.

Then came the first attempts to open the door with the wrong key.

Next, from the sounds and the way he opened the door, she could tell the state in which her father had come home that night.

If the door opened abruptly, only to be slammed shut straight way with a loud crash, the next thing would the sound of light but unsteady steps on the stairs, making their way towards the bedroom where her mother was pretending to be asleep. Curses, complaints and insults would be followed by blows and sobs.

Why does she put up with it? Why don't we get out of here? These questions tortured Moira as much as her father's violence.

If, on the other hand, after a few failed attempts with the wrong key, he finally succeeded in opening the door, a slow creaking of the rusty hinges was followed by a slight sound as it slammed shut; then the dull thud of his slow, shaky, stumbling footsteps was followed by the muffled sound of his shoes as he fell onto the bed. That would mean that tonight he was too drunk to start another row. He would collapse onto the bed like a dead man and stay in the same position for more than ten hours, to get up with a severe headache that he got rid of with a coffee and a couple of aspirins brought to him by his dutiful wife.

Those ten hours of anxious calm allowed Moira at least to sleep, if not to dream. She no longer had dreams at home, only hazy memories of better times in Lancashire, a past she never knew.

Moira couldn't put up with this for much longer. She didn't have the words to express how she felt, or the energy to do anything about it and get away. She threw herself headlong into friendships with other young women and men and spent most of her time out of the house that, for her, was a constant source of bad news and ill treatment.

From then on, instead of falling into despondency and depression, Moira seemed to escape into a flurry of activities that had no clear purpose, rushing about with no clear direction.

She was hardly ever in school. She found it very boring, because she had neither the interest nor the intellectual energy to pay attention for more than a few brief moments. She flitted rapidly from one thing to another, and that prevented her from sticking to whatever activity she undertook.

Moira's life was like a kaleidoscope of whirling images, with no sense of unity or continuity other than enjoying what she saw. Moira led an ephemeral existence, living only for the moment, because her personality was fragile, malleable and inconsistent.

"He went down as if he was struck by lightning. Wham!" said the landlord of the pub, where Joseph had a heart attack that killed him instantly.

"He was lucky he didn't suffer," commented others, who had no idea that he had suffered throughout his entire life.

At the beginning Moira took it well, perhaps too well. She was anxious, "too talkative," commented Sally, the landlord's wife, slipping in a tangential criticism. "She didn't shed a single tear," she added, with an insinuating look. But no one had the bad taste to join this insidious attack at the time. "It doesn't seem normal to me," she added, with a nasty expression of disbelief.

The truth was that Moira was confused. She had so often longed for the death of her father, but not in a literal way. When he actually died, she felt that in some strange way, her secret wishes had contributed to this result.

"Oh God, I didn't really want him to die, I just wanted him to leave us alone." But God didn't answer, and she took this divine silence as a reproach.

However Moira had no time to worry about the divine insinuations of gods she didn't believe in. She had more immediate earthly matters to attend to.

The funeral arrangements, the house, the form-filling and the many bureaucratic procedures shielded her in a sort of way. They kept her moving gently onward, further away from the pain and the guilt. In addition, her mother's grief and devastation helped Moira to come out of herself.

After Joseph's death, Moira and Dorothy, her mother, found themselves with no savings and no family to fall back on in case of need. In the Midlands of the nineties, it was almost impossible for people like them to get a job. Moira was too young and inexperienced, with no skills or qualifications. Her mother was too old, and her health was not good.

After a few weeks they had to confront the fact that there was no money to pay the rent. What little they had went on buying food.

After jumping through a series of hoops at the town hall and a visit from a social worker, they managed to relocate to a council flat and began to receive a few pounds benefit to live on.

Moira gave up college for good and began to take on occasional temporary part-time jobs that required as little experience as the pay they offered. It was better than nothing!

When she wasn't working, which was most of the time, she spent her time with her boyfriends in the street or in the pub. The attraction that these rough muscular boys held for Moira went further than the sexual instinct. There were other deeper, personal reasons.

She secretly envied them their physical strength. If only she had had it, she could have used it to restrain her father from the beginning. "A few punches would have sorted him out, and he would have left us alone. The old bastard..." she used to say to herself bitterly, over and over again.

The freedom the young men had to run their own lives and their resulting autonomy was something she and her girlfriends could only aspire to.

No, women aren't equal. It's all much harder for us, she thought to herself, admiring them from afar.

If she'd been a man, she'd have gotten out of this dump long ago. Anywhere would do, the further the better. But that would be dangerous for a woman. Girls could only imagine or dream of a better life. Boys could act, get away from it all....

V

FOLLOWING HIS RELEASE FROM PRISON, after serving a short sentence for theft, John Hanson became the one the local lads looked up to.

This sentence would be the first of many to come, but that didn't matter to him. In his world, the future was something abstract and meaningless that only the elderly were worried about. His horizons hardly extended more than a week ahead. John lived with an uncle, who was never at home but provided him with food and a roof over his head. John was fit, and he had no dependents. For him there would always be another day; life was everlasting.

John was not very bright, but he had the quick wits of the survivor. Graduating from the university of life, he had learned his lessons from mistakes and fights. So he was all set to make the most of the new status he enjoyed among his friends. John was the centre of attention, especially when regaling them with stories of life in prison. Some were true, but most were made up or adapted to what his limited audience would like to hear. It was the little details he added that captivated his friends and made them feel as if they had been there themselves.

Seduction was a skill that was highly prized on the streets. A good seducer could win over and control more vulnerable people without the need to resort to violence. Moira fell in love with John at first sight.

At home she did nothing but talk about John. Dorothy didn't like him much.

"Life is a dear school, but only fools learn in no other," she would tell her, as she patched up an old pair of tights.

This was water off a duck's back to Moira, because she was used to hearing it by now.

She knew that John was making up some of his stories, but she pretended to believe them and listened with such rapt attention that he reached the point where he began to believe them himself. Thus, over time, Moira made herself indispensable to John's continuing self-belief. She was intelligent and seductive, in her own way.

But John was not the only hooked to Moira.

He smoked half a gram of heroin a day. It was only two packets at ten pounds each, but every single day. At first he tried to hide it from her, but she soon found out.

"Do you mind?" he asked.

"No, not if you let me try it," she replied.

"Sure?"

"Yes; if you can do it, why shouldn't I?"

So it came about that Moira was initiated into the art of *smoking heroin* from a thin slip of aluminium foil.

The first hit that they shared was an experience that compared with lovemaking, not so much because it was pleasurable but because it was instinctive. The experience of doing illicit drugs together made them feel very close, creating a strong bond between them. They didn't know that in the end, this was the very thing that would drive them apart forever.

When Moira became addicted, and the first withdrawal symptoms threatened, an immediate problem arose. They needed more money.

After a couple of weeks, they were both on the same hit and needing at least forty pounds' worth a day. That was a small fortune.

The only reason Moira never went cold turkey was John. He always got her the hits she needed. However, the sharks he was dealing with only gave him enough money for his hits.

The need that heroin dependency creates is immediate and physical. The pain you feel from withdrawal is so intense and acute that you can't listen to reason or tolerate any delay. They needed more money, and they needed it now!

Although there were other reasons, John always insisted to his lawyer that it was his chief one for joining the gang. Like every new recruit, at first they got him to do small tasks. He didn't make much dough, but he got enough work, and he was good at keeping his clients.

One day the gang leader told him he had a plan and needed someone good to carry it out.

The plan was to infiltrate an area on the edge of Manchester, near Salford. The operation wasn't risk free, but if it turned out well, there would be plenty of money and a good commission to work the district.

"Have you got the balls for it?"

Johnny wasn't so stupid that he didn't understand what he was letting himself in for, but he was very short of cash, and his options were running out.

"Sure, why not? I'll do it."

A false smile and an untrustworthy handshake sealed the deal.

On his first day in the area, he succeeded in striking a couple of deals, but he also attracted the attention of the Salford dealers who worked the patch. It didn't take long for them to decide to get rid of the intruder and send a clear signal to his bosses.

He had made his new contacts so quickly that he got confident and began to think that this time, he had started off on the right foot.

"Things are going to be different," he thought, confidently.

He was right; things were going to be different – but not in the way he meant.

The next day he took an order for twenty bags and fifty pounds up front. The delivery would be made that afternoon in Blacken, known as the capital of *Gunchester*, an area as poor as it was violent.

Partly from excitement and partly as a precaution, John arrived fifteen minutes early at the agreed place with the gear.

A walk through the neighbourhood was enough to convince him that there were worse places that his own area. The streets were deserted and damp in the drizzling rain. Although mistrustful and cautious, he saw nothing to arouse his suspicions as he made his way to the corner of Primrose Hill and Church Street, the place arranged for the deal.

Almost twenty minutes after the agreed time, there was no sign of his new client. The place was completely dead. No soul could be seen on the streets except for an old lady with a stick, walking her dog, and a chap who looked like a Pakistani behind the counter of a little tandoori restaurant, which gave out a strong smell of curry and cheap vinegar.

Uncertainty was giving way to frustration and annoyance when John decided it was safer to beat a retreat to familiar territory.

He made his way down the street at double-quick speed, looking sideways out of the corners of his eyes, alert for any sign of the local police or an opportunist thief. What he had on him was too much to count for personal use, and if arrested, he would be looking at several years inside. He had walked just over a hundred metres when two hefty men came out of a side street.

John wasn't bothered, because they didn't seem like heavies, but he was soon to learn that you can't always tell what a heavy looks like. One of them was tall with short hair and wore a discreet jacket of dark brown leather. There was nothing particularly noticeable about him, apart for a small blue-and-red tattoo on his neck.

John couldn't say much about the other, except that he had a large metal ring that caught the light just before it smashed into his face, breaking the skin and exposing part of his right cheekbone. The blow knocked him out at once. Oddly enough, John thought himself lucky to have taken this blow, because it left him unconscious throughout the rest of his beating. This meant that most of his memories of were remote and indistinct, as if they had happened to someone else.

The unknown skinny black man didn't stop talking and jabbing his finger, but although he could see his lips moving to reveal large white teeth, John couldn't hear a word he was saying.

From time to time, he seemed to be laughing as he called to others to join him in this gruesome spectacle. Moments later John saw he was surrounded by brightly coloured shoes, the only thing he could see from where he lay on the ground.

"What the hell do they want?" he thought.

One of them bent over him, and John was not slow to realise that an eager hand was going through his pockets searching for valuables. Now he could clearly see thin, bony cheeks. This one had white skin, pitted with acne and covered with red pimples. His hair was short, and he had a broad nose. Instinctively John tried to stop him, but his arms wouldn't do what his brain was telling them.

Suddenly they all ran away as if in flight. The one who was checking him over, spit in his face before escaping.

"Shit," he could read clearly on his lips as he got a kick in the ribs.

A flashing blue light, indistinct at first, then growing bright, told him that the police had arrived.

The measure of John's return to consciousness was the degree to which he became wretchedly aware that he was in a bad way. He was injured and couldn't move, trapped in a body that he could only recognise as his own because of the pain that was starting to become unbearable. Resigned to his fate, he surrendered himself to the future; and in a strange way, that was a relief.

The cold afternoon contrasted with the warm liquid oozing from some part of his cheek and trickling into his mouth.

"Well, well, look what we've got here. Call the paramedics; first we've got to get him to hospital." Johnny was still lying on the ground, paralysed and motionless, but at least he could hear them.

Ridiculous as it was, at that moment John's main concern was not his precarious physical state but his boss. He would be furious when he heard about it. How could he explain the loss of twenty wraps, and how was he going to pay for them? *He'll kill me*, he thought, reflecting on a future beating while still suffering from the consequences of the present one.

"What's your name, son?" asked the officer.

"John."

"John who?" prodded the police officer, dividing his gaze between the prostrate body and the notebook he was taking it down in.

"I don't know. I don't remember."

"All right, don't worry. You'll remember soon enough," the officer said, looking around. A few minutes later an ambulance arrived. "All yours," said one of the policemen to the paramedics, who were quick to get him onto a stretcher.

Once in the ambulance he started to groan with the pain and asked for something to relieve it.

Many people have a different reaction to the prick and the needle entering the muscle, but John felt an immediate relief he could only compare with the soothing presence of a familiar friend at such a dreadful time.

"What happened to you?" asked the paramedic, trying to keep him conscious until they arrived at the hospital.

"I don't know. I think someone punched me in the face."

"Yes. I think they broke your nose, but what I'm worried about is the cut to the cheek. That's what we're going to stitch up first, so you stop losing blood."

"Is it a big cut? Will it leave a scar?" he asked anxiously.

"I think you'll need about twenty stitches at first. But later you'll be able to have plastic surgery, and it won't show so much."

The morphine was taking its effect, and Johnny felt more relaxed by the minute. The pain and anxiety were dissipating into a familiar, pleasurable haze. Before drifting off into unconsciousness again, he was able to think more calmly about two things.

One was the scar, that message written on his face—probably forever. Now no one would want to come near him.

The second was Moira. *When will I see her again?* he thought.

The punters hadn't wanted to wipe John out. That would have been easy enough, but not so much use for their ends. The message they had sent wouldn't be slow in getting around. They had also left a few small packets loose in the top pocket of his denim jacket, enough to ensure him a heavy sentence for trafficking.

They would think twice before they sent anyone else. Otherwise, the next message they would get would be in a wooden box.

On that ill-fated day, Moira also ended up in a hospital—a different one, and for different reasons. Without any money to buy heroin or any sort of substitute, her withdrawal symptoms were getting progressively worse. Moira was anxious, irritable, restless. By this stage she knew something had gone wrong with the deal, but that wasn't her main concern. Her body was desperately demanding the hits she had gotten used to, but which were now denied her. Her skin had turned pale, cold and sweaty, like a dead chicken. She turned cold and hot alternately. She felt a constant pain in her shoulder, and stomach cramps were accompanied by being violently sick. She didn't have to say much to the doctors to get a subcutaneous morphine injection that, in a short while, as if by magic, brought her back to a state that she would have described as "normal."

The doctors and nurses on duty were used to seeing many Moiras and Johnnys with withdrawal symptoms. Those crises were well within their experience, and they were very good at managing them.

Moira was taken to a recovery room where, two hours later, she was visited by a young doctor of Asian appearance and a friendly manner, who informed her with tact and delicacy of two things that were destined to map out the course of her life for the next twenty years: her heroin addiction and her pregnancy.

Dorothy Smith died without ever knowing her grandson, but she lived long enough to see her daughter embark on what was to become the first of many treatments to fight her drug addiction.

Although it all happened very quickly, nobody felt the least surprised. Her death was a predictable one. Joseph had gone to the grave, taking the greater part of Dorothy's life with him. Although Moira knew only the bad times, Dorothy dwelt on the happier moments they had once enjoyed. She lost the will to live, to carry on the fruitless struggle. Hers was not so much depression as a deep frustration and despair.

This time, Moira had as little chance to say good-bye to her mother as to Johnny. It was all as sudden and unexpected as her pregnancy.

Moira found herself torn between profound sadness at the death of her mother, a natural joy at her pregnancy and anxiety at what the future would bring.

For the first time in her life, she felt helpless but not alone. She had a child on the way. Holding on to him would be her lifeline. As if blindly, intuitively, following the often incomprehensible logic of our being, Moira was about to do for her son what until now she had never done for herself: look for a better life.

VI

MOIRA WAS NOW HALFWAY THROUGH her thirtieth year, though it seemed more like her fortieth when she began to realize that she wouldn't be able to carry on like this much longer.

After her son was born, it was impossible to find a job or a partner who was worth the trouble. She had lost contact with the father of her child years ago, and she had no family left. All she and her son had in the world was each other.

They had support from social services, they had a place to live and enough to eat, and when Moira occasionally earned a meagre salary, they could even have a little treat sometimes – if she wasn't too high on drugs. One hundred pounds a week could not buy much heroin, but it was enough to feed her habit.

A few months earlier, Moira had started again with her last methadone treatment. Eighty millilitres, under strict pharmaceutical supervision, formed part of her daily routine. That dose ensured she was fit enough to avoid feeling rough and keep her job, but in spite of this, she still continued to come up positive when they carried out a urine test to detect drugs.

The street they lived in was as drab as their own lives, a bleak range of greys and blacks that contrasted with the red brick of the damp and crumbling walls that had seen better times. One day, in the not-too-distant future, her area would be thought of as archaeological remains from the distant past, when the industrial revolution swept England.

Without her knowing it being able to even imagine it, her destiny was the same as many other people's in Europe, America and Asia, who lived in the urban slums that grew up around industrial complexes that were running down or already abandoned.

The capital that gave life and movement to that whole productive enterprise of men and machines vanished as quickly as it had come, without giving the time or the opportunities to adapt to the new realities.

Moira's father had been the first generation to fall victim to these changes, and soon she and young Johnny – named for his father – would join the endless list of those marginalised by complex economic and technological processes, which they didn't understand but had to put up with.

For that matter, they also couldn't understand where all these Africans, Pakistanis and West Indians were coming from and why. The brightly coloured clothes they wore, the food they ate and sold with its tempting aromas, the resonance of the foreign words of their native languages and their distinctive accents when they spoke English injected new life into the area.

Both Moira and Johnny might have noticed that they had much more in common with these recent arrivals than they thought. Everyone there was sharing their misfortunes but also their gains from the struggle for a better future and a past that they wanted to leave behind and forget. But by letting themselves be taken in by the superficial appearances, which were all they could understand, they ended up finding those people foreign and a nuisance.

The fine generosity of the British people welcomed them in and allowed them to look forward to their future with optimism, in many cases for the first time.

In spite of this, Moira was convinced that the part of Druslem where she lived was not the best place to bring up her son. Most of the young people were using drugs, injecting or taking methadone in doses that added a new dependency to their pre-existing ones. Street fights, robberies and raids for illegal immigrants were a normal part of everyday life.

Moira didn't know that her fate, that of her family and all those around her, was the result of extraordinary historical movements sweeping them along to destinies that no one could foresee. Besides, Moira wouldn't have been interested. She had had more than enough, and she thought that the only solution for herself and her son was to get out of there as soon as possible. Any place at all would be better than to continue exposing him to bad company and the risks of something she knew only too well.

It wasn't easy for people in a situation as precarious as theirs, depending for the most part on benefits and social security and now subject to the budget cuts that threatened them with reducing practical help for an abstract concept, useful only for political speeches but not for people in need.

Moira could not remember any better life to compare with her present problems. Only in her imagination did she picture the places conjured up from her father's words when he spoke of his Lancashire past, a past he yearned for and idealised with exaggerated simplicity. But this was enough for Moira to start building in her mind's eye a place that was mythical, a place that would allow her to dream of a better life. And there she went.

It is hard to say if it was that deep desire for a better life somewhere else or the youthful enthusiasm of Zarah, the counsellor who looked after her in the clinic, but the fact was that Moira stabilised and kicked the habit. She stopped complaining and blaming others for her problems and started to think seriously about moving on.

After several months she took a steady job working as an assistant in a supermarket. Although the salary wasn't much, it was enough to get by without outside help. With money in her pocket, and having overcome her fear of withdrawal, Moira's self-confidence started to grow and she began to plan her next moves.

Her main concern was Johnny. He had a lot of free time to waste.

Moira felt panic-stricken and guilty when she read on his arms the story that he had recently begun to inject. She didn't need to go to a fortune-teller to predict what fate had in store for Johnny if they didn't get out quickly. Once he became dependent, his dealer would always stay around, making it his business to ensure that he paid the price. She knew very well that the problem wasn't just to get the monkey off your back but to make sure the circus wouldn't come back to town.

Zarah was proud of Moira's progress over the last months and was sympathetic when she told her what was going on with Johnny. She was quick to realise that their two destinies were intertwined and that she wouldn't be able to rescue one without the other. After various conversations with her managers and the panel of experts that controlled the special treatments' budget, Zarah managed to get approval for the necessary funds to pay for Johnny to be sent to a rehab clinic for six months' treatment.

Thus it was that by a mixture of self-esteem, compassion, warnings and a detailed account of the media consequences that the council authorities would be exposed to, if a young man in their care were to die because they hadn't approved the funds for his treatment, Zarah and Moira achieved their objective.

Sometimes it's hard to understand how a mixture of so many bad things can result in something good. But that's how it turned out. After five months of intensive recovery focus residential treatment, Johnny was a very different person from the one who had come in.

His hope for a new life could be seen, reflected in the sparkle in his eye and his infectious smile. He had made a lot of friends and put on twelve pounds. The change in his life had exceeded all expectations. The Hanson-Smith genes were beginning to develop in a suitable environment, showing that hereditary determinism didn't apply, at least in this case.

But it would be wrong to say that Johnny had achieved all these outcomes on his own. No one lives in a vacuum; we always co-exist.

His mentor, Chris, had seen something special in Johnny, something that resonated with a past experience he couldn't identify and saw no point in trying to define. Something very profound passed between them, forming a deep bond.

Chris had made him see life very differently, making Johnny understand that some good can come even out of bad experiences, and that sometimes one can arrive at the right place even by taking a wrong path.

The truth is that there is neither path nor destiny, only enjoyment or otherwise as we go through life.

Chris knew that the acid test would come at the end of the residential treatment, that of the rosy lane that Johnny had travelled during the last months, only the thorns would be left. Going back home wouldn't be easy. The harsh reality that he had come from would still be there when he got back. The circus wouldn't leave the town.

Chris's many years' experience had taught him that miracle cures don't last long if they are not properly followed up on. Johnny needed more time to distance himself from trouble to have some chance. Chris did everything in his power to prolong his stay at the centre. Every day he presented him with new buddies to talk over his experiences with and provide mutual support. They were those who would build their own network of a protective shield by listening to and respecting each other and themselves. Out of this union and cohesion would grow the invisible hand that would protect them.

But Johnny's time was nearly up, and Chris still wasn't completely confident that he would make it on the outside.

That's how things were stood when, on a sunny summer's morning, two weeks before the appointed date for Johnny's leaving ceremony, Chris had an unexpected visit.

Two representatives from an international organisation to which they were affiliated came to visit them. They were promoting an international convention of youths in recovery coming from all over Europe. The event was funded by the Vernaux foundation, and it would take place in a resort in the hills of southern Andalusia.

The idea was to share their knowledge and experiences, which they could pass on and promote when they returned to their home communities. The emotional experience of such a convention would also strengthen the bonds between the participants and the organisations represented.

It was a win-win situation in every sense.

Just one word came to Chris's mind as he took part in the conversation: *Johnny*. It was a unique opportunity that he couldn't ignore. Without a doubt, the event would be forgotten in time, but Johnny could be vaccinated forever. One life, just one life recovered justified everything.

Six weeks of living together in a healthy environment filled with sunshine and surrounded by nature was a great opportunity to make new friends, to listen to other people, and to be listened to with respect. That was the energy needed to recharge Johnny's internal battery.

Chris didn't feel badly when choosing Johnny, because unlike the other candidates, he didn't have any financial or family support. Johnny and Moira needed it more than the rest.

Furthermore, Chris had a local contact down in Andalusia, whom Johnny could turn to if necessary.

His childhood friend Steve Dariet had recently settled in Marbella, and he was someone he could trust.

VII

MAYBE IT WAS SHAME, or maybe it was anger that catapulted him out of his temporary retirement and revived his hunting instincts. Steve was overcome with shock and grief and furious with himself, all at the same time. How could he not have realised that Johnny was going to have a relapse when he had seen him the day before?

He should have noticed something in his behaviour, his speech, a gesture, a look, the eyes…the eyes never lie.

"I'm losing my touch," he said aloud.

Steve had promised Chris to look after Johnny, and he had let him down.

Perhaps it was excessive vanity that made him feel responsible. He couldn't accept that Johnny also could exercise free will and was master of his own decisions. No, that argument didn't help to soften the feeling that he had let down *his* protégé and *his* friend.

Chris had been Steve's neighbour during his childhood in Buckinghamshire. They have been schoolmates and friends from an early age. It would fair to say they grew together. They shared similar tastes in music, beer and women. Chris knew Steve very well, and during their brief telephone conversation, he had exploited this weakness to make Steve feel personally involved in the case. He knew that if he were successful, Steve would do everything in his power to clear up the deaths and catch the culprits.

He went straight to Romero's office. If anyone knew anything, it would be him.

Without beating about the bush, Steve came straight to the point. "What do you know about what happened, Romero?"

"Not much, I'm afraid," was his reply.

Initial investigations among the onlookers, most of whom were under twenty-five years old, revealed what he had suspected: that a large quantity of ecstasy and such had been taken, along with some legal highs that came from China.

However, several paid informers were in agreement in pointing the finger at a group of five or six fair-haired men with rough faces, dark complexion and a nasty look. They appeared to be from Eastern Europe, but the fact that they weren't wearing designer gear or flashing gold watches suggested that they weren't Russians.

"What caught their attention was that these men were handing out some stuff they didn't recognise, or at least that they had never seen before. They weren't selling anything; they gave the drugs away to a few youngsters but then still hung around, as if they were watching them," Romero explained, with a puzzled look on his face. "It all happened very quickly. Our people keep in touch with the dealers that operate on Fontanilla beach. If they had known that Poles were giving out these pills, there wouldn't have been any deaths. They would never have allowed outsiders on their pitch. By the time they got in there and went after them, the Poles had vanished."

"They were Poles, then?" asked Steve.

"I don't know. Around here, we call all the fair-haired people Poles if they're not Russians, British, Germans or Swedes."

"I see now. Their clients got hurt. The Poles will spoil their business for a while."

"Exactly! The area is going to stay under careful observation, and it will be months before things get back to normal. Steve, you know how it works. We'll never be able to put a complete stop to illegal drug dealing. All we can do is try to keep on top of things so they don't get worse. Pin down what happens when foreign thugs get in...."

"Yes, I understand. We do the same over there," Steve replied.

"All right, so a bit of ecstasy is being sold and we know about it, but their dealing isn't large-scale drug trading," Romero went on. "They know that if there are problems, we'll come in and put a stop to it."

"So, apart from ecstasy what was the local dealer's business that night?" Steve asked again.

"Water. *Fresh* water," he repeated, emphasising the reply.

"Water?" Steve exclaimed in astonishment, staring at Romero with a frown.

"Sure, man, bottled water. There are a lot of stalls selling vodka, whiskey, rum and fizzy drinks, but they are the only ones who sell bottles of fresh water."

"But where's the profit in that?"

"Three euros for a bottle that they pay twenty cents for. You know, when people take ecstasy, they get dehydrated, and they want water – not alcohol, not fizzy drinks, just pure water. That night there was no water in the wash-basins. If you wanted it, you had to buy what they were selling and pay what they asked for or else walk a kilometre to shops that were outside the perimeter," stated Romero in matter-of-fact tone, as if he were explaining the relationship between the tides and the proximity of the moon. "The problems began some time before dawn," he continued. "We calculate that it was between one and two hours after those drugs were handed out. The two boys showed similar symptoms: some agitation, sweating heavily, vomiting, high temperature and raised heartbeat. One of them was bleeding from the ears. The doctors who treated them in casualty thought it was poisoning from ecstasy, cocaine and alcohol. They treated them with hydration on the spot, but when they didn't get any better, they were transferred to the Costa del Sol hospital. They have all the necessary equipment at their disposal there to treat cases like this. The boys didn't respond.

"The doctors took blood and urine samples and sent them to the Seville and Madrid Toxicology Institute. They have a lot of experience in these affairs. Some years ago the ITM analysed four thousand one hundred confiscated ecstasy tablets from a similar event in Madrid. The tablets contained the usual doses, but among them were around twenty per cent that contained up to four times more. Without knowing it, one day you could take three doses of thirty milligrams, but the next day three doses of a hundred and thirty.

"That's one of the reasons why the regular clients are loyal to their dealers and why we allow the monopoly to a controlled group. Better the devil you know than the devil you don't.... Live and let live!"

"A very pragmatic approach. In the Netherlands there are government laboratories that analyse the drugs you bring in, no questions asked. At least people know what they are getting and aren't taking undue risks," Steve replied.

"I would call our approach a realistic one" Romero went on. Over here, some influential people would be jumping up and down, tearing their hair out, if we were to propose what they do in the Netherlands. In this way we have to act more discreetly to control the quality. It's the influence of the ultraconservative hypocrisy…

"As usual, today we've got the rave organisers saying they regret what happened and blaming the police. But that doesn't bother us; we're used to all that nonsense. They always claim to have sold half of the tickets they really sell, to pay less tax and licenses."

And so It turned out. According to the organisers, they had obtained all the necessary permits from the local authority, and there were 116 security guards in charge of the event that night.

In a brief statement, the spokesman for the organisers said that the drugs had been bought outside the perimeter, and only a few people had brought them in. The Marbella authorities confirmed that the megarave complied with all the necessary regulations. However, because of what had happened, no further events would be allowed on the beaches.

An unofficial source stated that the event had been arranged for some eight thousand people, but possibly up to twelve thousand had succeeded in gaining entry through the perimeter, because some tickets had been photocopied. The organizers did not inform the authorities that the beaches were overcrowded, which they should have done; and because of that, the security guards they had brought in were completely overwhelmed.

Soon followed the usual exchange of accusations that served only to fill the headlines for a few days until some well-known triviality, sporting event or distant tragedy upstaged the local affair. By now everyone had heard so much about it that they were fed up with it anyway.

That was the precise moment when, under the shadow of forgetfulness, someone started to organise the next event. The permits needed? That could still be sorted out in due course.

"There is something else" said Romero with an enigmatic look.

"What else?" asked Steve.

"My people are looking into another lead in Estepona. A little two-year-old girl, a Roma child, died from poisoning by an unknown substance. The symptoms are very similar to those the boys had, but laboratory analysis couldn't find out what the drug was. At least, it isn't one of the known ones.

"One of our men found some pills that we are sending to our labs in Seville. Perhaps they won't tell us much more but at the moment it's the only lead I've got. I've got the feeling there's something odd about this."

"What do you know about the two Britons who died?" asked Steve trying to obtain some more detailed information.

"Man, haven't you heard?" replied Romero.

"Heard what?" said Steve with a hint of surprise in his voice.

"There aren't two dead, only one," said Romero.

"But the papers said there were two British dead," replied Steve now confused.

"Those hacks…you know what they're like Steve. They don't know what they're talking about. There was a journalist in the crowd who gathered round the kids and he thought they were already dead when they were taken away. The stupid arsehole was in such a hurry to get his scoop that he said there were two British dead. He was wrong, one was American and the other was British, they were both in a coma. Unfortunately the American died in the hospital, and the other is still hanging on. I don't know what they'll say now. One of the dead men is making a good recovery. Yeah, yeah." Romero offered this cheap sarcasm that got no response from Steve, who remained as serious as ever.

"I know one of the boys," Steve replied.

"I'm sorry. I didn't mean to make fun of it," said Romero trying to justify his lack of tact.

"That's OK, but who is the one still alive? Do you know his name?" asked Steve.

"I don't, but I can find out," replied Romero grabbing at random papers and documents piled on his desk.

"Don't worry about that, I'll go to the hospital. Is there anything else you can tell me?" Steve asked as he stood up.

"The two boys seemed to know each other. At least that's what we were told by the girlfriend of one of them. We're still interviewing witnesses and people who were operating on the scene that night. I'll keep you informed of any developments."

"Thanks, Romero. I owe you one."

"Forget it, man, I owe you more than that. Bye for now."

VIII

THE INTERVIEW WITH ROMERO FERNANDEZ had given Steve some slight hope. He drove as fast as he could through the dense traffic that jammed all the streets of the Costa del Sol on summer afternoons.

In the middle of a traffic jam, he drew up alongside a convertible with a group of boys and girls in it, laughing happily. Just a few inches separated their happiness from his deep, overwhelming grief.

Life went on just the same. He felt irrelevant, diminished, lost among those who were still carefree, enjoying the sun, sea and summer, knowing nothing of the tragedy that he and a few others suffered from.

Although only a few kilometres separated the police station from the hospital, Steve constantly found himself being held up by the permanent traffic jams. It took him almost half an hour to reach his destination.

He went in through the main entrance and walked down the corridors of white marble and glass, making for the intensive care unit.

At last, mingling with a small crowd of people roaming the spacious corridors, he reached the waiting room.

The place was small in comparison with the number of people waiting there for news of their families and friends, lying in limbo beyond the double doors marked "NO ENTRY."

Some were groaning anxiously as they waited for news; others were praying. Two gypsies were taking loudly, but either through fear or because it would be useless, no one asked them to lower their voices.

Steve went up to the door and knocked gently. After the third attempt, still no one came to answer his call. He started to lose patience too, and soon began to sympathise with the other people there.

When he eventually knocked more vigorously, the doors opened and a short, dumpy nurse appeared. She nevertheless had a commanding presence and started to call out she names of the names of the patients inside.

As she called the first name, the whole crowd surged towards her in unison. Steve was caught in the crush and couldn't move, say or word or hear anything. They were all calling out at once, shouting and asking for their loved ones.

At this point Steve realized that they all enjoyed a quality that he lacked. They knew how to behave in the Mediterranean chaos that the Greeks had once observed disdainfully three thousand years earlier.

The initial hubbub started to subside as the families went back to their original places once they were given an update about their relative's clinical condition. When there were just a few people left, he was able to get to the nurse, telling her that he was a friend of one of the boys who had been brought in during the night.

"Name?" asked the nurse, in a loud voice that sounded almost impertinent.

"Johnny Hanson, he is one of the boys that were brought here last night after overdosing in the beach rave. I'm not sure if he's the one who's still alive."

"Do you think you could identify him?"

"Yes, if you let me look at him," he replied, with a firmness he didn't feel.

"Come this way," said the nurse.

Steve could hear a new outcry behind him, protesting at the nurse and demanding to be let in as well.

When the doors closed behind him, the nurse let out a sigh of relief, and Steve couldn't help thinking about the difficulties and dangers inherent in her work. The sweaty heat of the waiting room contrasted with the temperature inside the intensive care unit that never went above twenty two degrees. Limbo was a cooler place.

Steve walked at a fast pace, trying to keep up with the nurse, who was hurrying to a bed at the far end of the ward. When she got there, she drew back a curtain and asked bluntly, "Do you know him?"

Steve hesitated a moment, because the body she showed him was covered in tubes and almost naked in a totally unfamiliar environment.

However, on closer inspection, he was able to make out his hair and general features. Johnny was still alive after all. There was a ray of hope.

"Yes, I know him. His name is Johnny Hanson. How is he?"

"He is stable at the moment. But I can't say more than that; we must wait and see how he turns out. Something poisoned him. These boys take stuff they shouldn't, and look at the consequences here." She spoke in a strident bossy tone pretending to sound friendly. "Do you know the boy's family?" she went on.

"Yes, his mother's called Moira, and she's arriving tomorrow morning from England. Is there any immediate danger?"

"I don't think so. He's still in a coma, but he'll take his time to come out of it. He's young, and that's a great help," she replied, with a ghost of a smile. Then she added, "Unfortunately, I can't let you wait in here. You'll have to go back outside, and I'll let you know how he is every hour."

"Thanks," said Steve, slipping his card into her hands. "My number's here with my details. I have to go back to work for a few hours, and then I'll come back and spend the night here. Please call me if anything happens."

"You needn't worry; I don't think anything bad will happen in the next few hours," she said, twisting the card between her fingers and looking at Steve in a way that made him feel awkward. "But leave me the card in case it does.... By the way, my name is Macarena, but my friends call me Maca."

"Thanks, Maca," replied Steve, following her lead with a seductive smile and an inviting look. He just wanted to be sure of a safe conduct through the chaos that lay in wait on the other side of the doors.

The first thing he did when he got outside was to phone Chris and give him the good news. This time, Chris was as pleasantly surprised as he was grateful. There was still some hope.

The news that Johnny was still alive seemed to have revived Chris and no doubt would do the same for Moira.

Steve thought of how Johnny's blood flowed not only through his own veins but his mother's too, and the same for his joys and sorrows. When someone is born or dies, there is also a birth or death in those who love them.

Those who had ended the lives of the other boy had messed with many other lives at the same time, and those helping Johnny to recover were also saving Moira, Chris and surely many others too.

That thought helped Steve to see his own situation in Marbella more clearly. He led a tranquil existence there, but he was alone. His friend had burst the peaceful bubble he had been living in, which he was now beginning to think of as a brief summer's slumber.

Johnny wasn't dead, and Steve hadn't let down his friend. At some point Johnny would get better and go back to his own world. That would also let Steve go back to his.

His world? What was his world?

Without knowing why, in a sort of way he envied Johnny, Chris and Moira.

Steve spent the rest of the day in the hospital. It was already past seven in the evening when, after waiting several hours among groans, whispers, shouts and curses, Steve continued to receive the same routine information: Johnny was in a stable condition, he must carry on hoping for the best. The stifling, oppressive atmosphere in the waiting room left Steve restless with gloomy thoughts. He knew that Johnny was in good hands and there was nothing more he could do for him.

That was when he decided to visit someone, he was sure, could give him more information.

The sun was beginning to sink below the horizon, and the yellow and red skies of the Andalusian sunset were starting to give way to a deep, velvety blue that was almost black. The refreshing scent of jasmine blossoms perfumed the Mediterranean night.

Coming out of the hospital Steve jumped into his car, a second-hand Audi A3 in reasonable condition with sixty thousand kilometres on the clock. It was no big deal, but it served its purpose.

He took the N-340 towards the Mediterranean motorway, but instead of joining it, he left it on the right and turned first left, then right. He made his way towards the outskirts of Marbella, in the Malaga direction.

Steve was heading for *Las Albarizias.*

He was looking for Chano.

IX

In 1978, when Spain was still under the rule of General Franco, the authorities made the decision to end the extradition treaty with the United Kingdom in protest at the stalled negotiations over the Rock of Gibraltar. This meant that British criminals could no longer be extradited back to their own country, with the result that a growing number of criminals settled in the Andalusia region, especially in Marbella. Hence, property prices went through the roof, and satellite antennas sprouted like mushrooms on the sumptuous villas and estates by the golf courses or the beach. From their newly legalised paradise, the gangland bosses could still control their operations back home while enjoying the sun, the sea, and the new business opportunities.

The South American drug traffickers were not slow to realise the potential offered by this new situation in the region, and with the funds they got from cocaine, they set up sophisticated trafficking networks for every type of drug taken in Europe, especially their star commodity.

In the beginning, they dealt with the Moroccans, who traditionally smuggled alcohol and tobacco; later they substituted these for hash, which was more profitable. Later on, the trade routes across the Riff of the Atlas Mountains and the western Mediterranean were to deal with new merchandise coming from the regions of sub-Saharan Africa: human beings, all trying to escape from the wars and misery endemic in sub-Saharan Africa.

Setting up operational networks is a very complex business, requiring two basic elements. The first is to make friends among the governing classes, so they open their doors to you and give you protection. The second is to get logistical support from the local traffickers with established networks. It was that second element that changed Nuri's life and that of his whole family for ever.

They were gypsies, *gitanos*, a proud race united by strong ties of kinship and long standing customs. Nuri knew everyone, and nobody messed with him.

A short while after setting up the operation with the Colombians, there was a change in the way money started to flow in. The hundreds painfully extracted in the streets of Marbella turned into thousands that gave rise to regular operations that were more complex and better co-ordinated. Nuri helped to set up a beachhead, solving all the logistical problems of reception, storage and regional distribution of all the merchandise.

Although he was for all intents and purposes illiterate, Nuri displayed his business acumen when, instead of a salary, he demanded a payment of 25 per cent of all goods delivered. With this, operations as well as his profits were guaranteed.

"Drugs are the most stable currency," he used to say.

Some years later, the accession of Spain to the European Community complicated the judicial framework in which Nuri operated, but he still kept up the international traffic, to the despair of the customs officers.

The frontiers had shifted from the Pyrenees to the Urals, and new alliances from Eastern Europe meant that his business expanded beyond his wildest dreams. Time went by, and although Nuri still made strenuous efforts to remain unchanged, both he and his family and friends were different. There are no two ways about it; money changes everyone and everything!

Las Albarizias, his birthplace, he only kept on as a headquarters where he felt safe. That was the territory where he held sway, where he was feared and respected. But Nuri and his family had since moved to one of the country estates on the outskirts of Malaga. He no longer drove around in second-hand cars with false licence plates but rather in the latest German models, which were considered the most reliable, according to Chano, his younger brother, minder and partner in all his deals.

Nuri's death was as sudden as it was unexpected. Amid heartrending cries, shouting and wailing for the deceased, that very same day Chano naturally stepped into the shoes his brother had just vacated.

Nobody missed the funeral or the chance to pay their respects to the new boss.

Chano appeared sombre, withdrawn, saying nothing more than that Nuri's death had come about from natural causes, and nobody had any cause for concern. Chano knew that was not the case, but he would take care of settling a current debt, and soon it would be business as usual. His closest contacts looked at each other with sullen expressions and agreed.

The next day three bodies were found at distant points on the outskirts of town. All of them had a deep cut in the throat. They bled to death. Barely twenty days earlier, they had been arguing with Nuri, putting his leadership in doubt, in front of his people.

No one asked any questions; they all understood what *gitano* vengeance meant. The account had been settled, and Chano had consolidated his leadership with action that spoke louder than any words. He was not prepared to tolerate disaffection or run any risks. Anyone who stood in his way knew of the danger he was exposed to.

Chano was a tall, thin man, dark eyes and an arrogant look. His long, wavy, black amber-coloured hair, glistened even in the dark. A white silk necktie at his throat and a number of rings and crosses of pure gold were the only accessories that stood out from his black shoes, socks, trousers and shirt. He seemed about forty-five years old, but nobody could say exactly, and nobody dared ask.

No one ever saw him on his own; a small group of at least four discreetly armed men surrounded him at all times since the death of his brother. A glance from him was enough to inspire respect.

Since the arrival of the Colombians, Italians and Eastern Europeans, everything had changed. Chano became very distrustful and decided to take precautions.

Barely more than a kilometre from the town centre, alluring Marbella showed a different side, with nothing quaint or glamorous about it.

It was a place that few people dared set foot in. Buildings that had once been housing estates had now been abandoned by their original inhabitants. Most of them were ruined, with doors removed and windows broken. Some showed large, black damp patches from the rubbish left behind inside.

The few remaining walls that still showed signs of what was once a white colour were covered in graffiti, sprayed with black or blue aerosol messages of love, hatred, anger, adverts or even direct threats. What hadn't been ruined had been set on fire.

Steve entered this territory with a lot of misgivings.

After a few metres, he could see a car without wheels or windows. Right behind the wrecked car, there was a standing man with a gun in his hand. He was a guard, posted to see who was coming in down this street. It was hard to imagine someone once buying this vehicle, filled with joy or at least with the enthusiasm that anything that hasn't been used before creates. Now this battered wreck had become an observation and control post, when it wasn't being used for target practice.

On all sides could be seen green plastic sacks containing every sort of rubbish, preyed on by wandering cats. They were scattered around carelessly, giving a warning that was more depressing than anything else that was so unpleasant about the place.

Steve thought it was all part of a revolting film set that was attempting to frighten or put off anyone trying to gain entry to the area. He continued moving slowly onwards, calmly, without paying attention to those who were watching him with menacing disdain.

Some hundred metres from the entrance lay a broken fridge with its door open, looking pathetically like something that had died. Nearby could be seen a rusty bathtub, full of all sorts of rubbish and broken plastic chairs, surrounded by green bins full of rubbish that some municipal workman had not had time to empty in the past, and now no one would risk it.

As Steve was reaching his destination, he could see a group of boys playing in the shadows in the middle of the road, underneath a streetlight that inexplicably still hadn't been smashed or shot at.

With his gun the guard pointed Steve a place to park his car. The boys stopped their game to watch him, as if they were seeing something quaint and foreign, and began to come closer. For a split second, all the activity around him seemed to stop. He felt uncomfortable. He was the focus of all this menacing scrutiny, even from those he couldn't yet see but intuitively knew they were there.

Like his elder brother, Chano controlled and ran all his illegal activities in the streets of Marbella, Malaga and several neighbouring towns from this spot. Nothing happened in his territory that he didn't know and approve of. Someone once said: "You can do anything without Chano's approval, but it will be your last act!"

Steve parked his car at the end of the alley in front of two black BMWs, immaculate with their seats of red leather, in shocking contrast to the heaps of scrap all around them. He switched off the engine and stayed in his seat, quietly looking ahead, waiting for a signal.

The boys came up and gathered noisily round his car. They were all talking and shouting at the same time, gesticulating and laughing. Some of them asked him what he was doing there and why he'd come, while others wanted to know his name. He would have no trouble finding someone to extort money from him to take a message or conduct him to where he wanted to go.

Steve ignored them and carried on waiting, impassive.

Soon a man came up from behind, out of nowhere. He cleared a path through the crowd, who still managed to be rather menacing in spite of being kids, and with a single shout got them all to run away and go home.

The man moved slowly all around the car, carefully examining the vehicle and its driver. He bent down to make sure that the interior contained no surprises, and when he seemed satisfied on that score, he gave a rough gesture to let Steve know he could get out. Steve opened the door in an unhurried movement, got out and stood up next to his car.

"Who are you looking for?" asked the *gitano*, in a tone that could hardly be described as friendly.

"Chano."

"You won't find him here. Better go back where you came from, if you want to get out in one piece."

"Tell him Dariet is looking for him. I need to talk to him," Steve replied, taking no notice of the threat.

The gypsy gave him a contemptuous look and seemed to mutter an insult or a threat under his breath. He looked Steve in the eye, spat on the ground and turned on his heel, making his way towards a group of men who had come out of one of the buildings and were gazing at them intently with suspicion.

Steve kept his cool. He knew that this was all part of the *gitano* security ritual, but all the same he was aware that he was taking a risk. These were no empty threats.

The men seemed to have a brief discussion until one of them took out a walkie-talkie and sent the message, awaiting instructions.

A few moments later, someone emerged from behind the group of men that were still keeping a suspicious eye on him. In the gloom of sunset Steve could only make out the profile of the figure, which was moving towards him with a slow, measured pace. As he passed the BMW, his fingers slid gently over the bonnet without taking his eyes off the person he had come to look for.

A quick flash of gold on the wrist and the gold crucifix on his chest told Steve that Chano had come out to meet him.

Without taking his eyes off his visitor, Chano stopped in front of him. The gap between them was so small that he could feel his breath. For a few seconds that seemed like hours, they held each other's gaze in a piercing silence.

Chano made a slight movement of his head and smoothed his hair back with his left hand. Suddenly, for no apparent reason, he landed Steve an unexpected blow in the stomach, which made Steve double up in agony, leaning forward and falling onto his knees. Instinctively he clutched his stomach and stayed still, lowering his eyes and looking at the ground as a sign of respect.

In pain and struggling to stay calm, Steve waited.

Soon, with the same right hand that had landed the well-aimed blow, Chano took out his favourite Sevillian knife. The combination of its huge, silver-plated steel blade, which could cut a watermelon in two with a single blow, and its black handle made it very elegant and dangerous. He opened it in a leisurely fashion and slid the cold blade over Steve's right cheek, leaving the tip as sharp as a scalpel resting gently just below his left eye.

Without moving his hand, which with a rapid movement could leave Steve blind or cut his throat, Chano leant towards Steve and, in a very low voice, whispered something in his ear that he alone could hear.

"It wasn't my people; it was the fair haired men. You'll soon find them, because they're looking for you. They followed you here, and they're watching us. If I hadn't humiliated you like this, we'd probably both be dead this very night. Take care, Dariet. Go with God, and may *Sara la Negra* protect you. You're going to need her."

Santa Sara la Negra was the patron of the gypsies, but Chano also called his Magnum .44 Blackhawk by the same name. He had both of them for protection.

Without a word, Steve slowly straightened up and got into his car, under the inscrutable gaze of Chano, who continued to stand tall in the same spot, showing that he was lord and master of Las Albarizias for anyone who wanted to see. Including the hard faced blond men watching from the distance.

X

CHANO'S WORDS WERE STILL resounding in Steve's head when he got back onto the N-340 and, glancing in his rear view mirror, saw a navy blue Porsche Cayenne driven by a man who, from the almost thirty metres that separated them, could have had fair hair.

That alone was enough to show him that Chano was right and knew what he was talking about. Steve took his warning seriously.

At first, he tried to get rid of his followers by making sudden sharp turns as he went in and out of the town. Given enough time, perhaps some blockage in the central zone might come between them. But it wasn't to be. He couldn't get rid of them, but they didn't get too near him, either. They just wanted Steve to know he was being followed.

They must have followed me from the hospital, he thought, while trying to shake them off. The last thing he wanted was for them to find out where he lived. He made a lightning decision to leave the town again and make for a cheap motel, near a beach that he knew very well. If they wanted to come for him, he would be ready for them.

After checking in at reception, he made his way to room 5. He parked the car right in front, so he could easily keep an eye on it. As soon as the door closed behind him, he took out his .38 Special and looked very discreetly through the window, hardly moving the heavy curtain so as not to be seen.

The Cayenne was at the other side of the car park. Although they were fifty metres away, he could see them very clearly in the yellowy orange light of a street lamp. There were three of them, two in the front and one in the back.

They had stopped, but they had left their side-lights on. The engine must still be running.

If they don't mind being seen, it's because they're not going to attack. That's a sort of warning, he thought, trying to keep calm.

After about ten minutes, they turned round and drove behind his car, directing a threatening look towards his room. Then they went back the way they had come.

Steve gently drew back the curtain, and for a few brief seconds his gaze met that of the man who was sitting in the back. Message received.

By eleven-thirty, everything was quiet, but Steve was still barricaded in behind a wardrobe blocking the doorway. He positioned himself in an armchair just opposite the main door, gun in hand, ready to fire on anyone who tried to get in uninvited.

Eventually he got up, went out and headed for the corridor, linking all the rooms, that led to the car park. He went down the steps and scouted round very stealthily, pistol in hand, ready to fire if he had to.

"They've gone," he muttered to himself. "For some reason they only want to scare me off. Well, we'll see about that. Tomorrow is another day."

Returning to his room, he barred the door, tipped up a chair and wedged it under the door handle to stop anyone from trying to force their way in. He lay down on the bed fully clothed and tried to rest. He laid the .38 on his bedside table and slept fitfully.

It was at half past three in the morning when a loud bang, blast and flash immediately following the explosion made him jump to his feet.

Stunned and confused, he grabbed his weapon and threw himself to the floor.

It came from the car park, but it had been a very close shave. He heard voices coming from outside, people running around and shouting. He went up to the window and looked outside, only to see his Audi A3 a mass of bright flames.

Message received, he thought. *These Poles, or whoever they are, may not speak the language, but they know how to make themselves understood.*

The warning was clear. They weren't planning to get rid of him, at least not that night. They just wanted Steve to piss off.

The sound of a small crowd gathering round the funeral pyre that was still giving off smoke from burning metal and rubber, combined with the arrival of the fire brigade and the police, would prevent him from getting any rest.

Without a second thought, he phoned for a taxi and went home. He had to calm down and get some sleep so he could think about it all more clearly.

Before going to bed Steve texted Chris. "*Due to new developments, I won't be able to pick you up from the airport. I'll explain you tomorrow. Sorry mate. S*"

What happened that day was only a foretaste of what was to come.

XI

IT WAS NOON and the sun was at the zenith in all its glory, making feel his scorching magnificence to all living creatures under the Mediterranean sky. Sweat clung stubbornly to Steve's damp forehead and the creases in his cotton shirt, which left a trace of every movement he had made that day.

He headed to the hospital to hear the latest news on Johnny.

Chris was there, looking drawn and haggard. After receiving that first call about from the hospital, he had gone for almost twenty hours without a wink of sleep. Moira had gone to the hotel to rest and was due back any time now to renew her vigil.

"Any news about Johnny?" asked Steve.

"They say his condition is still stable, but he hasn't regained consciousness," Chris told Steve.

"That's not so bad, then. How's his mother doing?"

"As well as can be expected, given the circumstances."

"I'm glad to hear it."

"She won't talk about anything except Johnny and her faith in his future. She feels very ashamed and blames herself for what happened. Last night she swore this time she was determined to quit once and for all. We'll see…that's what they all say."

"I'd like to see it. It's easier said than done," said Steve.

"And how about you? What about the developments you mentioned in your text?"

"In a nutshell, yesterday I was warned off by a contact and given a punch in the guts. After that, some people I don't know followed me and set fire to the car I'd just bought. Apart from that, everything's fine, no complaints at all!" replied Steve, pretending to stay cool.

"You're joking!"

"There seems to be a bit more to this than a straightforward case of an overdose Chris. Someone is trying to stop the investigation for some reason that I can't figure out. I must talk to Johnny as soon as he comes out of his coma. I need to find out what happened that night."

"I don't think he'll be in a fit state to talk for a while, even supposing that everything goes well and he pulls out of it," said Chris.

"There's a lot I don't understand in all this mate. Why did he take the drugs when he was recovering so well? It doesn't make any sense."

"I keep asking myself the same question. I'm really surprised. He was growing more confident; he had definite plans for when he got back home, and he suddenly throws it all overboard in a couple of hours. That's very rare," Chris replied thoughtfully.

"He called me just before he went to the party. We talked about the risk, but he told me not to worry. I didn't pick up anything unusual or hesitant in his tone of voice or his way of speaking. I have some experience in this kind of thing. I really didn't notice anything to worry about," Steve told him.

"Was he on his own?"

"He said he was going with an American lad whom he'd gotten to know in a peer group meeting. Apparently this boy had a girlfriend, Carol, who came over to see him from Florida. It seemed a bit unusual to me, but if she was in the same group, I assumed it was a safe contact."

"I didn't know anything about that," said Chris surprised.

"Yes, it's the other boy, the one they couldn't save. We've got to find Carol. She must know something."

"Yesterday night someone called asking after Johnny. She spoke to the duty nurse and said she was upset about what had happened and wanted to co-operate with the investigation," said Chris trying to make sense of the intriguing call.

"That must be Carol. You seem to have got hold of more information than I have, for all the punches and the car that I'd just got used to. How did you find out about her?" Steve asked, trying to avoid a professional manner.

"The nurse," answered Chris.

"Maca? The little plump one?"

"Yes."

The old friends exchanged knowing glances and laughed.

A few hours later, during the routine update to patient's relatives and friends, Maca told them that the doctors had taken Johnny off the ventilator. He was breathing normally by himself, and this was a good sign, a very important step forward. They hadn't yet received the results from the lab, but she promised to let them know as soon as they arrived.

"Thanks very much," said Chris. "You've taken a load off our minds."

"My pleasure," Maca replied, with a wink and a broad smile, as she closed the door.

"She's all yours," joked Steve. "You're doing a great job. We need someone of our own on the inside."

"Stop fucking around man," Chris replied with a sour glance.

XII

THE NEXT DAY when he turned up unexpectedly to Romero's office, Steve found him reading through a thick file as he sipped his coffee. To his right the rays of the early morning sun were pouring through a wide window, bursting onto the cedar desk and reflecting a diffuse, almond-coloured glow onto the white walls.

The classic furniture, with its darkly glowing lustre, burgundy leather armchairs, easy chairs, cabinets, leafy ferns, crimson carnations and Murillo replicas, was in sharp contrast with the austere simplicity of offices where other police chiefs worked in Northern European countries. But this was Andalusia, the South, the Mediterranean....

Romero abruptly broke off from his work and rose to his feet to greet his colleague and friend. "Hello, Steve, do you fancy having a *bocadillo* with me?" he said, inviting him to share his thirty-minute mid-morning break for coffee and snacks Spaniards usually have after mid morning. His long lunch break would come three hours later.

They made their way to the interior courtyard on the ground floor, cool in the shadow of the building and the plants.

"How are you doing, *amigo*?" Romero asked him.

"Surviving," answered Steve.

"Oh, yes, the blond-haired thugs. Well, I think they were just trying to scare you, so you'd get out of their way. If they'd intended anything more serious, you probably wouldn't be having breakfast with me now."

"That's what I thought. But I'm rather puzzled by it. In normal circumstances they'd have disappeared immediately. Why would they hang around to threaten me? How did they get the idea that I was involved with this case?"

"You're right. We don't know these people; they probably came from somewhere in Eastern Europe," Romero mused.

"Chano warned me. He knows something."

"Our friend Chano always knows much more than he lets on. That's why he's still alive."

"Any leads?" Steve asked.

"Not at the moment. We know they're not from round here; they have nothing to do with Chano or any of the other Russian bosses around here. That lot know the rules of the game. These deaths attracted media attention, and that's very bad for all business."

"I know," replied Steve.

"Marbella is no longer the glamorous place it used to be twenty years ago; even the French Riviera isn't any more," said Romero. "We've all been overtaken by the Italians. That's where it's all happening. At the moment.... All we've got left is middle-class German and English tourists and a few well-off upper-class ones, who don't move outside the closed circles of their golf and their mansions."

"Not forgetting to count some of your old acquaintances who turned Costa del Sol into Costa del Crime," added Steve.

"Bah, there's always someone like that," said Romero. "As long as they don't commit any crimes here, I regard them as peaceful residents, until they prove the contrary or I'm given an arrest warrant for them."

"OK, so none of them are involved?" said Steven sipping his coffee but without taking his eyes off Romero.

"There isn't the slightest indication that that's the case."

"So who are these men, and who are they working for?"

"I don't know, but I'm going to find out. We're working on it. Someone's bound to talk soon. Chano has promised to share anything he finds out. He wants them out of here as well. In this situation we work together."

Steve needed more detailed information, but he could see that the conversation wasn't leading anywhere; and for the moment, Romero seemed unsure as to whether to tell him everything he knew. Using his best manners, Steve quickly finished off his Serrano ham sandwich and drank the last drop of coffee. "Thanks for the coffee and for sharing your liberal point of view with me," he said.

"Don't call me that, Steve. I'm not a liberal at all. My father was assassinated by the reds towards the end of the Civil War."

"Sorry, Romero, I had no idea...."

"It's OK. Not a problem. A misunderstanding. I'm a pragmatist – at least, I try to be," replied Romero, still upset as he struggled with the last slice of fried chorizo before he gulped it down.

"You mean you're a pragmatic conservative."

"Exactly, you've got it. I'm not dogmatic. I'm flexible as far as possible."

"Sounds good to me. In our trade, pragmatists get to live longer."

"There is something more, Steve," Romero added, wiping his lips with an immaculate white linen napkin.

"OK, shoot."

"You remember I mentioned the death of a child in Estepona?"

"Yes, and...?"

"The drug that killed the child seems similar to the one that your *guiris* took. The mother, a prostitute by profession, says that a casual client gave it to her as a tip. She didn't know him, and he never came back to see her again, but she is sure that he was a Latvian, like herself."

"Interesting."

"We don't know what was in the pill, but it could be the same drug that the American boy's girlfriend handed in to us."

"Carol?"

"Yes, that's her. According to Carol, her boyfriend was given the drugs free during the rave."

"I see; they were handing small amounts to a few people. I don't think they were planning to start dealing – that would have been very obvious and very dangerous. Possibly it was something new that they were trying out," reasoned Steve.

"Exactly. That's the hypothesis we're working on. A marketing trial that went wrong. Carol doesn't know who provided it, but she saw her boyfriend talking to a large, fair-haired man with a red, sunburned face a little while before the accident. Carol doesn't take drugs, and because of this she got annoyed and went back to the hotel when her boyfriend got high. Without him noticing, she managed to take two pills from his pocket when he was high," said Romero.

"Do you know how many young people took those pills during the party?"

"No; it's very difficult to find out with any certainty, because no one wants to incriminate themselves. All I can be sure of is that there are no other victims, either dead or poisoned."

"Do you think Carol would know the dealers again?"

"Yes, I think so, but we have to catch them first. I can't see them coming back to look for any reason."

"We need to talk to Carol again."

"One more thing," Romero added. "It's about Johnny."

"What about him?" asked Steve.

"Johnny didn't slip. It was the other boy. He put two pills in Johnny's drink without him noticing it, for a joke."

"Some joke."

"Carol was really disgusted, and although she was worried, she felt there was nothing she could do to stop him and decided to go back to the hotel. She had no idea what was going to happen. She thought it was ecstasy. Now she feels guilty, because she feels she ought to have warned Johnny."

"Too right."

"Don't be hard on her, Dariet. They're kids; she didn't know who Johnny was, and she had no idea what would happen," said Romero, as if apologising for her. "They have no idea of the risks they are running when they take stuff they don't know about."

"Thanks, Romero. Keep me up to speed, and please let me know if the chemists find out the kind of drug we are looking at. It might help to speed up Johnny's recovery."

"Sure I will, don't worry."

"This is all turning out to be more difficult than I thought."

"My dear Steve, life is always more difficult than one thinks," pronounced Romero, as he shook his hand with a broad smile. "Otherwise, everything would be very boring and predictable. *Vaya con Dios.*"

XIII

ONE DAY FOLLOWED ANOTHER, hot, humid and full of uncertainty.

Steve didn't stop going to the hospital to keep his friends company and to get briefed on Johnny's condition. He would go in through the gardens that surrounded the main entrance, flanked with blue columns, leading to the spacious white marble reception area. From there he would make his way to the intensive care unit, where Chris and Moira were looking after Johnny.

She wasn't tall, but she wasn't short either, neither fat nor thin. It would be difficult to describe her physical appearance; being so nondescript meant she escaped unnoticed in any group of people, large or small.

Moira had mousy, fair shoulder-length hair that made her look thinner than she actually was. Her figure was conventional; she wore a meek expression, and she usually dressed in plain colours that stood out as little as possible. This made her almost invisible among the Andalusians around her, who were constantly gesticulating, all talking at the same time at the tops of their voices. Moira stayed impassive in her corner, not saying a word, awaiting the slightest sign of encouragement from Maca. Only the anxiety in her green eyes could reveal that the vigil was taking its toll.

When Steve saw her for the first time, her extreme shyness made him nervous. Instinctively he tried to comfort her, twice placing his hand on her shoulder, as much to reassure himself that he was talking to a real flesh-and-blood person and not a shadow. But in time he came to realise that first impressions could be deceptive.

Shortly after his arrival Moira filled him in on the latest medical bulletin. Then they waited together, sometimes in silence, sometimes reflecting on life, at others laughing together gently.

"I'm in no position to criticise my son, Mr Dariet," Moira said at one point, with a formality and respect that made Steve feel awkward.

"Don't be so hard on yourself; you did the best you could for him. Life hasn't been a joyful ride for you either. It was your taking him in for treatment that made Johnny get better. And Chris has done a great job. This was just...bad luck," Steve answered, trying to cheer her up.

"I've been so blind for such a long time."

"If I had a quid for every idiotic thing I've done, I'd be a millionaire by now. Stop blaming yourself, Moira; it doesn't help. Look to the future; soon Johnny will be well again and getting on with his plans."

Moira was going through hell, but she was hoping for redemption. Johnny was the one thing she had to hold onto in her life, and it wasn't hard to imagine what would happen to her if she lost him. He was the faltering flame that still kept her going. With head bent and downcast eyes, she would stare at the ground as the tears rolled silently down her cheeks, fists tightly clenched. Only when Maca brought some good news did her face light up.

During the few scarce moments they were allowed in to see Johnny, Steve had seen her caress her son gently as she lovingly gazed at him. It was at one of those moments that he noted with surprise that caring for Johnny was making her come alive, healing her soul.

Why do some people feel closer to life when they come face to face with death? he wondered.

Before his very eyes, which he thought had seen everything, Steve could see life starting to flourish in what not long before had been barren ground. So it came about that he started to get to know another Moira beneath the appearance and preconceptions that many addicts give rise to. Moira the mother. Moira the human being, hiding behind the *junkie* stereotype.

The love for her son made it easier removing her addict mask, setting her free from old painful memories.

It was an unusual experience for Steve. He had never felt emotionally involved with the cases he had to manage before. He was a pro. He could deal with indignation, anger or even rage. He had been trained to manage it. Those emotions put him on guard, arousing the hunting instincts that kept him alive.

Moira had no idea of the thoughts that were passing through Steve's mind, like a chaotic display of fireworks on a starry night. She hardly gave him a thought. Her mind was entirely fixed on Johnny.

Moira's heart only had room for hope, whereas Steve could recognise only his thirst for justice. For him, anger was still stronger than love or compassion.

XIV

OVER THE PAST FEW DAYS, Steve had tried to get in touch with Romero, but without success. Text messages, calls to his office and two e-mails had been in vain. This lack of response was suspicious. Given Romero's usual politeness and formality, his silence spoke louder than words. Something had happened. Romero couldn't talk. A week later Steve decided to take drastic action and go and see him in person, prepared to put up with a long wait as he hadn't made an appointment.

He was wrong.

"Come in, Señor Dariet; the inspector has been expecting you for two days now!" the secretary welcomed him cordially, as she opened the door of the office for him. Taken aback, Steve went through.

Romero welcomed him with a smile, this time without rising from his comfortable armchair behind the desk. "My dear friend, what's kept you?" he exclaimed.

"I'm sorry; it took me a few days to understand your message. What's happened?"

"I don't know; all the documents and files from the case have been requisitioned by Headquarters in Madrid. We welcome their help, but this is as far as we can go. Any new development will have to be passed on to the Central as a matter of urgency. From now on, they are in charge."

"Why?" Steve asked.

"My dear Steve, a long time ago I learnt that: *Ask no questions...*"

"*...and you'll be told no lies,*" Steve finished the saying for him.

"Exactly! You're a professional like me and all our colleagues in the capital," Romero went on, raising his voice, almost jocular, as he passed a note over the desk top to Steve with a broad wink.

Steve took the little white envelope and put it in his pocket without as much as a glance.

Someone was listening and possibly recording their conversation.

"I quite understand, it's just the same in London. Don't worry about it," Steve replied.

"Unfortunately, now I only hold a watching brief on this case. From now on, you'll have to get your information from London. You know the procedure," said Romero.

"Sure. Anyhow, it isn't my case. I'm retired, and I'm only trying to keep the family up-to-date," Steve replied.

"Then we'll let our colleagues take charge of the rest," replied Romero with a conspiratorial look. "From my point of view, they're doing me a favour. One thing less to bother with," he concluded, smiling insincerely.

"You're quite right. The only thing I've got out of this is a burnt-out car. Now I'll try to get the money back from the insurance and go back to minding my own business. The bottom line is, that's why I came to Marbella in the first place. I have to learn to enjoy my newfound freedom," Steve replied, going along with the game. "Thanks for everything, Romero. I'll tell the family that everything is in hand and that the perpetrators will soon be caught."

"You're welcome, Steve. And don't worry about it. Central will do a good job, as always." Romero's final words were not without a touch of irony as he accompanied Steve to the door of his office to see him out.

When they got to the door, he bent forward slightly to put his arm round Steve and whispered in his ear, "Take care; even Chano is scared. Burn the envelope after you've read it."

Then, raising his voice, "*Vaya con Dios,* Dariet."

"*Gracias,* Romero. One of these days we'll go for a drink together. *Adios,*" said Steve, in a farewell tone, as he winked back, and the door closed behind him. Steve walked out with a measured pace, relaxed and smiling affably at everyone he knew. He wanted to create the impression that nothing was bothering, him in case someone was watching.

As soon as he left the police station, he hailed a taxi and went straight back to his apartment, without making any calls from his mobile and restraining himself from opening the envelope.

Only once he was inside his apartment and had helped himself to a Scotch did he sink down onto the living room sofa and open the letter Romero had passed to him with such secrecy.

As he did so he saw a handwritten note in blue ink and a small vacuum-sealed packet of transparent plastic, containing a small quantity of clear grey powder.

Without any preamble, Romero had written:

Estepona: Lab results show a substance similar to morphine. It's a new drug that we know nothing about. They also found mephedrone, synthetic cannabis and diazepam in small quantities.

The same drugs were in the pills that Carol handed over to us.

The same drugs and concentrations were found in Johnny's blood.

The pills were sent from Seville to Madrid for analysis, but I saved one as a present for you. Perhaps your people can find out something else. If so, let me know.

The blond haired men have disappeared. They're not on my patch any more.

Take care and good luck!

Hardly had Steve finished reading the note when he got up and took it to the kitchen, where he set fire to it. Gathering up all the ashes, he threw them into the sink and ran water on them. He didn't want to take any risk that would affect his friend Romero.

Deep in thought, he went back to the sofa, picked up his glass of pure malt whisky once again and drank a large slug, almost without noticing.

It was at that precise moment that his mobile phone began to ring. Not the one he normally used in Marbella, but the other one. The one with the encrypted line that only his London colleagues could call.

"Hello, Steve, this is Mike. Remember me?"

Steve was not amused by the irony of the man who had been his boss for fifteen years, and answered stiffly, "Hello, Mike, what a pleasure to hear your voice."

"How are you?" Mike asked.

"Very well, thanks, and you?"

"Can't complain; getting on with my work, as always."

"Always working, you mean!" Steve corrected.

"It's the same thing, isn't it?"

"No, Mike, it's not the same thing. I don't need to be always working. Don't you know there's another life outside here?"

"Steve, Steve, you're starting to sound like my first wife."

"Is there some problem back home?" asked Steve, interrupting him drily.

"I'm sorry about the Johnny affair. He's very young, but he'll get over it all right."

Although it shouldn't have surprised him, it wasn't possible that Mike would know about Johnny if there wasn't something important going on. The whole business kept on spreading out its tentacles like an oil slick in the sea. It seemed to have no limits. "How do you know about it?" Steve asked.

"That's our job, Steve, don't you remember? Here we know everything…about everything."

"Thanks for asking. Johnny is recovering slowly, but as you will already know, he should pull through."

"I'm glad. Sincerely, I'm very glad." The word *sincerely* sounded strange coming from Mike. It was almost a contradiction in terms. "I've got something for you, Steve," he went on.

"No thanks, Mike. Not at the moment. I can't…"

"Listen, mate," Mike interrupted him without a trace of politeness and cut straight to the point. "I only want you to carry on with what you've been doing, but working for your old friends. This is bigger than you think. You'll need our support and protection, and we need you. You can't do this on your own. I'm sorry."

"Do you need information?" Steve asked.

"I've got enough, Steve, but we need something more."

"Who's the 'we' this time?"

"Your old family and some American cousins."

"Hmm…" Steve frowned and bit his lip. "What are my options, Mike?"

"Basically, accept my offer or get out of the way and forget this whole business. You know how it is when other agencies are involved."

"Thanks for reminding me of the limits to my freedom, Mike."

"Forget it. Come to London next week. We'll meet other family members."

"OK."

"We'll be discussing some aspects of this operation. You'll only be told what you need to know to carry out your mission. Nothing else."

"Only what I need to know."

"You know the rules, Steve."

"This is serious," Steve commented.

"I already told you that. Sometimes a limited knowledge is good for the health. You don't have to worry about things that are outside our remit."

"Let me worry about my own safety, Mike. I'll see you next week. Bye for now."

"Fine. That's my boy. Call me when you get here. Good-bye."

"I'm not yours or anyone else's," Steve muttered to himself, hurling the mobile phone onto the sofa.

PART II

*Methamphetamine, Black Mamba and
a lady from Massachusetts*

XV

MANY VISITORS TO LONDON think that the Big Ben, Tower Bridge, Buckingham Palace and other tourist attractions characterise it as much as the wet weather, but this can be a misleading stereotype in the summer. Heat and humidity aren't so good if you have to endure them away from the beach, swimming pool or air conditioning. London is geared up for cold and rain but not for a heat wave that can become oppressive.

But after a thirty-minute car drive north, in the suburb of the city where Mike's safe house was located, the air became a little less stifling. That was where meetings were held to launch special operations, his idea being that the agents should get to cover the ground from the start as they coordinated their roles.

It was a family house, surrounded by many others just like it, with parking space for two cars in the front and a small garden at the rear. Even the name of the street where it stood, Poets Corner, seemed to have been chosen as a cover for the activities that now took place there.

Actually, the safe house was three houses. Two at the front, with separate exteriors but converted to one on the inside, and another at the back, with an exit to a different street.

Most of the neighbours were young, professional couples who worked in the city and just came back home to sleep, amidst a little more space and a bit of green that they couldn't possibly have bought for the same money in Central London.

The homes were mostly Victorian terraced houses, mass produced, beginning on twentieth-century lines and renovated frequently through the years, though always carefully keeping to the same exterior style: red bricks, white walls and black slate tiles.

A cursory glance would show nothing to suggest that the safe house was any different from the rest, if it weren't for the fact that a little rear garden linked it to the adjoining house at the rear. The advantage was the exit to both streets. Nobody knew when it might be needed.

Another distinguishing feature that was hidden from view was the large basement, running the whole length of the building, doubling the available space that could be seen from outside. This was the bunker used to store arms, ammunitions and communications equipment. There was also a small strong room, with concrete walls reinforced with steel that could be used as a last resort – or to intimidate certain "guests" and get them to "sing." The rest of the house wasn't much different from the rest of the neighbourhood, apart from its décor and function.

On arrival, Steve gave his name and was immediately taken to the first floor, where Mike was expecting him. The atmosphere was almost informal. Three or four agents, all under thirty, looking fit in shorts, sneakers, socks and neatly mended polo shirts.

Steve thought that there couldn't be any "guests" in the house at the moment, so this must be a new operation in its early stages.

After a brief welcome, Mike took him to the conference room, where the other agents awaited them, sitting round a large, rectangular conference table, surrounded by ten comfortable chairs with black leather upholstery.

The fact that he had arrived on time but was the last to join the group led him to suspect that he was only taking part in the second half of a meeting that had started earlier.

Apart from some small bottles of mineral water with soda, glasses and coasters, there was nothing else on the table. The three empty bottles led him to believe that the meeting couldn't have been going on for more than an hour.

"Excellent, now we're all here, let's start with introductions," said Mike. "You already know who I am. Steve Dariet is the officer who will lead the operation on our side. James Stinger of OCA1 will keep us up to date on financial, political and a few other aspects, but none of his agents will be taking part in field operations. Agent Alison Riley represents our American colleagues from DTF (Drug Trafficking and Firearms) and will contribute technical, logistical and personnel information in operations outside the UK."

Steve said nothing but allowed himself a hint of a smile and inclined his head, his colleagues returning the same welcoming gesture.

"Let's start from the beginning," Mike continued. "Ali, if you would be so kind...."

Without more ado, Ali began to read her brief. "Five years ago, an important business meeting took place at the Burlington House Club in London...."

Ali was an attractive woman, not just on account of her features alone but because of the balance she displayed between beauty and intelligence. Steve listened to her attentively, trying to concentrate on what she was saying and drive inappropriate thoughts out of his mind.

Ali's temperament was calm and rational, and although she was capable of occasional passionate outbursts, they never got in the way of her reason.

She was wearing a designer suit, light indigo in colour, which set off her fair, straight hair and deep blue eyes to perfection. The care she took over her appearance down to the last detail revealed the attention she paid to the little things as well as the overall picture.

Perhaps it was the damp glow with which the morning rain had bathed her cheeks, leaving them soft and smooth. Or who knows what combination in the light of the room, mixing the sun's rays shining through the window and penetrating the white net curtains, lent a particular sheen that highlighted her delicate features, making her seem even younger than she actually was.

Whatever the cause, it wasn't easy for Steve to keep his professional detachment. He kept his gaze on her while avoiding direct eye contact. To catch her eye might have caused her to blush, and that would have been disastrous and humiliating.

"His guests were five international brokers who had access to funds in America, Europe and Asia," she said. "In the course of the meeting, Render announced that he was on the point of producing a drug that could generate billions, if it were put on the market at the right time." Ali continued describing Render's proposal in detail, taking care not to give away the source of such precise and detailed information.

During her presentation, Ali paused to sip mineral water from the glass in front of her. After she had finished, she replaced it on exactly the same small ring of damp that was left when she picked it up from the coaster. Steve couldn't help noticing this detail. Together with the impeccable tailored suit she was wearing, he thought it revealed a perfectionist streak in her personality.

"But if Render was working on a new morphine antagonist, how is it that he discovered the opposite?" Mike abruptly interrupted the presentation with his question.

"The answer is complicated, but I'll try to make it simple. Morphine exerts its effect by binding on to a series of specific receptors in the brain, the spinal cord and other organs. Think of the receptors as locks that have to open up to produce an effect, and morphine or other similar drugs as keys that can open up these locks. In order to inhibit some specific morphine effects you have to block the specific receptors/locks. Render was working on 'alternative keys' for these locks, extremely specific keys/drugs that could be used just to produce stimulant effects, but at the same time, preventing the dangerous ones, such as respiratory arrest, to happen by keeping their receptors/ locks blocked.

"This was all being developed using three dimensional computer modelling. In the process, Render built an original algorithm that led him to something unexpected, an ideal morphine, something approaching a real-life version of Huxley's *Soma*. Render thought he had found a very specific morphine-like drug that would induce a pleasurable sedation and prevent overdose risk. The potential value of his discovery was obvious."

"And he made it." Mike completed the sentence for her with an air of astonishment and admiration.

"Well, not exactly, and that's the problem," Ali replied. "He thought he had discovered a drug that was as powerful as morphine or heroin but as safe as candy. However, this wasn't the case."

"A very interesting and marketable sweet," said Steve.

"Dr Render started off by financing the investigation out of his own pocket for as long as he could, but his funds ran out before he could finalise the product. That's very expensive and needs many millions of dollars."

"He needed a little help from his friends...."

"Effectively, help of thirty million that could be called little in relation to the potential value of the product.

"It wasn't long before his potential investors began to ask specific questions about the product, and discuss investment formulas and business plans. From the beginning Render made it clear that he would only deal with two of them, no more. He thought that more than three partners was too many for this type of business. Three partners can make decisions very quickly, and if there are two contrary opinions, the third partner can have the deciding vote.

"After several months of tough negotiations, Render finally reached agreement with Newton Crowe of Morgan-Crowe-Sullivan associates in Long Beach, California, and with Werner Jurgen of Global Ventures Fund in Zurich, Switzerland. Each of them would pay fifteen million dollars as a deposit."

"So did Render sell his product for thirty million?" asked Mike, as he took notes.

"No." James spoke emphatically. "Allow me, Ali; this is where we come in."

"Sure, no problem."

"This aspect of the operation is important if we are to understand how Render managed to increase his profits quickly. The thirty million he asked for was only to get the first option for buying thirty-three-and-a-half per cent of the product at market value in two years time, when the research and marketing operations were sufficiently advanced. At that time, Render would sell three per cent of the shares in the new drug. It would be the market who will establish the final price that his partners would have to pay to buy their shares, minus the advance that they had already paid for the first option. This advance of thirty million would allow Render to finance and develop the drug for those two years, and the rest would be pure profit."

"By the end of the two years, everything was going very well," James went on, "and the experts talked of nothing but the advances in research and the importance of the project. At this point Render succeeded in selling his three per cent for three-point-six million, which automatically put a value of one hundred twenty million dollars on the project. His partners had to pay each forty-point-two million, deducting the fifteen million they had put up front. At this point Render had made eighty-four-point-three million that he could use to complete the project and make a huge profit. He also kept his thirty per cent of the shares and became the director general of the Virin Project, as he decided to call it. Any questions?"

Steve listened attentively, frowning with concentration and stroking his chin, as he tried to imagine what one hundred twenty million dollars would look like in small-denomination bank notes. Absolutely not a profound thought, in fact quite idiotic, but it was little things like this that used to help him keep his feet on the ground when unusually large figures or quantities were being discussed.

"Render seems be much more than a mere scientist," he commented.

"This is even bigger, Steve," James continued. "The operation entailed a degree of risk, and, as you know, without taking some risks you get nowhere. But Newton and Jurgen make risk their business. They use complex systems and processes to manage the risk in their investments. The financial mechanisms of leverage or increasing the value of investments are as complicated as the marketing operations that often accompany them. So Render contracted three medical authors to publish at least twenty-four papers a year in the main medical and pharmaceutical reviews in Europe and America. Constant references to Virin in the specialist media attracted more interest from investors all the time. About that time a *blue chip* from the sector opened up negotiations that concluded with the signing of a memorandum of intention to buy the entire Virin project when it was finished. Render and his associates started to think they were no longer looking at millions, but at billions. This memorandum, although secret, would increase the value of all the other projects that Render was involved in. The sky would be the limit for the value of Render's enterprises."

"So it seems the memorandum wasn't such a secret, after all," said Steve.

"It was, until they decided to go public with it a year later. That was a very interesting business decision that both sides did well out on. Even though that big pharmaceutical company hadn't yet paid a single dollar, the very fact of letting the market know that they would be in charge of a drug with such potential raised the shares value immediately. Hundreds of millions started to circulate around the fringes of Virin before the project would become a drug approved by the United States Food and Drug Administration."

"Smoke and mirrors...pure speculation," said Steve.

"One more to add to the many that fill the business world. If the highest-value enterprises in the world operate in virtual space like the Internet and consist of intangible goods called software, what are you surprised at? Nowadays nobody buys anything thinking of its current value, but what they think it will be worth tomorrow, or what they think they will make others believe it will worth tomorrow. It's a bet on the future," James replied.

"The value lies in the anticipation!" added Mike.

"More or less, instead of chips in a casino they operate with futures and derivatives" James said.

"Bits of paper..."

"No, that's old hat Steve. Today, all stock exchange transactions are electronic, many of them controlled by their own information systems that are designed to buy or sell in particular conditions. But the best thing of all is that those who place the bets never do it with their own money but with savings belonging to a lot of other people. If things go well, they win a lot of money, but if they don't, the government will bail them out of it with tax payers' money," James pronounced.

"Even if we don't like it, we all live off these bubbles and feed them. Render and his associates know the rules of the game and take advantage of them. You can hardly blame them," commented Steve acidly. "Many of these financial transactions are carried out in a murky grey area, and when a crime is committed, it's very hard to prove it," he finished, with an air of resignation.

"Think of Johnny, and many of these murky grey areas become clearer," Mike answered, with a knowing look.

"OK, we already know that Render financed his deal from my aunt's pension funds and that his drug has killed people. What else do you have? What has all this got to do with the deaths in Marbella?" asked Steve.

"As well as funds, Render needed time. He had promised to have the final product ready in around five years, but he advised them that the initial share value would be growing throughout that period" Ali said.

"And how did he think he could do this?" asked Steve.

"Throughout this period," replied Ali, "Render would continue to produce reports in various scientific and popular journals. He would also need distinguished professors and opinion makers to begin to mention the drug in their own publications and presentations at symposia and medical conferences. These pharmaceutical marketing ploys would attract interest from investors in biotechnology, pushing the price up even higher."

"All right, but I still don't understand what this has got to do with the American boy's death and Johnny still struggling for his life," Steve said.

"Plenty," Ali replied. "It wasn't just in Marbella and Estepona. We're investigating around forty-eight deaths in other cities in Northern and Central Europe. All related to the Virin project."

"But doesn't Virin create a safe addiction, so to speak?" Steve asked, his face showing bewilderment and some confusion.

"That was what Render meant to do, but in the process something went wrong, and he soon realised that he needed more time and money at his disposal to finance the project."

"What happened?" asked Steve.

"The mathematical and computer models, the sophisticated biochemical tests, studies with laboratory animals, appeared to show that the affinity of Virin with the appropriate receptors was very specific. However, when they started trials on humans, Virin didn't behave as expected. Although it didn't produce the side effects on the respiratory centre or other organs that could result in unpleasant symptoms or risk to life, Virin didn't produce the stimulation effect that the addicts were looking for, either. The more the dose was increased, the more the euphoric effects were blocked. Nobody would pay for such a useless drug. He needed more time and investment to develop it."

"Render is finished," observed Steve, lifting a glass of water to his lips.

"Render wasn't such a fool that he hadn't anticipated this possibility. He had a plan B that he had mentioned when he made his pitch at the Burlington dinner," Ali replied, revealing a touch of admiration for the man who had started all this mess. "Plan B was to sell Virin as a better version of the existing drugs that act as morphine blockers. Newton and Jurgen wouldn't get the profits they expected, but they would get back their investment in time. What Render failed to realise was that that wasn't an option. They could contain the economic losses and possibly break even, but what they couldn't tolerate was the loss of face in front of their clients, who had been promised a return ten times greater than their investment. No, Render's plan B wasn't an option."

James took over and briefly explained that brokers like Newton Crowe never took on losses due to the nature of the clients they dealt with. He went on to describe how they would make up for their losses and the risks of managing funds whose origins are shrouded in mystery. However, his explanation became too complex and abstract for Steve's taste, and eventually he broke in abruptly.

"Cut the crap, James. Come out with it and name names. We'll all be out there doing the job, and we need to know exactly who we'll be dealing with."

With a sigh, James seemed to look for a glance of approval from Mike, who, with a quick look of agreement, let him move on and show them data that could be useful for the field operations, although they could pose a threat to other international money laundering operations in which Steve wouldn't be involved.

"It's difficult to put a name to the money Newton controls, but we know that the funds come from an international bank based in Panama and Caicos, along with other very respectable banking sources in Mexico. The part of the fund that Jurgen controls gets investments from small banks in Eastern Europe and American biotechnology corporations, one of which is the CRO – Clinical Research Organisation – with an extensive net of laboratories run from Brussels and Amsterdam. There's also a small but significant amount of funds that come from private investors in the Middle East."

This news wasn't very encouraging. Still annoyed, Steve began to realise that the boundaries of this operation were extending much further afield than he had expected. "How far do you think they can go to get their money back?" he asked, unable to conceal his irritation.

"As far as they have to! But there's something else you need to know before we go on. When we started to investigate Jurgen and Newton, we realised that we have something in common: their clients. Some of them are our clients too. They are under investigation for laundering money coming from drugs and arms.

"We know that Brussels and Amsterdam Centrals are coordinating investigations into an extensive network of laboratories in Buenos Aires, Costa Rica, Caracas, Istanbul, Belgrade, St. Petersburg, Seoul and some North African cities," James went on. "This lets them launder the movement of people, money and drugs. All perfectly legal."

"It's not a very original scheme, but I have to admit I didn't know of that particular network," Ali commented.

"Up to now, we've no evidence that the investors have had any direct contact or participation with Render's operations or the Virin project, but we're still working on it," James concluded.

Mike was quick to remind them that even if there was no proof of it yet, from an operational point of view, they should assume it was so.

"That's a load off my mind, James. If the insurance doesn't pay up, I'll pass the bill for my car on to them." Steve spoke sarcastically but no one else smiled.

As the discussions went on, the objectives and risks of the mission became clear, but it still left a lot of unanswered questions; and Steve needed answers. "If their time's up for getting the results they promised, and they don't want to use Virin as it's been developed up to now, what options do they have?"

"We're not sure, but we think that for some reason, they're trying to modify the Virin molecule to reinforce its stimulating effects – to the detriment of those who think it is safe for consumption. That is something they could introduce into the market and quickly make a good return. In addition, only they know how to produce it, which would guarantee them an exclusive profit for a while," explained Ali, entering a realm of speculation in which she didn't feel very comfortable.

"Render's profile is one of an intelligent man, a risk taker, used to walking on a knife's edge, but always within the law. What do you think would push him over the edge?" asked Steve.

Ali thought that for some reason Render had reached the point of no return and from then on was working under pressure. He didn't have any option other than to accept the conditions imposed by Newton and Jurgen.

"OK, so we now have the basis to charge him and put him behind bars. I imagine that's what we're talking about. Catch him and arrest him. I doubt if there'll be much resistance; he'll be safer with us than his partners," concluded Steve.

"I'm afraid that won't be possible, Steve," murmured Mike in a serious tone of voice, looking down at the notebook in front of him.

"Why?"

"Because Render is dead," Ali replied drily.

XVI

THE ARRIVAL OF SANDWICHES, fruit, tea and coffee for a light refreshment break interrupted their discussions, reminding them that they had already spent three hours in the meeting, and the world outside was still turning. A world that business deals, ambition and greed made go round. A world that spun at a speed that made some people fall down, finding it almost impossible to stand up again, like Johnny's family; or even people like Render and Newton, when they lost control of the movement that they started.

Some people think that this is the price we pay for progress, the chaotic development of humanity, from which, all too often, the same few make the profit while many others pay the price. But the fact is that if Render hadn't thought of Virin first, someone else would have; and if he couldn't complete the project, someone else would.

Although Render and Johnny had never met, they were both products of the same system, although fate had assigned them different and predetermined roles.

As soon as Mike announced a short tea break and proposed to resume the meeting in thirty minutes, Ali got up and, reaching into her briefcase, took out her mobile phone. Watching her leave the room, Steve wondered whether she would be checking her calls, or who it was she had to speak to so urgently. She was surrounded by an unseen aura that seemed to keep her in some way aloof from the group, even though she was playing an active part in the organisation. In spite of the recommendations of his boss, Steve was not entirely convinced that she was to be trusted.

Ali was outside, probably talking to her boss, perhaps filling him on the details of the meeting or getting her orders. Meanwhile, James excused himself for a couple of minutes and went out for a cigarette in the garden. Mike and Steve were left alone in the conference room.

"I have to admit this is bigger than I thought, Mike."

"You do your bit, and leave the rest of it to the others. Your job and mine is to catch these people and bring them to Justice."

"Nick was an American citizen. Johnny is recovering, and the crime was committed under Spanish jurisdiction. Why don't we leave it to the Americans and the Spanish?"

"The American boy's mother is British, that's another reason for us to get involved."

"Don't give me that crap, Mike. What else is going on? Why I have to work with Ali?"

"Orders from higher up, very high up. The Spanish will do their bit, but the snakes' nest isn't there. This lot have come from a different territory."

"From where, exactly?"

"Various parts of Europe and Africa. I can't hope to get rid of all of them, but at least we can strike a blow at the heart of these great serpents that are poisoning our people and their backers. Ali needs proof to get Newton arrested."

"What do you know about her?"

"Not much, but she comes with very good references. She's good at what she does, very professional."

"There's more to this than meets the eye, Mike. I don't know what it is, but I can smell it. She's got a hidden agenda. She's working on it right now."

"And so what? Since when did you worry about hidden agendas? She's an agent the same as you are; she's got her orders, and she's carrying them out. There won't be any conflict of interests."

"How do you know that?"

As if to emphasise his point, Mike looked Steve straight in the eye, smiled and placed his right hand firmly on Steve's shoulder. "I know," he replied.

There was only one way to interpret Mike's gesture: accept the rules of the game or get out. Steve had to make a decision quickly, based only on his trust in his boss and his own instinct. Mike wasn't a friend of his, and he didn't particularly like him, but many years of working together had taught Steve that Mike was someone he could trust. Furthermore, to quit at a time like this, after he had accepted the proposal, was just not his style.

When the meeting reconvened, Ali told them that Render had died in a plane accident, when the Cessna 172 in which he was flying had crashed in the Colombian jungle north of Medellin, near the Sierra Nevada coast of Santa Marta. They didn't know what he had been doing there or what had caused the accident. That was something that was under investigation by her team. The terrain was very hard to access because of the jungle, the mountains, the guerrillas and the other armed groups that were operating independently in the area.

"A joint operation of one of our teams with Colombian army special forces managed to reach the site of the accident ten days later. It wasn't easy to find any remains, because by the time they got there, there wasn't much left to recover. Parts of the plane, Render's documents including his passport, his clothes and some burnt human remains were mixed up and scattered over a radius of five hundred metres.

"The local experts confirmed that this always happens, because whatever isn't finished off by vermin, the termites will get to in a matter of just a few hours.

"So that's it; there were a few remains stuck to some bits of clothing that we were able to analyse in our laboratories, and it showed a hundred per cent match with Render's DNA. As far as we're concerned, Dr Kurt Render is definitely dead," she concluded, placing the report she had been reading from onto a table top that was now littered with folded serviettes, fruit and scattered crumbs.

Ali then helped herself to a glass of water and remained silent.

"Is that all?" asked Steve.

"Yes, that's all that we know about him," Ali replied.

The mysterious Render was now a dead end. What had caused the deaths and who was backing him were questions that hovered in the air.

"We think that there must be a different version of Virin out there, more addictive and dangerous. They are trying it out and won't stop until they have recovered their investment. Someone has taken Render's place and is playing at filling his role of the old alchemist," said Mike.

Steve now understood his role with greater clarity: to find Render's substitute. But who could it be, and where could he find him or her?

"We'll be in charge of European operations. Ali and Steve will report directly to me, and I'll be communicating directly with Ali's boss. James will be our contact with OCA1's Financial Crime Department and will let us know of any new intelligence findings. Is that clear?" Mike said.

Silently, the three nodded their agreement.

Mike was a good professional, and he hadn't spent years on the job for nothing. He knew how to sum up a colleague's worth almost at first sight, like the synergy that was now beginning to work in a coordinated way between Steve and Ali.

After some discussion of various technical aspects of the operations and the agents taking part, they got to the point of looking at initial priorities.

"Does the name Mel Cooper mean anything to you?" asked Mike.

Apparently, none of those present had ever heard of him.

"I want to start with him. He used to be an old friend, very close to Render, and they went through a lot together, both personally and professionally. Cooper is a doctor."

"Do you know where we can find him?" asked Steve.

"That's quite simple. You'll find him in Helfen prison, where he's serving a long sentence for manslaughter. HMP Helfen is a high-security establishment."

Ali sighed, and Steve made a gesture that showed his disappointment. Render dead and his best friend in a high-security prison. All the paths seemed to lead to a dead end.

"Perhaps Cooper doesn't have any direct information, but he certainly knows more about Render than all of us put together. I've heard he's an intelligent man, though cynical and a bit twisted. He's not dangerous, or violent, but take care," Mike said staring at them with a penetrating look.

"Next I want you to go to Brussels and Amsterdam. Apart from seeing the tulips, you'll be able to gather local intelligence. We think that the drugs are being produced in some laboratory in the region, either above board or underground."

Steve suppressed a smile. Suddenly, the Venice of the North seemed an interesting place to visit with Ali. Another inappropriate thought, considering the circumstances.

"For the moment, that's the plan," Mike concluded. "We'll be deciding what comes next as the events unfold and we get more information."

Without further ado, Mike thanked them for coming and dismissed them, not forgetting to warn them of the possible risks, especially after what had happened to Steve in Marbella.

"Thanks for the warning, Mike, but in the last ten years, I've done much more than intelligence operations. I've been working in the field nearly all the time. If I'm lucky after this operation I'm hoping for a more peaceful life in DC, more meetings and fewer airports" Ali replied.

"That's what I had planned, but you never know," said Steve.

Ali slowly turned to face him, and with a broad smile, in which Steve perceived a touch of irony, she answered, "That's true, you never know."

She was right. Steve had no idea of what he was getting himself into.

XVII

In 1948, David Koperinsky arrived in England under the Polish Act of Settlement of 1947 that gave almost ten thousand Polish Jews who had fought under the British High Command the right to settle in Britain. The allied forces had won the war, but Great Britain had paid a very high price.

Memories of Montecasino were still fresh in his mind when he met Ruth. The battle for reconstruction had just begun when they decided to get married and carry on the struggle together as a family. Life was very hard, but they were young. After what they had been through in the last few years, even the area they settled in seemed like a bed of roses.

They were not well off, but their difficulties hardly showed at all as long as the rationing of food, clothing, furniture and fuel lasted. The clothes they wore made them practically indistinguishable from the rest, but they were happy.

In those years, very few differences were visible between neighbours; a strong community spirit bound them together across the divide.

Mel was the only son that Ruth had the joy of giving birth to and feeding at her breast. The simple, austere life they had lived for many years never caused them any discontent. Mel grew up in a neighbourhood that was partly in ruins, but as it was the only world he knew, he never saw it as a problem.

They lived in a small, red-brick, terraced house with a black slate roof and a little porch in front; it was very hard to distinguish from two hundred others that were all identical.

As there were only the three of them, Mel had a room of his own, where he could read and paint in splendid isolation.

Although he enjoyed going to school, he was never interested in sports like football or rugby. He sometimes played tennis…unenthusiastically.

Mel had a certain type of precocious intelligence that made him a bit arrogant from an early age. But in reality, this arrogant attitude was a façade behind which he hid his insecurities. During his school years, he had been physically and verbally abused by thugs who took advantage of his emotional unsteadiness, making each day a little hell.

Mel lacked of the physical strength needed to fight the bullies, but what he had not in muscle, he possessed in brains. That *belle indifference* towards his enemies led some people believe he was an original thinker, and others to believe that he was eccentric, while the majority just thought he was arrogant.

This created some controversy around it, an aura of mystery that very often made him the centre of many conversations, but also helped him to regain his pride. However, although he had many friends, only a very few got to know and accept the real Mel. Kurt Render was one of them.

Mel was very sensitive person, but the continuous mistreatment he was subjected to for so many years left an enduring mark on his character.

As time passed by, that feeling of abandonment by those who should have protected him turned into anger, resentment and intellectual challenge against any person or institution representing an authority.

Kurt never shared Mel's confrontational attitude towards the academic *establishment,* but he always admired him for his original ideas and his loyal honesty. Once he asked him what his real name was. "Cooper doesn't sound very Polish to me," Kurt said.

With a surge of frankness unusual for Mel, which only Render was privileged to hear, Mel explained to him how Koperinsky had become Cooper. Shortly after the end of the war, when his father settled in England, he decided to take the opportunity of changing his name to one that sounded more British. Cooper was the one that came closest to the original.

"He did it because he wanted to forget the horrors of the past and start again. And besides, my father was a practical man, and he realised that over here, Cooper was easier to pronounce than Koperinsky."

Mel's complex personality had deep and varied roots and there were many gaps in his past that he tried to fill with made-up stories that served to feed the haze of mystery that surrounded him. With time, fake ancestors, aristocrats and philosophers, were added to the legends with which he regaled his friends and acquaintances.

Mel went on to study medicine, specialising in clinical neuropharmacology. He had started his pioneering work with heroin addicts in the seventies. At that time, sedatives and doses that many doctors feared to prescribe for treating opiate withdrawal were routine procedures for Mel. He always loved play with dynamite!

Years later, his treatment protocols had become textbook procedures, embraced as standard and studied by new generations of doctors. Some of his papers were even quoted in medical journals.

Mel Cooper had reached heights where he achieved almost universal recognition in his specialty. And as usually happens in such cases, he was admired by some, who considered him a leader in the field, and loathed by others, who only saw him as an arrogant maverick.

Treatment for alcohol and drug dependencies is not influenced by scientific evidence only. There are a lot of prejudices, subjectivity, financial and political interests involved, which usually play a decisive role in the way society approach these complex problems.

There are three ways in which treatment for drug and alcohol addiction can be compared with football.

1. Most people have an interest in it, and everyone has something to say about it.
2. It arouses passionate opinions, mostly based on either prejudice or nothing at all.
3. Few people have the understanding or humility needed to admit that. Just as in football, at the beginning of a match, it is very difficult to predict the outcome. Everyone looking for help presents with different circumstances. This is because they are not just patients, service users, alcoholic or addicts. They are individual human beings. They are persons.

For these very reasons, the politics and strategies for addiction treatment vary widely from one country to the next; and in almost every case, they are subject to the vagaries of public opinion polls and electoral swings.

Methadone is the cheapest and most common medication for stabilising those who are dependent on heroin or similar opiates. This medication was discovered in Germany during the Second World War, but more recently, from 1964, it began to be used to treat heroin addicts in New York.

The idea is simple. Instead of prescribing heroin to stop withdrawal symptoms, doctors prescribe methadone, which is also an opiate but stays longer in the bloodstream, so it only has to be taken once a day.

Replacing heroin with methadone has achieved a reduction in the number of deaths from overdose, viral infections, such as hepatitis C and AIDS, and also in criminal activities that addicts have to get involved in to be able to buy their daily fix.

This last point is extremely important to reduce crime, because, to get hold of the 80 to 150 dollars on average that an addict needs every day (to avoid withdrawal symptoms), he or she has to steal goods worth around five times that amount. That is one of the many reasons medical treatment always turns out to be much more economical than criminalising use.

The introduction of methadone for treating addicts has been a great advance in addiction medicine.

The first clinics in Britain to offer treatment for heroin injectors with methadone opened around 1968, but the arrival throughout the seventies of heroin from the Middle East, allowed people to smoke it (chase the dragon) instead of injecting. From then on the numbers of heroin addicts grew exponentially, and the use of liquid methadone became the standard for treatment. This was the beginning of what was to become known as the *British system*, characterised by an approach that was more permissive, comprehensive and humane.

Mel wasn't slow to join the pioneers in this field, finding his niche in operating at the limits of what was permissible.

From the very beginning, he threw himself into it wholeheartedly, never letting anyone – not even his closest colleagues of the time – question his part in a movement that was making history.

However he had a change of heart when this therapy became part of *the system.*

Mel always lived like a petite bourgeois, but he hated to admit he was part of any *system*, because deep down he felt an outsider, anti-system, a nonconformist. So it came about that he began to experiment with variants and procedures that were still under investigation, had little scientific support and were consequently unlicensed.

By nature, he was inclined to push the boundaries beyond the accepted limit. He didn't want to be, or perhaps couldn't tolerate being, one of the crowd. Yet again, his attitude began to attract notoriety especially in liberal thinkers' circles, and along with it a lot of criticism from others who found him reckless and arrogant.

As usual, Mel only acknowledged those who agreed with his methods and disregarded the rest.

Many of his treatment protocols included regimes that were more lax and flexible, lacking in supervision. By using combinations of very powerful sedatives at higher-than-recommended doses, he was bringing the therapeutic levels perilously close to the toxic.

But Mel thought that his patients required special care, and most doctors could not understand their suffering.

At this stage he was someone who could pick and choose his patients, and the majority of his colleagues already considered him a loose cannon. He had passed the point of no return, and problems weren't slow to follow.

It was a Friday afternoon, and Mel was driving his convertible to his office in Harley Street after having lunch with a friend. He was running late.

After crossing Baker Street and passing Madame Tussauds Museum Mel was approaching Park Crescent. At that point he made a fast turn, before the bus coming in the opposite direction blocked his way.

Neither the rain that hindered visibility nor the group of tourists standing in the middle of the road justified his reckless driving.

It was not just the fact that Mel had hit a pedestrian, he had also failed to stop until three people stood in the middle of the road fifty yards ahead. The level of alcohol in his blood, just above the legal limit, contributed decisively to deteriorate his legal position. But that wasn't all.

The accident victim died a few days later because of complications of a heart condition she had been suffering for years. To make things even worse, she happened to be the mother of a very traditional member of parliament, who was well-known for opposing any policy that could result in a raise of the social budget, mainly the provision of treatment for *junkies*.

Mel had found his nemesis.

Quickly, his opponents and detractors came to offer their condolences to the family of the deceased, and their assistance to provide the necessary evidence that would facilitate the public execution soon to come. Everything indicated that Mel would be expunged by the establishment he hated so much, and none of his enemies wanted to miss the show.

Eight months later, Mel was sentenced to pay a compensation of two million sterling pounds and serve a sentence of seven years in HMPS Helfen.

XVIII

HER MAJESTY'S PRISON SERVICE establishments are classified according to the level of security required to lodge their illustrious guests. These included high-, medium- and low-security prisons, as well as some open prisons, where some prisoners are allowed to go out to work in the daytime and come back at night.

Dr Cooper had been sent to a high-security prison about thirty-five miles outside London, where Ali and Steve made their way to interview him.

Prisons are strange places, always full of individuals who are innocent but whose fate was sealed by an unfortunate combination of false accusations, *vendettas*, twisting of facts and a dose of bad luck. That was what Mel and his closest inmates thought, anyway!

Even in prison he was considered a special case. To be treated as one of the crowd would have been one more blow to his damaged self-esteem. Surrounded by internationally known terrorists, multi-millionaire traffickers, politicians and celebrities who had fallen from grace, Mel would have many more stories to add to his arsenal of unlikely anecdotes.

From a distance, HMP Helfen seemed more like a university campus than a maximum-security prison. The broad green spaces and peaceful living quarters surrounding it made it hard to imagine that it contained some of the most notorious prisoners in the United Kingdom.

It would be wrong to think that these prisons are cheap hotels!

The average cost of a place in high-security prison in England and Wales was around thirty thousand pounds sterling a year.

To penetrate the concentric circles of security barriers was not easy. It took Ali and Steve almost twenty minutes to get from the main reception to the interview room, where Cooper was waiting for them.

It wasn't so much that their prison escort was slow, but after so many years of working there, he had become one more cog in an extraordinary security apparatus. Everything in prisons is large, heavy and oppressively bureaucratic.

Prison structures have to make their presence felt as overwhelmingly superior to every individual there, whether prisoner, visitor, officer or governor. Everyone, absolutely everyone, has to be subordinate to the routine procedures that control the rhythm of life inside. The underlying message is simple: no one can escape from the system.

To get through the first perimeter fence, they had to take off their shoes, belt and other metal objects before being frisked by the guards.

"Do you mind if I examine you?" the female officer asked Steve.

"Not at all, go ahead."

"Anything to declare before I examine you?"

"No, maybe a few sins to confess."

"That's between you and the priest, not me. I'm only looking for metal, sharps, mobiles, cameras or recording equipment."

"No, love, I've got nothing like that on me."

"Then go to hell. I mean, go ahead."

"Thanks, my dear."

"Pleasure, Mr Dariet," the officer replied with a wink.

Mel had been inside Helfen for two years by the time Ali and Steve visited him. Because of his good behaviour, he was allowed to spend his mornings working at his own request in the library, while in the afternoons he contributed to the group meetings that were set up to help new arrivals to settle in. Both tasks helped to keep his mind active and made him feel useful – and perhaps would also count for something when he came up in front of the parole board

"Did I know Kurt Render?" Mel asked with a smile. "Well yes, just a bit," he said ironically. "It must be about forty years ago now that we first drank mescal together, in the deserts of northern Mexico, near the Texas border. Some months later we took part in an initiation ceremony in San Pedro, in northern Peru. It was at dawn on a Tuesday," he went on, speaking slowly as his gaze lingered on an imaginary horizon where he was trying to recreate his memories of long ago. "Did you know Tuesday is a sacred day in Inca culture?"

"No, no idea," replied Steve, trying to remember the difference between the Incas, the Maya, the Aztecs and the names of other Andean cultures that sprang to mind.

"Well it is, at least according to the old shaman who was our mentor in this experience," Mel said.

It was at the beginning of the seventies that Kurt and Mel, two young men hungry for new experiences, had embarked on their adventurous journey.

However, they weren't guided only by romantic ideals.

Their British education had been very down to earth. Adventure to them meant experimenting with new ways of living that would enrich their personalities and also perhaps their bank balances, if they came across a new substance that they could market when they got home.

Unlike other travellers in the Andes at that time, they had no dreams of freeing the world from capitalist oppression or imposing extreme ideologies by force. They had no inclination at all to risk their lives for insubstantial ideals and people that they knew nothing about. Kurt and Mel had their feet planted firmly on the ground and had a healthy respect for cultures they didn't know. They didn't see themselves as visionaries, but they were not uninterested in the people they met on the way.

"During this trip to Latin America, we were lucky enough to live for a few weeks with the Kogui Indians in the Santa Marta range of the Sierra Nevada, north of Colombia. They were very suspicious of white people, because the atrocities committed by the Spanish *conquistadores* five hundred years earlier are still fresh in their minds.

"The Kogui had lived in the mountains for generations, and their contact with civilization is very restricted and under government protection."

Alison listened in silence, occasionally making a few notes.

"We found a checkpoint at the bottom of a hill, at the entrance to a path leading up towards the villages. According to the Kogui, no one was allowed to go up these paths. The only exceptions allowed are in the event of an emergency, and that was exactly what happened when we were talking to the guards on duty.

"A man had come down in a panic, asking for urgent medical help, and the guard didn't know what to do. The phone lines to his HQ were down, and he wasn't allowed to leave his post. On the other hand, any delay in making a decision could cost a life up there, and that was also something his superiors might be disinclined to overlook.

"Speaking a bit of broken Spanish and using signs and gestures, we offered to help. Although he didn't like it, the Kogui didn't have much choice, and we didn't want to miss this opportunity. So there we were!

"According to what Aluna told us on the way – that's what he was called – his wife was about to give birth, but she was having severe pains, and the child wasn't making any progress. Time was running out, and they knew that if something wasn't done very soon, both mother and child would be lost.

"Don't ask me how made ourselves understood, because I don't know. It was a desperate situation for us in a very exotic place. We communicated like children do, with signs, gestures and basic words that we tried to associate with concrete meanings. This system worked well all the time we were there.

"Under different circumstances, they would have thrown us out, but what with Aluna's panic and the guard's fear, the gates were opened for us to a world that very few people know of. A world two thousand metres high up the Andes mountains.

"It took us eight hours of non-stop walking to get to the first village. The Kogui used to do it in only three, but this time Aluna had company.

"We arrived at last as it was getting dark. His wife Ayahuma was lying on a blanket on the ground, in a hut no more than three metres across. Three old women were standing over her, they seemed to be praying or chanting a prayer that repeated her name, Ay Ay Ay Ayahuma....

"When I examined her, I realised that labour had started several hours before, but the foetus was lying crosswise in the womb, and it would be impossible to give birth without changing its position. To do this would run the risk of the umbilical cord getting twisted around the neck of the foetus, so it would die of asphyxiation.

"However, not doing this would mean the death of the mother and possibly ours as well. Making a mistake wasn't an option, but I was too busy concentrating on what I was doing to think of the consequences or feel any fear.

"The old women kept a close eye on what we were doing while Aluna stayed silent, not saying a word, his face impassive, almost stoical. God alone knows what was going through his mind, because the Kogui keep themselves to themselves, although they are very sensitive.

"After a couple of hours of agony, on my part as well as the mother's, I succeeded in turning the foetus, and the baby was born.

"A few minutes after the birth, the baby was bouncing and the mother worn out. But Ayahuma was young and strong, and with the other old women looking after her, she recovered completely after a few hours' sleep.

"As a sign of his gratitude Aluna invited us to stay in one of his huts for as long as we wanted. He told us that from now on we were part of his family, which meant part of his tribe.

"Word got round among all the neighbours, and as time went by, more and more people came to request our 'white magic' services.

"After a couple of weeks we were ready to go back to our own world. A large crowd of people came to say good-bye to us. As we went away, we couldn't stop looking back and thinking of the friends we had made, whom we wouldn't see again."

As Cooper finished his story, he was almost talking to himself as he went back over past times that, in this case, were undoubtedly happier.

"I don't know why I'm telling you all this. Perhaps it's because there isn't much to do here, so when things are quiet you either go to sleep or start reminiscing...."

Ali gazed at him attentively, wide-eyed, then asked if they had succeeded in identifying any interesting plants to complete their project.

"We didn't find that, but we found out a lot of other things and became great friends.

"The Kogui chew coca all day; it's an integral part of their culture and their beliefs. But there was nothing new in that discovery, only our personal experience of it."

"Your story is certainly fascinating, but as far as finding a new drug is concerned, it turned out to be a wild-goose chase." Steve's voice was expressionless, his face more suited to playing a hand of poker than listening to an interesting story.

"Mr Dariet, you often find worthwhile stuff when you are looking for something else," replied Cooper.

"Virin, for example." Ali fired it at him point-blank, without any warning.

Mel smiled and, with a sigh, he said in a fatherly manner, "Yes, Virin for example. But we'll come to that later."

Cooper wouldn't give Ali the chance to control the tempo of an interview. Without taking any more notice of her interruption, he continued his account in a pleasant, courteous tone.

"Some months later, we decided to go to Africa, where we lived for a time among the Babongo and the Mitsogo. They initiated us into the *Buiti* ritual, and we ended up hallucinating like the devil, vomiting and losing all muscular coordination. We didn't gain anything positive from these experiences, apart from some ghastly memories of ibogain intoxication.

"We never gave up our search for the *el dorado* of pharmacology until Kurt finally found it, and he had to pay a high price for it," Mel concluded, lowering his gaze and putting on a sad face. "You did come to talk about him, didn't you? If you want to understand Kurt, you must start by getting to know how his mind worked.

"Kurt was a rich man, but he also had a wealth of original ideas. His outlook on the world and on life was a very individual one. He never let himself be influenced by avarice or greed."

"Sometimes the boundary between scientific and personal ambition can be very hard to establish. Don't you think so, Dr Cooper?" asked Ali, biting her lip.

"At first sight, the distinction may seem a bit blurred, but even if it can't be seen clearly, it's always there, dividing the waters. Besides, what is a man without ambition? Nothing. We all have our ambitions and our secrets, don't you think, Miss Riley?" he asked, looking her straight in the eye and rubbing his hands together.

"You're right, Dr Cooper," replied Ali, smiling and self-controlled. "But we'd better leave his ambitions till later."

Now it was she who was back in charge of the interview.

"OK, that's fine with me," he replied. "I still remember the days we spent in the El Prado hotel at Barranquilla after our adventures in the Sierra. One day we were in a hut and the next in a palace built in nineteen-twenty-seven.

"When we got there, we were thin and haggard, dirty and exhausted. It took us a week to recover, both physically and mentally."

"Who paid the bill, Cooper? It must have been a very large one," asked Steve.

"Kurt paid. He was the only son of a very wealthy family. It was nothing to him.

"When we got back to England, Kurt joined a big multinational pharmaceutical, and I went to work in the National Health Service. It wasn't surprising that, after these experiences in South America and Africa, neither of us could adapt to the bureaucratic routine of our new jobs. We were bored and disillusioned with working in vast institutions, which had no room for personal initiative. We also had to battle against an army of managers who lived by and for the system. They didn't care about real people. The system they revere and represent always comes first."

Cooper was so carried away with his reminiscences that he failed to notice the fact that his listeners were still working for very large and bureaucratic organizations. However, if they had their own doubts about the *system*, they kept them to themselves.

"After a series of temporary jobs here and there, Kurt decided to invest part of his family fortune in setting up his own facility for clinical investigations. At around the same time, I started to treat my first private patients."

"So you had more than a shared past in common," said Ali. "You are very similar in your way of thinking and feeling."

"You're right, but all that's ancient history now. We're here..." Mel threw his arms wide as he spoke with a rather dramatic effect, "...and Kurt is up there," he added, looking upwards. "He's left us for good." It was a cheap attempt to distract their attention, which neither Ali nor Steve were inclined to buy into.

"I didn't put you down as a believer in God, Dr Cooper," said Ali. The statement was put naively but was full of irony.

"Oh, no! Well, not really. But I believe that this is such an immense, extraordinary and chaotic universe that it's even possible that God may exist," he replied, with a pensive sigh.

"And do you believe that Virin exists?"

"Virin…" he replied, showing his teeth. "Hmmm, yes, I believe it exists. Perhaps not in as pure a form as Kurt wished…. But I thought we were going to talk about that later.

"You know, Kurt was inspired by one of his girlfriends, called Virina, to name his new drug after her. He always felt contented and safe with her. When he told me about it, I roared with laughter. I thought he must be joking, but he was quite serious. Poor old chap!"

"He can't have been very much in love with her," Ali commented.

"Kurt in love? I don't think so!" Mel replied with a smile. "He was too busy with his projects to fall in love. Virina was his drug, and he managed to turn her into a pill," Mel replied. His manner completely belied the profound sentiments he was speaking about.

"Yes, I see," Ali replied, with a sidelong glance at Steve.

Cooper continued to talk nineteen to the dozen, but the useful information that came out was proportionately much less. He did say that creating a drug like Virin had been his own idea, but it was his friend's genius that had brought it to fruition.

Kurt Render was not a man just to be content with good ideas, he put them into practice.

Towards the end of the 1990s, Kurt and Mel were working on two projects aimed at producing psychoactive substances that could be taken with a high margin of safety. One of them was to develop wines and beers containing something that wasn't alcohol but had the same effect, and which could quickly be blocked by another drug that could be taken afterwards. So you could enjoy a night on the tiles and take a drug afterwards that would avoid the after effects of alcohol consumption.

This was certainly a great idea from the pharmacological point of view, but it would never be accepted by heavy drinkers for one very simple reason. People who drink too much can recognise *excess* in others but never in themselves. That's where you get the definition of the alcoholic that some people propose: the alcoholic is any patient who drinks more than his doctor!

Kurt and Mel knew all about the brain but very little about the mind. This project never got off the ground.

The other project aimed to create a drug that would produce the same effects as morphine but little or no risk of overdose.

"At the time of prioritising the projects we came to the conclusion that the market for alcohol was much bigger than for opiates, but the commercial resistance we would meet would also be colossal," Mel explained. "On the other hand, a powerful sedative like morphine but with fewer risks would be welcomed by everyone. With time, it would be possible to substitute it for other opiates, including those currently being used in addiction treatment, or even those like oxycodone that so many Americans are dependent to.

"If we succeeded in substituting opiates with Virin as the drug of preference for addicts, it would make it easier to develop an addiction that isn't dangerous. It would lead to a dramatic reduction in deaths from overdose, viral infections such as hepatitis and crimes linked to drug usage.

"Governments would welcome this new drug with open arms and would distribute it in the same way as they do methadone or buprenorphine, but without the safeguards that have to be introduced."

"But the number of addicts would go up enormously," Steve said, with a frown.

"That's right...yes, but it would be a harmless addiction," came Cooper's reply.

"Safe as long as they are taking the drug that you are producing and your governments are promoting. In the long run, they will be all dependent on you and your masters," Steve pointed out.

"And what's wrong with that?" demanded Mel. "Wouldn't it be better for them than drinking alcohol, stuffing themselves with junk food, smoking tobacco or injecting with drugs when they don't know where they've come from? Can you think of a better solution to reduce the number of patients with obesity, diabetes, cancer and viral infections, all these conditions that come from today's lifestyle? The consumer society is consuming itself!"

"You and Kurt dreamt of coming up with something that would change the social behaviour of millions of people, is that it?" asked Steve.

"It sounds a bit ambitious, but why not?" replied Mel.

"Contentment and social control. Widespread dumbing down and dependency," added Steve.

"That's taking things to extremes. That wasn't what we originally intended, but it's a side effect. The use that politicians make from a scientific discovery is a different matter. Nuclear energy wasn't developed solely to make bombs," replied Mel.

"If it's used in the same way, Virin would be an extremely clean bomb. For domestic use only, so to speak," Steve said sarcastically while Ali stayed silent, listening intently without taking part in the discussion.

Mel couldn't hide a smile and, lowering his head, said almost proudly, "That's right, after a while we'll come round to this point of view. Virin could have been the drug of the future, a unique vehicle to maintain social order in areas convulsed by the economic crisis and unemployment. What's wrong with that? Have you got a better alternative?"

Cooper went on talking, moving his hands as if he was trying to create some object in the air; his eyes were wide open, and from time to time his gaze was unfocussed. Ali and Steve decided to give him some rope and let him open up so they could get to the bottom of his ideas.

He talked about the global underclass, the increasing drain on energy resources and the excessive demand for foodstuffs in a world in which the workforce is completely devalued. "Anything machines can't make in America or Europe can be made by someone in Asia for a fifth of the salary. How can they correct this imbalance without violence?"

Steve tried to listen to him, but by now he was beginning to lose his patience.

"Miss Riley, you know that eighty-four per cent of world heroin is produced in Afghanistan. Besides the twenty-seven billion dollars wasted on the war and the high cost in terms of human life, heroin production there increased by thirty-one hundred per cent. In 2011, they produced one hundred eighty-five tonnes and ten years later an incredible five thousand tonnes. In 2011 alone, production rose by sixty-one per cent, and the street value fell by fifty-one per cent.

"Virin is a great contribution to humanity! It could even put an end to international drug trafficking..." he added, with a burst of idealism that didn't fit in with his personality.

"I'm afraid the problem is more complicated than that, Dr Cooper," said Ali pleasantly. "We're not here to save the world, you know. We've just come to talk about Virin and stop more people dying from taking it."

"It's not Virin that is killing people," countered Mel. "Kurt couldn't complete the project. He would never have allowed anything like this."

"And just how do you know what it is that *is* killing people?" Steve asked, struggling to control his aggressive tone.

"The answer to that is very complicated. The first laboratory trials of Virin had had positive results, as had all the tests with laboratory animals that had been carried out in Brussels and Amsterdam. Tests of tolerance and toxicity also showed that Virin was safe. However, we knew that the real challenge would come when we used it on humans. Mammals have very similar organs and physiology. A guinea pig has a very similar liver and stomach to that of human. The big difference lies in the nervous system and the brain.

"Five years after the project began, we started the first human trials with a small clinical investigation company based in Colombia and Costa Rica. They offered very high-quality services at very reasonable prices, and we were assured of their discretion.

"By the end of six months, Kurt realised that something was wrong. The results were not what we expected.

"The first thing we noticed was that Virin induced certain types of withdrawal symptoms – vomiting, stomach pains and goose bumps. Next, that the pleasurable effect was weak. Virin behaved like a partial agonist drug in approximately half of the subjects. The symptoms were not so much severe as very irritating. That was why we couldn't detect them in the laboratory trials."

"Animals can't talk," said Steve, stating the obvious with some sarcasm.

"Well, if you had known some of the project backers, you'd probably change your mind. Some animals do talk!" Cooper replied.

"Which of them do you mean?" asked Ali.

"Newton Crowe. He's a very powerful animal who put pressure on Kurt all the time. 'I want results, I don't give a shit about the technical problems' he used to say, when he realised that more time was needed to perfect Virin.

"It was obvious that Newton was very worried about his partners' reaction. It seemed they couldn't accept failure and only wanted the returns they had been promised."

"How often did you meet them, Dr Cooper?" asked Ali. The ballpoint pen she was using to take notes was poised on her lip.

"I never met them. Kurt told me everything that happened, because it was really getting to him, and I was the only person he could trust. He soon began to realise that doing business with Crowe had been a mistake."

"Are you sure that you never met any of the others in person?" Steve insisted.

"Well, I may have bumped into one or two of them when I visited Kurt in his office. These were very brief and informal meetings. I had no direct involvement with the Virin project."

Cooper bent forward, coughed two or three times, and tried to regain his composure, resting an arm on the table.

"Are you OK to continue, Dr Cooper?" asked Ali.

"I'd prefer to stop now and carry on tomorrow or next week, if you don't mind."

Steve's face darkened, and he looked daggers at Cooper. He knew he was trying it on, and this indisposition was all a pretence.

"This is a very important matter, Cooper. Stop playing games. We're not here on a social visit. Out there, people are dying," he said, pointing to a window. "We want to know who's killing these people, and who is behind it all."

Cooper seemed to have difficulty getting his breath and looked worn out.

"I'm sorry, Mr Dariet, I'm not in a fit state to carry on. I don't feel at all well. This prison is killing me. Why don't you come back on Monday? I'm sure I'll feel better by then."

Ali's smile was almost sympathetic as she said "I understand perfectly, Dr Cooper. Today is Friday; would you agree to us carrying on with this conversation in forty-eight hours' time? We need this information, and we're prepared to recognise your contribution in clearing up this case."

"Thank you, Miss Riley, I think we understand each other," answered Cooper, suddenly better. "I know you need me, but have you considered that I need you? I've been put into prison unjustly, and this prison is killing me. You're worried about people dying out there," he added pointedly to Steve, "but perhaps you ought to worry that I don't die in here."

"Up to now there have been forty-eight deaths relating to Virin, Dr Cooper. You can't ignore this fact," Steve replied.

"That can't be true. Virin didn't achieve what we hoped for, but it's still a safe drug. These people must have been killed by something else."

"Such as what?"

"Please, let's continue on Monday. I don't feel well. Please give me some consideration and give me the weekend to think things over. I deeply regret what's happening out there, and hopefully I might be able to do something to put a stop to it, but you should have come before. Neither Kurt nor I is responsible for this. But I need to have a rest now to refresh my memory. I'm dying in here. Have I made myself clear?"

"As daylight," replied Ali, with a conciliatory smile.

"I'm glad you understand, Miss Riley. It's not about what I want but what I need, and what you can do to help me."

"We didn't come to haggle, Cooper. We need information, and you're going to give it to us," Steve said sharply.

"Just a moment, please." This time Ali spoke to her colleague. "This is too important for us to decide by ourselves, Steve. I'll speak to my bosses and I'll see what I can do. But I want to make it quite plain that I'm not promising anything further than that. Just to speak to my superior officers."

"Thank you, Miss Riley, that's all I can hope for. A bit of understanding and help," Cooper replied, playing the victim.

"You're playing with fire, Cooper," said Steve, without taking any notice of Ali.

"So what, am I going to burn up? What are you going to do to me, lock me up? Don't make me laugh, Mr Dariet. You've come to beg me for what little life and thought I've got left. I say no, no, no. Thanks for nothing!"

"You've made yourself very clear, Doctor. I'll see what I can do," replied Ali seriously, as she slid her documents into the leather briefcase she always carried with her.

"Thank you, Miss Riley," replied Cooper with a smile. "Have a good weekend."

"Thank you, and the same to you, Doctor."

Cooper smiled and shrugged his shoulders.

Steve rose from his seat. "We'll meet again on Monday, Doc. We want the whole story."

"Sure, Mr Dariet, sure. Good-bye."

XIX

STEVE FELT A MIXTURE OF CONFUSION and annoyance at the same time. Why had Ali been so conciliatory and accommodating towards Cooper? She could have put more pressure on him to get a result. On the other hand, Ali wasn't a weak sort of person to allow herself to be manipulated in this way.

"There's something that I don't understand here, Ali. Why do you think your boss in America can get concessions for a prisoner in a British gaol?"

"He has his contacts," came her enigmatic reply.

"Where is your boss?"

"In Washington, DC."

"Is that where you live alone?" Steve said lowering his voice, almost whispering while giving Ali a straight sexy look.

"Oh, please, Steve," she answered, continuing to arrange the documents in her briefcase.

"Sorry, I didn't mean to…."

"Yes you meant to, but that's OK; it's a natural reaction. You're a man. It doesn't matter."

"If it doesn't matter, then answer my question."

"I live on my own in DC. Anything else?"

"That'll do for now," was his smiling reply. "We'll get to know each other in time. There'll be plenty of that before this business gets sorted out."

The weekend passed without any major developments. Steve tried to read through more of the documents and confidential reports about Render, Cooper and the brokers who were financing the Virin project with money that came from dubious sources.

Monday morning found Steve and Ali back at the main gate of the prison to continue with the interrogation. When they got to the room assigned for the interview, they found Cooper waiting for them, leaning both arms on the table and linking his hands.

That morning he wouldn't be working in the library. He was on his own, downcast and pensive, but he sprang to his feet when he saw them in the doorway. He looked perky and seemed to be in good spirits and a co-operative mood.

"Hello, Cooper, I hope today's meeting will be more productive than the last one," said Steve, taking his seat.

"Sure," Cooper answered. "But first things first," he added, fixing Ali with a piercing gaze.

"OK," she replied. "I've got some documents here that I want you to read carefully. Take ten minutes. If you agree to it, we'll sign and talk afterwards. If you don't, that's it. There's no more bargaining. Take it or leave it!" she went on, showing a tough side that hadn't appeared during the previous visit.

Steve was astonished at what was going on in front of his eyes. Ali had not even spoken to him, let alone consulted him, about either the offer or the negotiation. However, professional discipline made him swallow his pride to avoid having an argument in front of a key witness.

Without another word, Ali went over to a two-seater settee, made of wood and upholstered in a blue vinyl fabric typical of the products that came out of prison workshops.

In spite of his perplexity, Steve followed her like a zombie, sat down beside her and looked her in the eye.

"You needn't think that I'm in charge of this negotiation, Steve. Our bosses will approve the offer. I'm only the messenger.

Cooper knows a lot more than he is saying. We need to know some of this right away, whereas the rest will be more important later."

"Why hasn't anyone said anything to me?"

"Remember the deal. You'll be told what is strictly necessary to complete your mission and nothing more. They don't think it's important to involve you in the negotiation. You and I just have to use it to achieve our objectives. What happens afterwards isn't our problem."

"I get it," he answered with a frown, nodding.

"In general terms, they've offered to transfer him to a special unit, if the information he gives us turns out to be useful. However, if he gives us something very important, Mike promises to write a letter of recommendation to the parole board that will decide on his release terms and conditions."

"You've managed to secure these terms in just two days over a weekend?"

"Yes."

"But to do that, you need to reach agreement with the Ministry of Justice, the prison service, the Home Secretary and their lawyers. The bureaucracy is enormous. Normally, if everything goes smoothly, it would take at least two weeks."

"Not this time. All the departments you mentioned answer to the same person at the top, don't they?"

"Number Ten?"

Ali smiled without answering.

"So your boss can contact the Prime Minister's office just like that?" he asked, snapping his fingers.

"Perhaps it's someone higher up. It's not my problem."

"You never cease to surprise me, Ali."

"It's not me. It's just the case that we're investigating."

"All right," Steve answered, pursing his lips and lapsing into deep thought. Ali's reply, far from clarifying his uncertainty, had left him more confused than ever. A lot of things were going through his head at the same time as he was keeping up a fluent conversation. Besides, it wasn't the time or the place to discuss such complicated issues.

At the end of the ten minutes, Ali said, "Time's up."

Once again Steve got to his feet and followed her.

Although the room was well lit, he felt as if he was groping in the dark, and his only consolation was the thought that Mike had never yet played a dirty trick on him.

When they got back to the table where Dr Cooper was reading the agreement, it was clear that the situation had changed. Ali was in the driving seat, and Steve was the passenger. It was a situation that his macho attitude didn't let him feel very comfortable in, but he judged it to be more prudent. He decided to let her take the initiative and see where it led.

At first, Cooper seemed a bit put out by the vagueness of the terms. However, at last he agreed that the agreement seemed fair and accepted it. They signed the documents and sealed the pact with a handshake.

Recognising that he had no more room for manoeuvre, Mel decided to cooperate and share all his remaining knowledge. "I'm all yours, Miss Riley. What do you want to know?"

"Let's start with the project backers." She was getting ready to take notes.

Cooper told them how, after the famous banquet, offers started to roll in, and Render had discussed them with him. After evaluating each one of them, they both agreed that Newton and Jurgen offered the best terms.

Kurt was the official negotiator and always had the last word. Cooper did not exert any influence over him other than that of a confidential advisor.

"Virin was my idea, but I had nothing to do with the project development or the finance side. Put it this way: my role was just a marginal one.

"Jurgen, like a typical Swiss, was very formal and methodical. Perhaps this was why he never trusted Render blindly or allowed his ambition to interfere with his professional judgement. He was willing to take risks, but always and only when he exercised total control over the determining factors.

"Jurgen was the only one to use mathematical algorithms to evaluate the financial risk, the probabilities of failure and its consequences. He used to monitor the risk margins all the time and had decided on a limit, beyond which he would pull out of the project.

"Newton Crowe was a completely different type," Cooper went on. "He was attracted by risk; it gave him a special sensation, a tension that he could only control by drinking like a fish, snorting cocaine and throwing himself into his work.

"When Kurt told them of the initial failure of Virin, alarm bells started ringing for Jurgen. He asked for heaps of data and finally reached the conclusion that Plan B should be implemented immediately. He told us that, given the circumstances, he would rather lose some of the money than all of it."

"Was Render the only source of information they had, or was there anyone else who could give them inside information, too?" Ali put the question without looking up from her notes.

"They had people to tell them how things were going in Brussels and Amsterdam. They kept on top of all the developments there, but Kurt was the only one who got information from all sides and could see the whole picture.

"During the last months, he spent a lot of time travelling and visited both the central laboratories and the smaller ones, where they were studying details of the drug's bioavailability, its concentration in different organs, toxicity, absolutely everything. He didn't leave anything to chance. He checked the data two, three, even four times to be absolutely sure. Kurt was fully conscious of the financial implications of the laboratory results.

"He kept his private notes in a little exercise book bound in light brown leather that he took with him everywhere. He never used a personal computer or notebook to write down his ideas, conclusions or details that seemed important to him. He didn't trust them. He said they might get hacked."

Ali didn't let him get away with anything. "Have you any idea where these notes or this exercise book might be?" she asked, with feigned indifference.

Cooper gave a cynical smile. "I'm not sure." He looked her straight in the eye without blinking.

"How come you're not sure?" she asked with irritation, taking the bait.

Cooper appeared to be enjoying some game, in which Ali had inadvertently shown her hand.

"I can't remember now, Miss Riley, but I think that the manuscript is irrelevant at this stage. Our priority must be to avoid more deaths. That's what you said on Friday. That's why you're here, isn't it?" His eyes gleamed unnaturally bright, like those of an old eagle. He had trapped her, and now he was toying with his prey.

"Sure, that has to be the first priority," Steve answered. Without really knowing what had happened, he recognised Mel's game.

Render's manuscript was Mel's final bargaining tool. It was too important to hand over without further concessions. That was his ticket to freedom, and they both knew it.

"Right, so what did Jurgen and Newton do when Render asked them for more time and money?" asked Ali, trying to steer the conversation in a different direction.

"As I said, while Jurgen wanted to implement Plan B or get out of the deal, Crowe was willing to double his stake. That same afternoon, Newton offered to buy out Jurgen's shares for fifty per cent of the nominal value, but they finally settled for seventy-five per cent. For the first time in the negotiations, Newton raised his voice in a threatening way.

"Jurgen took a loss of twenty-five per cent to get out of a project that was beginning to unravel, and from then on, Newton Crowe would have complete control of the Virin project. Kurt wasn't happy that the deal had turned him into one of Crowe's employees."

Cooper told them how one of the first measures Crowe adopted was to name another chemist to work hand in glove with Render, who was under express orders to share all his data with him. Crowe had no idea that Render had the handwritten notes; otherwise, it would have been a different story!

"The chemist he appointed was a Dutchman, with a lot of experience but a bad reputation. He was called Tygo Gillis," Cooper told them.

"Kurt neither liked nor trusted Tygo. But all this happened eighteen months ago. I remember one of the last things Kurt talked to me about was how he planned to keep him busy and away from his notes. For this reason, he got him to work on a modification of the chemical structure of Virin that he knew wouldn't work, but it would take Tygo several months to find that out."

"Do you think that Tygo could have realised the trap before Render disappeared?" asked Ali.

"I don't know. A little while before the accident, Kurt's visits became more and more infrequent, and the information I got was scarce. What I did hear was that since the accident, Tygo has taken Kurt's place."

"How do you know this?" asked Steve.

"That doesn't matter. Least said soonest mended. The important thing is that Tygo must have given into the same pressure that Kurt couldn't tolerate. Newton must be forcing him to produce something that will lead him to a quick return on his investment."

"Such as what?" Steve pressed him.

"Something like a variant of Virin with more stimulant power, and not so safe. That's the most logical conclusion. For a long time he made a living producing illegal substances in clandestine mobile laboratories."

"You mean that the deaths and toxicity are due to trialling that drug?" Ali asked solemnly.

"It's very likely that they are trying out more than one variant of Virin at the same time to see what works. This could be also the beginning of an operation that could spread to America," Cooper warned.

"America? Why America?" Ali asked, in surprise.

"If the funds that Crowe controls come from drug suppliers who operate over there. A new synthetic drug that they alone control would be a big opportunity for deals in the markets they control."

"I understand; it would flood in from the South and soon spread rapidly to California and the rest of the US where it would become a substitute for the *Oxies* and *Vikes*," said Ali, referring to oral oxycodone and hydrocodone.

"You get the picture, Miss Riley." He winked at her. "Have you not had any similar deaths over there?"

"As yet, no, but it would hardly be surprising."

Steve broke in. "Wait a minute, all this is just supposition. This would be a very sophisticated operation, and Render isn't in charge any more. Tygo wouldn't be capable of organizing something like this."

"Newton and Tygo are a very dangerous combination. Who knows where their greed and lack of scruples might get them? On top of that, they have to answer to their shareholders. They stand or fall together, in a way. They're fighting for their lives, and they don't care about any number of deaths, provided that, in the last resort, they save their own skin."

"That must have been a problem for Render before he died," Steve reflected.

"He probably never expected things to get that far," Ali added, thoughtfully.

"I assure you, Kurt would never have allowed it. He didn't know where the funds that Newton controlled came from. But Kurt is no longer with us...."

"Do you know what he was doing in Colombia when the accident happened?" Steve turned the topic to Render.

"No idea. His death took me by surprise. He'd already distanced himself from me when things started to go wrong. He hardly came to visit me at all during the last phase," Cooper replied.

"We shall have to investigate that accident more fully," Steve decided.

"Yes, but this is not the right time," was Ali's response. "At the moment we have other priorities, like catching Tygo before he can kill more people."

"Do you know where we can find him?" It was Steve who asked the question.

"Amsterdam," came Copper's immediate reply. "But it won't be easy. Tygo is a very slippery customer. If he's involved in producing something illegal, he's bound to be very well hidden and employing heavies for security."

The conversation started to drift off into different channels, and the points they discussed were not as vital as those they had just dealt with. Cooper seemed to have given them most of the worthwhile information that he had in his possession and didn't have much left to negotiate with.

Now the investigation was moving forward, and pieces of the jigsaw puzzle were beginning to fit into place.

A complex web of interests existed, uniting drug barons in Mexico, with financial brokers from California and Zurich, European and American scientific networks, Latvian gangsters and gypsies from Andalusia.

All this without taking into account the political implications of the product they were trying to fabricate.

There was no doubt that globalisation had not only cut down geographical distances but also the gaps separating social, political and financial structures.

The interests behind the Virin project were very complex, and its workers were operating in a broad twilight zone, where the boundary line between legal and illegal was so blurred as to become almost indistinguishable. Steve was no longer sure of the way forward.

Instead of keeping his head up to look into the distance, his horizon would be limited to what was in front of his nose, where he could be sure enough of his ground to inch forward step by step, without plunging into the mire.

From this new perspective, he realized that the wary attitude of Romero and Chano was evidently inspired by their instinct for survival.

XX

WHEN ALI AND STEVE MET UP with Mike in his office again, Tygo Gillis was at the centre of their discussion.

As far as they could tell, Tygo was in charge of the technical side of the project, while Crowe exercised overall control from what he thought was a safe distance. Their problem was to find out who was carrying out Newton's orders on the ground and how they communicated. The fair-haired men from Marbella had provided a clue, but it was a very indirect one.

For the time being Tygo was all they had, and they had to start from there. Mike had already been in touch with his contact in the Netherlands, and he was now coordinating the next steps in the operation with Ali's boss in Washington DC.

Ludger Brecht was the veteran head of NSOS, the Netherlands Special Operations Service based in Utrecht. Mike had known him for many years, ever since they were both young officers cooperating over the issues and uncertainties of the last days of the Cold War.

Now Ludger was nearer to retirement than to the beginning of his career, but he was still exercising his role as lead of the intelligence network for the eleven operational services of the Netherlands Police Agency.

When Mike mentioned the name of Tygo Gillis, Brecht couldn't hold back a chuckle. He knew that name very well. Gillis was one of his regulars, always coming up in the lists of suspects or contacts linked to drugs and organised crime in Holland.

Tygo Gillis was a biochemist with an unstable character. He was forty-five years old and had graduated *cum laude* from the University of Utrecht. His main field of professional and personal interest was addictive drugs. After he got his degree, he had worked as a postgraduate in University laboratories in Bristol, Cologne and Paris.

His mother had died after being abused for years by her alcoholic husband, who didn't survive her for very long. Once his wife was gone, all his aggression turned to himself and he ended up literally: drinking to death.

It was not hard to see how so many years filled with constant conflict and instability had left their mark on Tygo, and it was a deep and twisted one. As he grew older, the hatred and resentment he had felt against his father turned into extremist, almost anarchist views. Tygo reacted badly against anything to do with authority and regulation.

Towards the end of his university career, Tygo had played an active role in helping to coordinate students' anarchist activities in various European capitals. However, he had stayed out of prison, because almost all the marches were pacifist demonstrations against capitalism or the *establishment,* usually organised by groups of young idealists from the universities and pretty women.

Up to now, his radical tendencies were still largely ideological, never going beyond harmless protests and interminable discussions in cafes that went on till the early hours. By this time, Tygo was already smoking cannabis every day and taking amphetamines fairly regularly.

When he finished his studies, he moved to England to take up an internship. This was a little over a year after he had lost his mother and father.

Perhaps to fill the void, Tygo got involved with a girl he described as a siren. "She has a beautiful face but drinks like a fish." It was probably to keep her company that he decided to jump on the bandwagon and started to drink hard as well. True to his extremist tendencies, one night he had to be taken to hospital after binge drinking.

If Tygo was interested in something, he had to throw himself into it wholeheartedly, with the same passion with which he hated his father, the same intensity with which he drank, and the same ardour with which he always searched for the causes and solutions to his problems somewhere outside himself.

Bristol had become a place that had left him with bad memories, so he decided to take a job in a research lab in Paris, working on chemical compounds to mitigate the effects of cannabis on the brain.

In the two years that he worked in Paris, Tygo learnt a lot about the effects of illegal drugs on the nervous system and the way they could be modified to reduce the side effects. His apprenticeship was carried out not only in his laboratory work but also by personal experiences in the city bars. He was still smoking hash and drinking vodka every afternoon, as if nothing had happened. He thought he had everything under control, so much so that on the weekends he started smoking heroin.

Tygo now tried to convince himself that these experiences were necessary for an in-depth understanding of the problems of addiction. Seeing himself as a guinea pig was preferable to accepting that he was turning into a *junkie*. Tygo could deceive himself, but these lies were not enough to convince his body when withdrawal symptoms started to appear.

So it came about that he got to know buprenorphine, the drug most commonly used in France to treat heroin addiction. This was a new experience to him, both as a patient and as a chemist, and it was to become fundamental when he was recruited to join the Virin project.

During his stay in Paris, he lived with Huong, a Vietnamese girl eight years younger than he was. She was very gentle and had lovely manners. Although in a rather twisted way, like almost everything else in his life, Tygo fell in love for the first time.

Huong did everything she could to wean him off drugs, but when she felt it was all to no avail, instead of leaving him, she began to use them herself as well.

Tygo was deeply upset, because he couldn't bear to see her falling into a heroin-induced stupor. Her ready smile turned into an expression of complete indifference, and her lively personality had disappeared. Now Huong no longer bothered about Tygo's rants but only about how she could get her daily fix.

He was very angry with this ghost called Huong. He was no longer her centre of attention, and for anyone as self-centred as he was, this was very hard to bear. But he still needed her.

Six months after she had started to *chase the dragon*, Huong began injecting in secret. By the time Tygo found out, it was already too late. Huong did everything possible to hide her arms, but at last the inevitable happened. The skin that used to be as smooth as amber velvet had become like orange peel, punctured with pinpricks, scars, and thin dark brown lines that once had been her veins flowing with life.

Although blind to his own problems, Tygo couldn't bear the grief that swelled up in him when he realised of Huong's addiction was now running out of control on a cliff edge. He started to hurl abuse at her, calling here names that she had never even heard of but could understand what they meant. For a moment he even raised a threatening hand against her, but he never dared to hit her. He knew that if he did so, he would lose her forever.

The ominous shadow of his father hovered over him. History was repeating itself, and there was no means of escape.

One night he locked himself into the bathroom so Huong wouldn't see what he was doing, although she knew very well. It was part of an established ritual every night at the same time.

Tygo was doing his night dose. But he didn't see that as a problem because "he could handle it."

From inside the bathroom Tygo kept on shouting and raging at her, whilst indifferent to his diatribe, Huong got together her paraphernalia of needles, syringes, spoon, lighter, and left.

Tygo was a hypocrite, a living contradiction, a caricature of the man he once was, the one Huong had loved with such patient devotion. Silently, with the care and delicacy which she still did everything, she went out and closed the door behind her as he continued shouting incoherently.

A few minutes later, Tygo realised that he was talking to himself. She had stopped listening to him a long time ago, but she had always been there.

Now, for the first time, Huong had walked away. That was something he had never expected, could never imagine.

He ran wildly down the staircase, shouting and cursing. He ran through the streets like a madman, searching for Huong, but all he found was a French policeman, who eyed him suspiciously.

"C'est quoi ce bordel que tu regardes?" ("What the hell are you staring at?") he asked, in a tone that the gendarme decided was insulting. Tygo had to spend a night in a police station to realise that the limits of his abusive behaviour had gone beyond his front door.

He would always remember that night, the worst of his life until that moment.

The police inspector decided to let him go the next day, after he had gone through the necessary formalities to start proceedings against him for causing public disturbance under the influence of drugs. That would mean losing his job, on top of losing his girlfriend.

Tygo went back home that afternoon. He was anxious, bathed in sweat, and his hands were shaking uncontrollably. He needed a hit, and he needed it now!

A few moments after injecting he fell asleep.

Six hour later Tygo woke up to a violent headache, a noise that was drilling into his eardrums and wouldn't go away. His eyes still closed, his hands flapped about in an uncoordinated way, as if he were trying to get rid of an irritating fly that was disturbing him with its buzz.

It was the phone.

"Yes, this is the number," he replied, to a woman who then started to ask personal questions before identifying herself.

"Are you family or friend of Mme Nhung?" she inquired.

"Yes, I'm her partner. Who's speaking?"

"Does Mme Huong Nhung live there?"

"Yes. Who is this?" he insisted now showing some anxiety.

"I'm calling from the police station in district thirteen. There has been an accident, and we have to contact Mme Huong's relatives. Can you come here as soon as possible, please?"

"What's happened? Is she alive?"

"I'm afraid I can't answer that question. May I have your name, please? If you can't get here under your own steam, we can send a patrol car for you."

This was enough for Tygo to know that Huong was dead.

They had found her at dawn. Her body was lying up against a wall in a narrow alley near the Avenue de Choisy. Everything pointed to death from an overdose.

Tygo remained devastated and never got over Huong's loss. However, his arrogance wouldn't allow him to admit any fault, to feel any guilt or shame. What he felt was an immense anger, which turned into paranoia after a while.

He was incapable of feeling any grief or giving way to tears. Nor could he learn anything from the suffering he had undergone during the last few years. Tygo blamed the low-quality heroin that Huong had injected, the police who hadn't found her in time...anything else that wasn't himself.

He had reached his point of no return. From then on, the intelligent but daredevil chemist was to become a man with a mission, to find a drug that could have saved Huong.

Tygo had lost his work, his girlfriend and what little professional reputation he had once possessed. Alone and ruined, he knew the only things he had left to cling to were the loyal companions that would never desert him: alcohol, drugs and neurochemistry.

There was nothing more to keep him in Paris. Once again his sole desire was to get away from his bad memories and what he considered a long run of bad luck. This time he decided to apply for a low-level job in a lab in Cologne. They didn't ask too many questions because they had a post to fill that had been vacant for some time. No sooner had they accepted his application than he left for Germany, as quickly as possible.

Cologne stands in the industrial heart of Germany. Gone were the days when Tygo would go for long walks with Huong on the banks of the Seine, he smoking and talking incessantly while she listened with the patience that she showed right up to the end.

Now he was alone by the bank of the cold Rhine, flowing ceaselessly through his native Holland back to the North Sea.

Tygo felt that he was completing a circle from which there would be no escape.

He had been looking for some low-profile work when he found this convenient seclusion, with its routine tasks. He lived a life locked in his cocoon, wanting to forget and be forgotten.

But old habits die hard.

So it came about that one day, he found himself saying more to his *dealer* than he should have. As soon as this man found out that his new client was a chemist who knew a lot about drugs, he asked him if he was interested in some special work that paid good money. As usual, Tygo was as short of funds as he was of scruples, so he decided to give it a go.

A week later he met with Goran, his dealer's boss. Goran wanted to set up three rolling methamphetamine labs and asked him if he was interested and capable of managing the operation.

This was the first opportunity he had had for a long time to take charge of a project; and the fact that it was illegal, far from putting him off, gave him a thrill.

Tygo had a few technical questions about equipment and the supply of phenylacetone, a substance now strictly controlled in the European Union but which was easy to get hold of in those days. "No problem," said Goran, and assured him that there would also be a regular supply of the ephedrine that forms the essential basis of methamphetamine production.

At the end of the month, Tygo handed in his notice at Cologne and left for Amsterdam, where the whole operation had its base.

The circle had been completed.

Tygo had plenty of work with the three vehicles that had been adapted to function as rolling labs. The plan was that they would circulate through the south of Belgium and Holland, delivering their production in some area around the triple frontier near Liege, Maastricht and Aachen.

Most of the time, the vehicles cooked up methamphetamine in two small farms that they had leased near the river Maas. It was one of the precautionary measures that Tygo had adopted to avoid the risk of a potential explosion produced by the flammable gases used during the process.

When the vehicles were stationary, they were camouflaged and decorated with a bit of mud and straw to make them look as agricultural machinery from the distance.

The operation started towards the end of 2001, with three second-hand motorhomes adapted for the job. As these became damaged by the corrosive fumes, a special team was entrusted with breaking them up for scrap and burying or burning the parts outside on the farm.

By the end of the winter everything was running smoothly and well-managed. Production was stable, and distribution extended as far as northern Germany. Goran was making a small fortune, and Tygo was regaining his self-esteem, although in a rather warped fashion.

A year later, buoyed by the success of his operations, Goran decided to take a bigger risk and built a permanent lab in the bigger of the two farmhouses. As one of the key elements in methamphetamine production is ammonium anhydrate, a product used in agriculture as a fertiliser, the move made a lot of sense.

As he had calculated, this expansion attracted more offers and more money but also more attention. Without knowing it, Goran and his team had come onto the radar of NSOS, the National Police Intelligence. They had had them under observation for several months and were now ready to take action.

But things didn't work out according to their careful plans. A few days before the planned raid, someone alerted Goran to the imminent danger.

In a sudden move, he crossed over to Morocco, taking all his funds in with him in cash, and Tygo had no option but to escape alongside him.

When the police went into the main farmhouse, only a few lower-ranking employees were found working there; they were arrested and their vehicles taken out of service.

The majority of these were unemployed peasants from the Baltic countries, who hardly understood anything of what was going on, because they couldn't even speak the language.

Even in Goran's absence, they kept their mouths shut. They believed his promises.

"I will send you my lawyers and you will be out of prison quick. They will sort it out," he said. But he was just buying time to cover his tracks.

Even though they failed to capture the big fish, the police operation was a media result that hit the headlines for two weeks. After a while everything started to cool down, and news of the operation was eclipsed by the forthcoming Champion's League Final between Ajax and Bayern Munich in the colourful Amsterdam Arena.

That was when Goran started to plan for his return in search of new opportunities.

XXI

MIKE GOT STRAIGHT TO THE POINT. "Our friends at NSOS have told us that after his enforced exile in Morocco, Tygo Gillis has now come back to Holland, but they don't know exactly where to find him.

"Goran Shirkov divides his time between Marrakesh and Agadir, but he also moves about freely through other African countries. We think he sent for Tygo to complete the Virin project and possibly to prepare the ground for his return.

"We also know from other sources that he is making a large amount of money organising consignments of ephedrine coming from Southeast Asia to supply the Mexican cartels."

"What has this got to do with Newton Crowe?" asked Ali.

"We're not entirely sure, but we think it could have been through Newton's associates in Mexico. Goran isn't a priority at the moment. He's just the executive arm that controls Tygo. He's our man," answered Mike.

"How can we get hold of him?" came Steve's response.

It was Ali who replied. "Our intelligence suggests that the most logical supposition is that he will go back to the same system that he relied on before. They think he must be constantly on the move between Brussels and Amsterdam by the southern corridor through Ghent, Brussels, Louvain, Liege, Little Switzerland, Eindhoven, Nijmegen and Amsterdam."

"What's Little Switzerland?" Steve studied the map he had in front of him.

"There's a very pretty area in the southern tip of Holland that the Dutch call Little Switzerland. It's very green, and although it's hard to believe, it has little hills full of hotels and spas. Technically it's called Drielandenpunt, or the point where the three frontiers meet, between the Netherlands, Germany and Belgium. Brecht's agents think they must be spending their weekends in that area." Mike was reading a paragraph from a briefing paper he had brought along with him. He stopped and, moving across to the big screen fixed to the wall, he enlarged a specific area on the map, which showed in detail the E40 motorway and the region he had just been describing. "I think the best thing would be to keep a base in Maastricht and another in Amsterdam, from which we can coordinate the operation." He fixed the spot by pointing with the shadow of his index finger. "If we get hold of them in the south, we can get them back from Liege airport; if we trap them in the north, we can board them at Schipol airport in Amsterdam. Our agents are already in the area, looking for information."

"Then we need to cover the corridor. It's only about three hundred kilometres long," Steve said, and glanced at Ali.

"You're going to take the Eurostar to Brussels, where Ali's friends will be waiting for you. They'll be running things in continental Europe. The mission consists of bringing Tygo in for questioning. That alone will be enough to rattle them and start a panic. It will certainly be enough to halt their operations until we can get on top of them," Mike concluded.

"I don't think Tygo will put up much resistance. He'll be safer with us. From the moment Goran finds out we're after Tygo, he'll give orders for him to be taken out. Tygo knows too much," reasoned Steve.

"What about Goran? Perhaps we could bring him in too, so we can arrest Crowe," added Ali.

"That won't be at all easy. We know he's been moving about a lot recently, perhaps because he isn't feeling very safe. Protection costs are going up all the time, and the local bosses are getting fed up with him. He's attracting too much attention. I think that, one way or another, he's going to disappear any moment now. His caution has always made him a very slippery customer," said Mike.

"Until the time we get him, too," said Steve, confidently.

"Yes, but our priority is to get Tygo and avoid more deaths."

"You're right, Mike. When do we leave?"

"Tomorrow morning. It's two hours from St. Pancras to Brussels Midi. They'll be waiting for you in the main hall. Jeff Davis will be in charge of the support team."

"Fine," said Ali, getting ready to leave. "We'll be in touch. Good-bye."

"Good luck," came Mike's reply. "Good-bye for now."

"We'll get Tygo, don't you worry. Cheers, mate."

XXII

SINCE STEVE HAD MOVED TO EUROPE, whenever he came back to the UK, he went to stay with his father in Buckinghamshire. It was only thirty-five minutes by train from central London.

The next day when he got to Euston, he couldn't help thinking about old times, and he decided to walk to St. Pancras, which is not much more than three hundred metres away towards Kings Cross.

After crossing Euston Square, he went past the fire station and the British Library. He knew that the last hundred metres would be the most difficult.

Hundreds of tourists, just arrived from the continent, were walking in the opposite direction towards him, dragging heavy, wheeled suitcases. Steve tried to get round this human tide, but he was unable to avoid getting stuck between a young Chinese man and his girlfriend he was trying to photograph posing in front of the imposing red brick monument to Victorian Gothic that would become the St. Pancras Renaissance hotel.

Click. Steve was momentarily taken by surprise and almost blinded by the flash, but like a true native, used to making his way among the tourists gawping at London attractions, he just smiled and bade them welcome to his city.

The last thing an Englishman of his generation would want to lose would be his courtesy and style.

When he arrived at the pub they had decided on to rendezvous, Steve ordered a lager. A full pint would be too much to start off the day. Just as he was draining his glass, he saw Ali appear out of nowhere.

"Hi. Would you like a drink?" he asked.

"No thanks," she answered pleasantly. "Let's go to the platform. We can board the train now."

Twenty-five minutes later, they were drinking a Blackberry Crush cocktail and a Stella Artois as they went through the tunnel linking Folkestone with Calais at three hundred kilometres an hour. No prizes for guessing which one had ordered the beer!

Ali, charming as always, was wearing a black jacket and skirt with a beige silk blouse that went beautifully with her hair.

The skirt offered a discreet glimpse of her legs, enough to distract a man's attention whenever necessary, but without being provocative.

Steve felt an immediate attraction, but all his attempts at bridging the distance between them came up against a wall that, for the moment, seemed impenetrable.

On arrival at the Gare du Midi, they met two short-haired, muscular young men, dressed informally, who took them to a black Range Rover with darkened windows.

"I'm Jeff Davis; welcome to Brussels." He said extending a hand from the front passenger seat.

When they set off, they were escorted by a silver grey BMW 520, in which the rest of the team was travelling. "We'll go to Sablon, the European quarter, Ixelles, St. Jacques and then take the E40 towards Liege," were Jeff's instructions.

"Roger," came the reply.

"We want you to get to know Tygo's old haunts. That's where we're concentrating our search," explained Jeff.

Steve nodded, looking out of the window without saying a word.

Ali asked if any of the reports suggested that Tygo might be gay.

"No, why?" Jeff asked in surprise.

"You mentioned St. Jacques."

"Oh, so you know the city already."

"No, just doing my job." Ali's reply was curt.

"There is a large gay community in St. Jacques, but there's no indication that Tygo has links with it from personal motives. There must be some other reason that we don't know about yet," Jeff replied. "We just want to show you the territory that we're combing."

"OK, let's go."

"We've got people, informants and agents, operating in these areas. As soon as any information surfaces, they pass it straight on to me."

"Good," said Steve approvingly, without attaching any more importance to his explanation.

When they arrived in Sablon, Ali couldn't resist the temptation to get out and walk. The most important antique shops in Europe were grouped around the main square, behind the church of Our Lady of Sablon. Her interest was twofold, from a point of view that was both artistic but also professional. The art and antiquities market offered extraordinary opportunities for money laundering. Several of the exquisite shops in the area, full of works of art but empty of customers, could only exist for that purpose.

Steve was amazed by the *choclateries* dressed up as boutiques that exhibited their wares as if they were jewels – and seemed to be priced accordingly.

The trip through the rest of the districts strengthened his feeling that the cosmopolitan nature of Brussels made it an ideal place for Tygo to hide. His conventional appearance and his fluency in five languages supplied him almost perfect cover.

When they had finished doing the rounds, Jeff asked if they would like to continue with their trip around the city.

"No, thanks," Ali replied. "Let's go on to Liege. We've got time to get there before dark, get something to eat and then carry on to Maastricht and spend the night there."

"Right, lads, you heard the lady. Take the E40 to Liege," Jeff told his men.

On the way, Steve explained to Jeff that he had decided to keep the Dutch police out of this operation, because the objective was to *persuade* Tygo to accompany them to London. Using force would mean an arrest or a kidnapping, and that was the last thing they wanted.

If their colleagues at NSOS were involved, they might feel obliged to arrest him, and from then on everything would be placed in the hands of some duty magistrate. That scenario would definitely not fit in with the orders they had to carry out from London and Washington.

Giving some leeway to NSOS would protect them to some extent. If anything went wrong, they could always blame the British and American services for running operations on their patch without authorisation. That would create a diplomatic problem that would have to be resolved at a different level.

However, they had to take into consideration the fact that a few years earlier, Brecht hadn't been able to prevent Goran and Tygo from getting away before they were arrested. Someone had tipped them off before the arrest took place, and Mike didn't know if the informant had ever been identified.

At all costs they had to avoid any leak. They would only get one shot. Failure wasn't an option.

"Mike call Bretch in due course," announced Steve.

"We know that the Amsterdam police are already asking questions. I think they already have an arrest warrant out over the methamphetamine labs," said Jeff, trying not to dampen his enthusiasm.

"All the more reason to move quick then. Our position is a bit different. We think Virin was made on the outskirts of Amsterdam, but it wasn't distributed in their jurisdiction; and there are no Dutch citizens affected. Almost all the fatalities took place in the Baltic States and Byelorussia. To my way of thinking, they don't have the right to investigate a crime that wasn't committed here, at least until they receive a request from some court inside the European Union," Steve continued. "In any case," he went on, "we need to avoid Tygo being arrested in Europe at all costs. If he's sent to prison here, Goran will ensure he'll remain silent forever."

"And how do you think you can persuade him?" asked Jeff.

"By making him an offer he can't refuse." Steve's answer raised a smile from his colleagues.

"And what might that be?" asked Jeff.

"Wait and see. The secret of a patient man is to keep himself busy with something else while he waits."

"Don't worry, Steve. We won't have long to wait," Jeff answered, with a smile on his lips.

XXIII

MAASTRICHT IS THE MOST COSMOPOLITAN CITY in the south of Holland, always crammed with foreign students, tourists and one-and-a-half million Belgians and Germans per year, coming to buy cannabis legally in special cafes.

The Netherlands is the only Western country where the sale of cannabis has been legalised, and yet only 13 per cent of young people take it. This is a lower percentage than the United States or France, countries that have much stricter drug policies. The price is even lower than in Belgium, where people are allowed to possess up to three grams of cannabis for personal use, although supplying the drug is still illegal.

During the group's evening meal it was impossible to avoid talking about these issues, which Jeff was expert in, since he had been stationed in the region for three years.

Netherlands law allows the sale of cannabis from licensed shops but restricts the quantity that can be bought. A mayor of Maastricht compared this inconsistency to letting bakeries sell bread but restricting the amount of flour they are allowed to buy. The pressure created by this unsatisfied demand has resulted in a thriving black market, exploited by criminal gangs operating in the region.

The extraordinary profits generated by the cannabis trade attracts the organised crime but also corrupts certain groups of professionals, especially lawyers, estate agents and bankers, who find themselves tied up with the subsequent operations of money laundering.

The Dutch police estimate that illegal cannabis growing is a cottage industry worth some 2,700 million euros, almost half of what is produced by the entire horticultural industry of the country.

On the other hand, enquiries show that 80 per cent of the Dutch people are opposed to the closure of the 730 cafes where marijuana can legally be sold and which pay a sales tax of 52 per cent. This contributes some three hundred million euros annually to government coffers.

However, their neighbours in Belgium, Germany and France are not very happy. They accuse Dutch laws of creating unnecessary problems in their peaceful border towns.

Jeff underlined the fact that most of the crime and violence was not at all related to the authorised outlets but to a growth industry in which the criminal gangs were fighting among themselves for the goods and products.

"A good example of unbridled capitalism," Steve joked, sipping his coffee.

"You don't have to buy cannabis from Morocco anymore," continued Jeff. "They say here that only forty per cent of the cannabis grown in Holland is needed to satisfy demand in the local shops."

"Do you think Goran and Tygo are linked to these activities?"

"We know that Goran controls one of the farms and some greenhouses that we've got under observation. Probably Tygo spends one or two days there on production management to report to his boss. We'll be waiting for him.

"Most of the people we shadow are foreigners," Jeff went on. "There aren't many Dutch involved with these mafias' activity. However, this region is home to a lot of international cartels carrying out drug trafficking operations, smuggling illegal immigrants, bringing in human beings for sexual exploitation, trafficking arms and stolen vehicles, you know what it's like.

"A growing number of Romanians and Bulgarians are getting involved. As you know a lot of European agencies are keeping a close eye on them."

"Recently, the Dutch and the Finns made it clear that they are still strongly opposed to including Bulgaria and Romania in the Schengen agreement, until they can produce evidence that they are making progress in the war against corruption and organised crime," Ali commented, slowly sipping the rose wine that still lingered in her glass. "In the last twenty years, there have been more than one hundred fifty contract killings of high-ranking Mafia bosses in Bulgaria, most of them carried out in broad daylight."

"Yes, in most cases they're the hired killers contracted for these operations," Jeff agreed. "The brains of the operation stay outside the country, directing one of the well-known international networks, but it's far too difficult to prove a link to any actual operation. Even when you do find specific evidence, it can only incriminate the people who are involved in the operation at ground level." Jeff's frustration clearly showed in his voice.

"The way we're fighting them is like trying to cut down a tree with a pair of scissors," Steve said in a resigned tone. "Cutting off the leaves first and occasionally a branch or two. But the tree is so big that while you're dealing with one branch, a whole lot of others are growing and expanding."

"That's true. Stopping them from being part of the Schengen agreement isn't going to do very much to reduce their criminal activities around here. Goran is a typical example of how the Serbian mafia has grown to such a point that they're taking over from the Russians. Some of them are commando groups, organised in exile, trafficking ecstasy and heroin from the Balkans," said Jeff.

Steve looked at him with some disdain. This was one of his specialties. "Don't kid yourself, Jeff; arms trafficking is still their main activity. Anything else is secondary."

"Do you think Tygo is working with them?" Jeff asked him.

Ali jumped in before Steve could reply. "No, I don't think so. Tygo is involved in a more sophisticated operation. They're still at the experimental stage."

"Is there anything that points to the Italian mafias?" asked Steve.

"Not at the moment. The clans from Calabria, Naples and Sicily operate in the Netherlands through the port of Rotterdam because it's so close to Germany. They invest their gains there or go underground when arrest warrants are issued in other areas. They operate in the north, not down here. It's just a transit zone for them," replied Jeff.

"The thugs who were working in Marbella, including blowing up my car, were fair-haired and looked as if they came from Northern Europe. They could have been Latvians or Lithuanians, like Goran's rolling labs workers," added Steve.

"Yes, we're thinking along the same lines. However, most of those are controlled by the Russian mafias. It's possible Goran is working for the Russians and employs some of their thugs. But if you think about it, he is a small fish for negotiating with Mexican cartels. More likely it was the Russians who had financial links with them, and Crowe is the link. Goran must be his local foreman," Ali explained.

"That's an interesting theory, a bit complicated, but it explains a lot," Steve replied. "What's the plan for tomorrow?"

"The plan is to tour the routes that these groups use to cross the frontiers, visit a couple of places in the Drielandenpunt. If you like, we can talk to some of our men on the ground," Jeff suggested.

"Sounds interesting, but I don't think it's necessary. We'd prefer it if you kept us informed."

"That's fine," said Jeff.

"We're going to set our strategy and priorities according to the intelligence that we receive, while you carry on with operations on the ground," Ali pointed out.

"That's fine by me," Jeff replied, putting his glass down on the table.

"OK, let's go to bed. We've got a big day ahead of us."

"Yes, best get a bit of shut-eye. Breakfast at eight on the dot?" Ali tried to make her order sound like a suggestion.

They all agreed.

XXIV

THE TOUR THROUGH THE AREA BROUGHT nothing new, apart from the unexpected pleasure of visiting a part of Holland that many of its own countrymen don't know about. At the end of the day, they decided that Ali should stay in Amsterdam while Steve went back to Maastricht. From these two points, they would coordinate the movements of Jeff and his team, who continued to comb the area in search of information that would lead them to Tygo.

By the end of the first week, the few bits of information they had obtained were very vague and came from sources that weren't particularly trustworthy.

On Wednesday morning of the second week, Steve got a call from Ali. He could detect a worried note in her voice. Her tone was more serious, and her repetition of expressions like "I think…it seems to me…we ought to…" showed a hesitancy unusual in her.

She had just heard from Washington that Goran had been found dead in Agadir. Only one shot, a 22-calibre bullet, straight through the temple. No one had seen or heard anything.

Forensics had found less gunpowder than usual around the entry wound. This suggested that the assassin had removed half of the gunpowder content from the cartridge, to reduce the sound of the explosion when the shot was fired, but leaving enough for the bullet to penetrate the skull at its weakest point.

The job was very professional, but that wasn't the whole story. In America, a joint operation between the Mexican marines and the DTF had succeeded in capturing a dangerous local drug baron. In the course of the operation, they had confiscated a substantial quantity of methamphetamine and fifty capsules of a substance that, on analysis, gave the same results as they had found in Marbella.

The link between the American and European rings, that one that Cooper had warned them about, had been confirmed.

For some reason or other they no longer had any use for Goran, but would they also get rid of Tygo?

Now it was just a question of time. His fate was sealed.

Steve knew that the so called *war on drugs* was an absurd pipe dream, but to look on with his hands in his pockets was not an option that he could accept.

He felt sorry for Ali, as this would certainly make things more difficult for her to collect evidence against Newton. But that wasn't his problem. To him, this new evidence meant they had to redouble their effort to catch Tygo before he was eliminated. That was the only thing that could help them dismantle the local network of laboratories that were still experimenting with the new drug. At least that way they could save a few lives, "and afterward…then we'll see," he said gravely, gripping the phone with all his strength, as if he wants to crush it.

"I know, Steve. Let's leave the generals to take charge of the war and limit ourselves to our own little battles. With a bit of luck, we'll get something," answered Ali, despondently.

That very afternoon Steve received an unexpected visit.

Mike had arrived from London to get up to speed with developments on the ground. Just as in the old days, Steve had prepared a detailed report on everything that had happened until then and what progress they were making towards achieving their objectives.

"Our intelligence thinks Goran's assassination had to do with something rather different. One of his jobs was to secure a constant flow of ephedrine to be shipped to America. To do this, he was constantly having to create new routes and complex systems. That meant massive expenditure and very complicated logistics. The Mexicans were willing to pay the agreed price, but it seems that Goran had kept some of the change. Now he won't be keeping anything anymore," explained Mike.

"And what do you think will happen to Tygo?"

"That's very difficult to say. Now that Goran is no longer part of the picture, they'll put someone else in charge of the Virin project. Tygo will stay alive as long as they think the drug he's making will be profitable in the short term. But the fact that the same pills have been found in Mexico suggests that some other technician is involved. Perhaps they're planning to continue the development in America. I don't know."

"That will be a DFT's problem."

"Yes, another one."

"Do you think Tygo is still in Europe?" asked Steve.

"Definitely. They must be guarding him under very strict security. But don't worry, you'll find him. One way or another...."

The conversation turned to the American services' concern at finding the new version of Virin in Mexico. Cooper's prophecy made good sense. It was no longer a question of *if*, but when and where they would start to test the markets. They could no longer prevent it, but perhaps they could do something to gain time and take preventive measures to minimise the impact in the United States. No one, not even they, could prevent these drugs from being introduced into a market that demanded them.

"We're pissing into the wind, Mike," said Steve, crestfallen.

"Oh, come on, do you really want Tygo and the ones who poisoned those boys to carry on with their work and do it all over again?"

"No, of course not."

"Then stop messing around with cheap poetry and get him before it's too late."

XXV

LITTLE DROPS OF DRIZZLE THAT COULDN'T decide whether to turn into rain splashed upon Steve's face, making him blink. *There must be lots of people on the beach now*, he thought to himself, as he crossed the canal, hands deep in the pockets of his mackintosh.

Ali and Steve quickened their pace, dodging tourists, passers-by and sightseers. Now the facade of Amsterdam Central Station was coming clearly into view, and they could make out the white lions holding up the shield with the third lion, gilded like the crowns that transformed them into symbols of monarchy.

The leaden skies of the end of September couldn't prevent the coloured building, with its mixture of neo Gothic and Renaissance styles, from appearing majestic.

Everything had happened very suddenly. Only the professionalism of Jeff and his rapid response team had stopped them from losing that unexpected opportunity. Steve was in town when he got the call.

"Tygo is on the Amsterdam train. Double confirmation and positive sighting. Looks as if he's coming from Utrecht, where he's been spotted, and he's being followed. But he's not alone; there are two fair-haired men with him."

Ali and Steve were waiting at the end of platform 5, where they knew the train would pull in, while Jeff and his team were guarding the station entrance. On the surface their communications equipment looked like ordinary smart phones and MP3 players, but they worked on a special frequency with an encryption system, making it impenetrable.

The agent on board the train had told them that they were travelling in the third coach. To avoid being recognised, Steve suggested they should go towards platform 4, on the other side of the same platform, where the trains left in the opposite direction.

They stopped short only ten metres from the door where Tygo and his companions would get out. They had never seen him in person though by this stage he already felt like an old acquaintance.

For several weeks now, they had been memorising all the photos and videos in his dossier, right down to the details of his gait, his speech and his gestures. They also knew that he was wearing a black leather jacket and matching cap, red cravat and dark blue corduroy trousers. As usual, he had on high boots of dark brown leather. The agent on the train also described an unusual detail: on his chin was a few days growth of stubble.

According to plan, when the train pulled in, they merged with the crowd of people getting off, but without losing visual contact.

"Third carriage, second door, flanked by two men a bit younger than he is. He'll be the second passenger getting off."

"Got it," replied Steve.

They both identified him immediately.

A quick glance and discreet signal to the agent tailing Tygo, was enough to making him understand that from then on, they were in charge. Straight away Jeff's man went off in the opposite direction.

Tygo went down the steps leading to the tunnel that connected all the platforms with the main concourse.

"We're coming out through the tunnel. You'll see him in thirty seconds."

Jeff was waiting outside with five of his men. Two in the BMW 520, two others in the black Range Rover and two more on bicycles.

As they went out, the cyclists approached so they could get a good view but avoided contact with Ali and Steve. One of them was Jeff. During the operation the team in the car would give logistical support and the men in the Range Rover would be involved with transporting personnel and equipment, while the agents on bicycles, the most appropriate way to get around in Amsterdam, were ready to intervene at any time or any place they were needed.

The nearer they got to the exit, the more people they met going here and there. Some of them were drinking coffee or eating sausage prepared in the little bars lined up all along the length of the corridor; others were buying provisions in the mini-marts before they went home.

Steve decided to move in closer, but Tygo suddenly stopped and, for no apparent reason, turned round.

Steve continued to walk on as if nothing had happened, and went into a tobacconist's shop a few yards ahead. Ali immediately slipped into the newspaper kiosk on the right and started to leaf through some magazines, discreetly trying to hide her face in them.

Steve could see clearly what was happening from inside the shop. "We're fine. He's buying sweets. He may be going cold turkey and needs some sugar to calm himself down. Stay where you are, Ali," he murmured into his microphone.

"Roger."

Tygo popped some sweets into his mouth, opened the can and drank a few drops of cola, almost at the same time. Then he continued on his way, but now he seemed hesitant, as if lost in thought. His companions followed him patiently, without saying a word.

Steve asked Ali to go ahead and wait in the main station concourse until they arrived. Steve went back to tailing him, but now only five metres behind. The two cyclists were already there, waiting for them outside, ready to join with them or take up their post.

Something made Steve think that Tygo was on the alert, but seeing him close up made him realise that this wasn't so. His pale, sweaty face told Steve that he just needed a fix to calm himself down.

Tygo arrived in the main concourse of *Amsterdam Centraal*, crossed the hall and left the building, making for the tram terminal on the other side of the street.

"Line 1, white and blue tram," said Steve, without taking his eyes off his prey.

"Roger."

The cars moved forward two stops and waited there. The cyclists waited for the tram at the other side of the bridge over the canal that went round the station.

Ali got into the same carriage by a different door, while Steve stayed in the carriage behind that gave him a clear view of the men. Trams leaving the Central Station were always full, and this was no exception. The risk of being spotted among so many people was negligible.

As the crossed over Damrak bridge, the cyclists began to follow them a short distance behind.

Jeff could keep an eye on the three from his bicycle, and Ali and Steve could identify him from his yellow and white helmet.

Tygo was sitting down, trying to read a paper, but his eyes were flickering too rapidly and rather abruptly. He almost felt sorry for this pathetic caricature at the verge of collapse. The men looking after him stayed silent, completely indifferent.

As they got near the Keizergracht, Tygo jumped up like a jack-in-the-box.

"Next stop," said Steve, noting a furtive look from Ali.

"Roger."

The three men got off, waited for the tram to pull away and then crossed the road. When they reached the opposite pavement, they made for the Herengracht canal.

"I've got a good view of them," said Jeff, who was following them from the other side of the canal. "They're going towards the river Amstel."

Thank God for the bikes, thought Steve, following them from a safe distance.

Two hundred yards ahead they stopped in front of a three-storey building. Tygo retrieved a key from his pocket and opened the door of a small but pretty house facing the canal. He seemed familiar with the place.

The vehicles were making slow progress, because the traffic flow was in the opposite direction from the way the rest of the team were going. Steve realised that only one bridge near the house was big enough to let cars get close as planned.

After many twists and U-turns, they managed to get over a bridge that was only seventy yards away from the house.

Ali and Steve breathed a sigh of relief at their arrival. This time luck was on their side.

"Take up your positions," ordered Jeff.

He deployed his agents rapidly, according to plan. One vehicle fifty yards ahead of the objective and another fifty yards behind, near the bridge.

Jeff, Ali and Steve met near the Range Rover to talk over the next phase of the operation. Tygo Gillis had been flushed out, they had tailed him successfully and now they had him cornered.

The house was an elegant, black brick building with wide picture windows looking onto the canal, and no one seemed to be keeping watch from inside.

They waited for an hour, and the place seemed quiet. No one had gone in or out during that time.

"We're going to give him a bit of time to get his dose and quieten down. I want to talk to him when he is calmer. I don't want him to make the wrong decision so we have to take him by force," Steve said without taking his eyes off the house.

"I'm with you," said Ali. "What do you have in mind?"

"I've already told you. I'm going to knock on the door and make him an offer he can't refuse," Steve repeated, a smile on his lips.

"Are you joking?"

"No, I really mean it. Everything ready?" he asked, turning to Jeff.

"Yes, the transport network is ready," he replied.

"Our contact in the embassy has confirmed that the bird is ready to fly as soon as we get to the airport. They're awaiting their orders," Ali added.

"Great. If everything goes according to plan, we'll be in touch with them in about an hour."

"What are you going to do if he doesn't want to come?"

"I'll have to improvise, but I couldneed help. Let me go in on my own, and don't stop keeping an eye on the main window. I'm going to try and stand somewhere near there, where I can see you and be seen."

"Fine," said Jeff, "but I think your plan is a very risky one."

"We don't have any choice. There isn't much time. Breaking into the house is even more risky," said Ali.

"I'm going in. Wish me luck."

"Good luck! You're going to need it," she answered with a nod.

"Thanks," Steve answered with a smile. He seemed to be enjoying the thrill of the moment.

XXVI

WITH A FIRM, DETERMINED STEP, Steve went straight up to the main door.

They might have seen him coming, but it no longer mattered. He was confident in the backup that Jeff's agents offered, and he would do his best to avoid any violent situation. He just wanted to talk to Tygo and convince him that his best option was to come with him.

The only problem would be to neutralise the bodyguards, who were sure to be armed. He had no idea how many there were, or what sort of weapons they were carrying, but on the other hand, he didn't want to create a problem that would attract the attention of the local police. Everything had to be done quickly and discreetly.

He ran up the eight steps and rang the bell.

Silence. No answer.

He rang once more and started to wonder what he would do if no one came out to open the door.

After a few seconds that seemed like hours, he heard the metallic sound of a bolt being drawn and the slight squeak of the heavy wood door being opened.

A man of medium height, with blue eyes and straight blond hair, came out to meet him. With a rough look he raised his head and mouthed a gesture without saying a word.

"Tygo. I've come to find Tygo. Tell him I want to talk to him," said Steve, looking him straight in the eye.

"Who's Tygo?" he replied in English, with a strong accent that sounded to Steve as if it came from northern Europe.

"Cut the bullshit. You know bloody well who Tygo is. I'm not the Dutch police."

Almost as a reflex, the man took a step backwards and tried to slam the door. Steve leapt forward into the doorway to stop him. The man tried to grab a weapon that lay on a small table by the front door, and Steve had no choice but to get in and seize him by the arm and twisting it into a position as uncomfortable as painful.

Quiet. I only want to talk to Tygo. Nothing more. Just that, do you understand me?" he said without lessening his grip.

With his eyes half closed from the pain, the man said that Tygo wasn't there. With a rapid movement, Steve twisted the arm even more still holding a firm grip. The man groaned with pain and cursed in an incomprehensible tongue.

"I told you to cut the crap. I saw him come in; tell him I've come with people from Virin. They're waiting for him outside," said Steve, indicating the window with his head as he threw him against a wall with a strong punch.

The man got up slowly, clutching an injured shoulder, and looked out of the window, only to see Ali, Jeff and three of his men stationed just in front of the house on the other side of the street.

"We don't have much time. In ten minutes the police will be here, and neither you nor I want that, do we? Now, go and get Tygo for me."

Steve was playing a difficult hand, betting on the fact that the thugs in the house felt they were at a disadvantage. They should have to decide whether to confront Steve's group or the police, and they only had ten minutes.

"Wait," said the heavy, going towards the inside of the house and clutching his right arm, as if it were going to drop off.

Property on the canals in the centre of Amsterdam had always been very expensive. For four hundred years the price was set according to the length of the frontage. That is why the buildings are usually very tall and narrow. These limitations require very specific architectural solutions; for example, they all have large windows at the front and a hook at the tip of the gable where the tiles meet, from which they hang pulleys to take up anything that they can't get in through the door or up the stairs. Steve went into the living room and stopped by the central window. He looked out and made eye contact with his team. A brief nod told them everything was going well so far.

Tygo did not keep him waiting. He came in right away, accompanied by the same guard who had opened the door and another fair-haired man who stood behind him, arms folded and looking as if he meant business. It was the same pair who had accompanied him from the station to the house, and who had possibly been in Marbella.

Tygo seemed calmer now and was walking better, although his movements were a bit slow. From the short distance between them, Steve could see that his pupils were very small. No doubt he had just had his dose.

"Who the fuck are you?"

"I'm your best shot, Tygo. We had a common friend, his name was Kurt Render. But we have to talk on our own. Tell this lot to fuck off."

Taken by surprise, Tygo looked at the thugs and gestured to them to leave him alone.

They gave him a doubtful look and talked among themselves in a language that sounded like Russian but it wasn't.

The house wasn't large; Tygo had opened the door with his own key and the men who were in there were the same ones he had arrived with. Steve was almost certain there was no one else inside. If things turned out badly, he would only have to contend with these two. Tygo was still so weak, he looked as if a puff of wind would blow him over.

"What do you want?" he asked, unsure whether to be annoyed or surprised.

"Look Tygo, we don't have much time, and it'll be better if we cut the crap and go straight to the point. I know who you are and what you've been up to. But someone has just got rid of Goran, and you are next in their list."

On hearing this Tygo turned even paler than he was before. "You seem to know a lot. Who are you?" he asked again, taking a battered packet of tobacco out of his pocket and starting to roll himself a cigarette.

"I work for a British agency. It's about the Virin project and the drug you've been producing. I'm investigating the deaths of British citizens in Marbella."

"Why didn't you come with IPOL?"

"Because I haven't come to arrest you. I've come to invite you to come home with me, so we can talk. We might arrest you afterwards. You and I know that if you stay here your days, maybe your hours are numbered."

"I haven't killed anybody. It was them – Goran and the American. I told them –"

Steve interrupted him sharply "Look, right now we're only talking about getting you out of here. You saw how they dealt with Render, and now they've got to Goran. You're bound to be next on the list. It's only a question of time. We need information, and in exchange we're offering you protection. Your cooperation will be taken into account in your trial, but you've got to decide quickly. I've got my team outside waiting for you."

Tygo stared at him and remained silent as he pondered the offer from this stranger who had turned up so unexpectedly. His whole life had been nothing but chaos, and this situation, although bizarre, didn't surprise him in the least.

"Your friends are calling their bosses right now to get their orders," Steve went on. "These lines are being bugged, and it's only a matter of minutes before we hear the first siren."

"Fuck off. Who the fuck do you think you are?"

"Right now I am your best option. I'm the only one who can rescue you."

"They've got nothing on me in Holland."

"They've still got a warrant out for your arrest for the rolling labs. You were lucky I got to you before they did. If you end up in prison, you won't last a week. They're going to silence you right away like they did with Goran...."

"You're making this up...it's a lie."

"I'm telling you to cut the crap. You know I'm right, and your time's up. We've found your pills in Mexico. You know what that means? They're looking for someone to carry on with what you started. As soon as they find him, they'll make you redundant."

"You're bulllshitting me," grunted Tygo.

"Right then, if you think I'm lying, you can take your chances. My being here will speed things up considerably. Now they know we are after you."

Tygo was no longer looking at Steve. His head was lowered and he was looking nervously at the flawless, handsome floorboards of Slavonic oak.

He seemed to fall to pieces as he clung on to the thin cigarette he was rolling between his fingers.

Steve was quiet for a while to let him stew on a slow burner, but time was running out.

"Go to hell, I'm not going." Tygo spoke without looking up.

"OK, OK. It's your decision." Steve turned to the window as he spoke.

"Why should I believe you? How can I be sure you haven't come here to get rid of me?"

"If I'd wanted to kill you, I'd have done it by now. I don't like wasting time, and I didn't come here for a chat. I've got my crew down there and a jet waiting at Schipol. If you come with us, in a couple of hours you could be safe in England. If I go, from the moment you step outside, your life won't be worth a fig. You already know that. "Don't get me wrong, Tygo. Right now, a friend of mine is fighting for his life in a Marbella hospital because of the shit you've been making. I'd like to put a bullet between your eyes at this very moment, but I can't. I've got different orders."

Tygo raised his head, and when he met Steve's gaze he decided he was telling the truth.

"I'm going to need half an hour to get my things ready. And what do we do with these?" he asked, with a sideways look at the two men waiting in the other room.

"We haven't got a minute. By now the police and your friends' reinforcements are on their way. Is there anyone else in the house?"

"No, but you're right – they could get here at any moment."

"Let's go, then. I'll take care of these two." Steve opened the door and pulled out his pistol. "Get out and go to the black Range Rover on the corner. My men are down there. Go with them."

The bodyguards came out as soon as they heard the sound of the door. Without a word, one of them hurled himself at Steve and tried to grab him by the throat. Tygo ran quickly down the steps, scared to death, looking backwards and forwards. He didn't know where the bullet would come from. When he saw him, Jeff came over and took him by the arm. "Come with me."

Steve managed to dodge the attack that was launched at him with a swift movement to the left. The thug lost his balance, and Steve managed to take advantage of this by throwing him down by the arm he was still holding in front of him. He could feel something crack under his hand when he gave him a strong, sharp blow to the throat.

At the very moment that the first thug fell to his knees, clutching his throat as if he was trying to strangle himself, the other one appeared, gun in hand. Without a moment's hesitation, Steve fired two consecutive shots into his chest.

From the street, Ali heard faint sounds of gunfire, and her professional instinct made her to run towards the shots. At the front door, she came face to face with Steve as he came out, panting heavily.

"I'm fine, but I had to put down one of them. Let's get out of here, the police and these guys' friends will be here any minute."

"We're leaving. Let's go now!" ordered Ali through her microphone.

The incident would be investigated by local officials and eventually precipitate a diplomatic crisis, but that was not their problem now. They had got Tygo and, for the time being, had avoided a confrontation in public. Mike and Ali's boss would deal with the Dutch. If the thugs' friends got there before the police, they'd probably deal with the body. The last thing any of them would want was to attract any attention.

When Ali and Steve got into the vehicle, Tygo was anxious and breathing heavily.

The blue BMW swiftly came up behind them and followed a short distance away. The two cyclists also followed them, weaving in and out and trying to delay the traffic that came up from the back to help their escape.

As soon as they got onto the main street, the cars gained speed and were immediately lost to view. Jeff drove towards the A10, the Amsterdam ring road, his escape route towards Schipol international airport. Ali talked nonstop into her phone while Steve tried to calm Tygo by telling him that everything was going according to plan. In a few minutes they would be heading for London. Tygo seemed to be shaking, but this time it was from fear.

"The transport's ready. They're waiting for us in hangar 9," said Ali, as she finished her call.

It took them no more than twenty minutes to get to the military sector of Schipol. There, a Learjet 85, white and marked with a double stripe of dark blue and gold, was waiting on the tarmac, engines running. American personnel were watching out for them at the entry post to facilitate their identification and rush them to the plane.

Jeff pulled up a few yards from the boarding ladder.

"Good job. See you around," Steve said, and held out a hand to him. Then he took Tygo's arm and got him on board the aircraft without giving him any time to think about it.

Ali gave Jeff his final instructions, and at last she, too, held out her hand to him. "You'll come out well in my report, Jeff."

"Thanks, Ali. Pleasure," he replied, and, putting his hand on his heart, he bent slightly forward and gave her a mock bow.

The aircraft taxied slowly towards the runway. It was third in the queue for take-off. Jeff and his men watched closely until the jet was lost to view among the clouds. Now their task was over.

"Everything's gone well so far." Ali breathed a quick sigh of relief. Steve sat with an expression approaching a smile on his face as he drank a scotch to wind down. Tygo stayed silent, sinking low in his seat, deep in thought, staring vacantly into the skies that, at this height, were completely cloudless.

No doubt he had plenty to think about.

Fifty minutes later they landed in a small airport in Bedfordshire, England. Penshurst airport only had one landing strip, three buildings and two hangars. It was small, secure, discreet and convenient to use, both for private fleets and special operations. No airline or commercial transport took off or landed there.

As the jet reached the head of the runway, it taxied towards the terminal building, where two cars were waiting for them. With a firm but elegant movement the hostess opened the plane door and lowered the gangway. Almost simultaneously, Mike got out of one of the cars. "Welcome home!" he said.

"Thanks," Ali said with a smile. "But I still have a long way to go before I get home."

"Well done, mate," said Mike, holding out his hand to Steve. Steve shook his boss's hand, smiled and started to walk towards the vehicles without letting go of Tygo. "Mr Gillis, I presume," Mike went on. "My name's Mike. You took the right decision to come here, you'll be safe with us. But don't worry, we'll have time to talk tomorrow. Today you'd better rest. You'll find all you need when we get home."

"*All* I need?"

"Yes, all. We won't let you feel bad. A doctor will examine you when we get there, and he'll give you what you need."

Tygo's only response was a sort of grunt that Mike chose to interpret as appreciation.

The cars made straight for the house where they had held their first meeting some weeks before. All of that seemed so long ago now.

On arrival, Mike's men took Tygo to his room. He looked completely worn out. Inexorably, his fate had caught up with him, and now he had to face the consequences. This time there would be no escape, but at least he had got away with his life.

XXVII

NEXT MORNING ALI AND STEVE were back in the same room where they had received their orders a few weeks earlier to start their operation, but that this time they were meeting to debrief on the procedures and the results they had obtained.

Mike had a lot of questions and wanted to know all the details, especially of the incident in which Steve had fired the shots. The Dutch were furious and threatening to cause a major row.

"I had no choice, Mike. He was trying to reach for his gun, so I had to defend myself. It was him or me. If I'd been hurt, the whole operation would have been a failure."

"OK, we'll discuss it later when I get the details from the Foreign Office. They and the Americans will have to sort something out to pacify the Dutch. They knew that one way or another, something of the sort was likely to occur."

After breakfast, Tygo was brought to the room that served as an interview centre.

The general impression was discreet, with just two cheap Turner reproductions on walls that, apart from that showed nothing in particular. A bronze candelabra with five branching arms ending in green lampshades, hung right in the middle of the room, exactly over the centre of the solid oak table with its six very solid, comfortable chairs.

Everything in the room combined to give an impression of serenity and established, old-fashioned solidity, exactly what the people who were going to be interrogated there needed.

Most of the guests had spent their previous days overwhelmed by profound emotional crises, deciding how much to give, and if they had got as far as this room it was because at some point along the way they had decided to collaborate. No one thought of this as the best decision, just the least bad one.

They called it the *soften room*. It was a special place, destined to facilitate the initial stages of interrogations that usually lasted for several weeks. Its purpose was to relax the guests and make them feel safe, calm and ready to talk to anyone who could help them. As in Tygo's case, that help almost always meant protection.

Generally these sessions didn't last more than twenty-four or forty-eight hours. The stage of the interrogation that went deeper and lasted longer was left in the hands of intelligence service personnel based at Headquarters.

Steve and Ali were waiting for Tygo when he entered the room. He seemed a bit calmer and was looking better.

The meeting was polite but not cordial. They offered him tea, coffee, orange juice or water, trying not to let his mouth dry up; if that happened, it would make him aware of his own anxiety, triggering a panic attack and causing unnecessary disruptions.

For the time being he was all right, but he felt he would need a shot before midday. "No problem," he was told.

To start off, Steve made some comments about the events of the previous day and cracked a couple of bad jokes about the jet they travelled on and Ali's finances. He tried to appear relaxed and carefree during the interrogation. He played on Tygo's prospects, hoping that his anxiety would turn into the need to talk. At that point they would "naturally" move on to specific questions.

After a few minutes, Goran's name cropped up in the conversation.

That was the moment.

"How did you meet him?" Ali enquired.

They both knew the answers to all the initial questions, but Ali and Steve wanted to ease the conversation and test the credibility of the answers. Tygo gave his version of the events of the last ten years in Bristol, Paris and Cologne. Increasingly he came through as a victim of circumstances or of the system. In his twisted view of the facts, Goran represented both.

Almost with resignation, he told them about the meth labs and the escape to Morocco, but never mentioning of the Virin project.

Tygo addressed Ali primarily, with an occasional glance at Steve, who remained silent so as not to interrupt the flow of the interrogation.

Like a child running round and round the edge of a park, Tygo talked about all the peripheral subjects. As the hours passed, his confidence grew, and he got ready to step into more difficult territory.

He touched on his relationship with Goran in Morocco, giving a detailed description of how he became involved in the organization with an online system for distributing and selling different legal highs and a mixture of herbs with Blue Lotus and Bean Bay, sometimes known as Spice.

Goran was in charge of the operation overall, and Tygo was only paid for working in the office and keeping the web pages up to date. Anyone else could have done the work, but Tygo thought that by keeping him out of Europe, rather than getting rid of him, his boss was making an investment for the future.

He denied knowing anything about the relationship between Goran and Newton and insisted that the first time he heard the name was in Morocco.

They didn't believe him, but they had to leave it for the time being.

It seemed that Newton didn't trust Render, and he needed someone capable of working closely with him to learn all his secrets until the Virin project was completed. Both Goran and Newton agreed, Tygo would be the appropriate candidate to take over the project.

That was the opportunity that Goran was hoping for to repay his investment, and for Tygo to get away from there.

Tygo had very specific orders. The first thing was to familiarise himself with all the technical details of the project and any other information that Render was keeping to himself.

Returning to Europe was Tygo's only chance to escape alive from Morocco. He joined Render's team at the very moment that found them in the throes of a big strategic dilemma: whether to stick to Plan A, which was to continue searching for a safer source of endless pleasure and social control, or implement Plan B, which meant making a few improvements to the existing molecule and selling it like an alternative new drug without much considering safety issues. After interminable heated discussions, they reached a compromise solution: to implement Plan B in order to finance Plan A. That is to say, they would use the money coming from the dirty molecule to perfect and complete Virin.

Now the only remaining issues to resolve would be the time needed to finalise the project rather than the money.

"I know it was a crazy idea, but Render was so brilliant that he managed to convince everybody that it was the most convenient solution. That old dog Newton didn't believe him, but what other choice did he have?"

Render now had six months to show results or face the consequences. Newton had never threatened him directly, but a word to the wise is sufficient.

"I stayed on the fringes of all these negotiations, and I didn't want to lose Render because I was learning so much, and in a way, I felt sorry for him," said Tygo.

The man was a genius, but he'd got mixed up with the wrong people.

The new drug they began to develop was perfect in theory, but the reality was very different. Though Render worked day and night, I always had the impression he was plotting something.

The design of a drug starts from mathematical and chemical models, then it moves to biochemical testing and finally, if all goes well, it is tested on laboratory animals.

"Goran said he didn't have time for all this. He wanted results yesterday! No doubt those were Newton's orders."

Steve looked up from his note-taking and asked him, "Wait, do you mean that Render bypassed the most elementary safety precautions and started to trial the drugs on real people?"

"No, it wasn't him," Tygo answered. "The world was turned upside down, and the animals took over the laboratory. We were making progress slowly but surely, but this wasn't enough for Goran. There was a lot of tension in the team. Every day there were threatening messages from Morocco that scared me stiff. It was then that Render disappeared and cut loose with all that stuff…" finished Tygo. He slumped forward onto the table, head in his hands.

An uncomfortable silence fell in the room as Steve offered him a little water. Tygo made no acknowledgement but sipped it slowly. Ali asked if he knew when and where they had started to trial the new drug.

"That came a bit later. At that time, the work was going on in Render's main lab near Brussels. One day he told me that he had to go to an urgent meeting. I didn't think too much of it. Three days later, the accident happened."

Tygo stopped for a few moments, lost in thought. He helped himself to a drop more water and drank it in two gulps. Although his glass was now empty, he kept it in his hand and continued his story as if he was glued to it.

"After Render's death Goran was desperate. He increased the security measures and put two full time guards on me. Soon they began to take lab samples and try them out on some *junkies* in the Moscow suburbs. That's what I was told by an assistant and one of the thugs who was with me in Amsterdam when you arrived. I never left the lab."

"And who was checking up on Render's movements?"

"Kurt was free to go anywhere. There was a plenty of money invested in the game, and most of it was his own. If the project collapsed, he had a lot to lose. On the other hand, nobody gets away from those people. It was different for me. I'm just small fry."

Tygo continued to explain in detail the places and names of those involved in the operation while Ali took notes and asked one or two questions. Later on, some of that information would be passed on to the Dutch authorities after being filtered by the British and American agencies.

With his description of facts and circumstances, Tygo was trying to establish the basis of a defence that he would make use of later when he came to trial. "I'm a professional chemist, not an assassin," he kept saying.

As hours passed by, Tygo became confident and was no longer afraid. He sang like a bird for the rest of the morning, supplying them with all the names and places that he knew of.

He had no choice but to cooperate without keeping anything back.

"I think we've got enough for now," said Ali. "The operation to arrest Newton in California will start this afternoon."

"OK, Tygo, you can go to your room, have something to eat and get some rest. We'll carry on this afternoon," said Steve, closing his notebook and indicating that the session was at an end.

Ali and Steve went back to the main dining room, where Mike joined them for a drink and to discuss the results of the initial interview.

So far so good" said Mike looking very pleased with results his team was obtaining.

They had corroborated part of the information that they already had, and in addition had learnt some new names and places that would be used to continue the operation and as incriminatory evidence in court.

However, they needed to go deeper into several technical details. For example, how far had they got with the development of Virin? Which specific compounds had Tygo manufactured? Who was working in the labs?

"You'll need a technical expert in the interrogation team," Mike added, not having the courage to look Steve in the eye. "Someone will be along in the next session."

"Someone?" Steve replied in surprise, trying to hide his annoyance but unable to stop himself from turning red. This was not a decision to be taken lightly. The teams on both sides of the Atlantic would have had to agree on a strategy and a name. Why hadn't he been consulted?

"Our bosses made the decision," said Ali, preparing to drop her bombshell.

"Who is this 'someone'?" Steve asked

"It's an old acquaintance," answered Mike.

"Ah, so you know him."

"Yes, we all know him. It's Dr Mel Cooper from Helfen prison," Ali shot back.

"What...!"

His face grew even redder, not so much surprised as completely gob-smacked. Where did all the indulgence given to this man come from? What more had he got to give? Mike owed him some answers. "What the hell's going on, Mike? Why, Cooper, why not one of our own?"

"Our Washington cousins want him in the room. They think Cooper can clear up some grey areas in Tygo's statements. It's part of the Helfen agreement."

"Why didn't you tell me before?"

"The decisions were only made at the last minute. You've done a grand job in bringing Tygo here and interrogating him, but your part in the mission will soon be over, and you'll have to step aside. Let the people who come after you make the long-term decisions. OK?"

Steve felt sick, or maybe it was indigestion from having to swallow too much pride. However, it made him remember why he had left the job.

"Shit. What the fuck!" he muttered to himself.

He knew that Mike was right; perhaps he was even protecting him by limiting his knowledge and his role in the operation. "It's not for soldiers to reason why, theirs but to do or die...!" he used to say. But Steve didn't feel like a soldier anymore. He had too much experience to refuse to see the truth without asking questions. At this stage in his life and career to go ahead like that would have shown an attitude more closely approaching cynicism than duty. Somehow or other he found it soothing to think that the only reason he had got involved in this mission was because of his loyalty to the friends who were waiting for him in Marbella, even though others higher up had been using him for their own ends that he would never know and he didn't care, but he was curious about.

Mike went away, leaving Steve perplexed. This state of mind was not new to him. There had been many times when he'd had to go forward, groping in the dark, carrying out orders that made no sense, like a pilot flying blind through a stormy night, trusting in his instruments. However, everything was different now. The greater freedom that he was enjoying meant he was able to ask some questions, however awkward they might be. "What is it you're really after, Ali? Come on, tell me," he said, as he sipped his malt whisky.

"I've already told you. We're going after all of them, starting with Newton."

"You don't need Cooper to get those people."

"I need him to clarify a few technical aspects about the process and get a better understanding of the ramifications of this case."

"And that's all?"

"That's all. Ask your boss if you don't believe me."

"He wouldn't ever tell me."

"If he won't tell you, what makes you think I will?" came her bright and breezy reply.

Steve said with a smile, "My British cool?"

"I can't see anything cool about you at the moment. Maybe you need to spend more time in Marbella. The climate's better!" Ali sipped her vodka Martini.

"I think you're right. The Mediterranean climate is more relaxing."

"You're lucky to have it. In a little while you'll be back at the seaside again. I'd like to go there too, but I've still got a lot of work to do in colder climes," came back Ali's grim reply.

"You sound as if you're moving to Transylvania."

"No need. There are plenty of Count Draculas where I come from."

"That sounds blood-curdling, Ali, but you're trying to sidetrack the conversation because you won't tell me what's going on.

"Let's get something to eat and find some nice wine to drink while you tell me all about the Mediterranean. Let's forget about this business for the moment."

"Oh, Ali, oh, Ali, why can't I resist your charms...."

XXVIII

STEVE GREETED COOPER'S ARRIVAL WITH a disgust that he tried to pass off as obeying orders but, underneath it, hid resignation.

He hardly recognised Cooper, because he was very smartly dressed for the occasion, in a blue jacket with a white shirt, grey moleskin jeans and dark brown suede casual shoes.

If he hadn't seen him earlier, he would never have thought he came from a prison. Ali gave a welcoming smile, but Steve merely held out his hand coolly, stony-faced. He couldn't find any justifiable reasons for this.

"You've got to put on a bit of an act," Ali whispered in his ear.

"Trust me, I'm making a huge effort just to stay in the same room with him."

"I don't believe you. You want to get to the bottom of this as much as I do."

"All right then, I'll try," he answered with a sardonic grimace. "Aghh."

Cooper joined the group and ignored Steve completely. He felt as if he had come back to life, and he was deeply grateful to Ali.

An hour later they went into an adjacent room, where Cooper was given instructions about his participation in the interview. Ali set out to him very clearly why he had been brought in, what she expected from him, what he could say and, most important of all, what he should not say. Cooper agreed without demur and listened carefully, but his apparent submissiveness didn't succeed in convincing everyone present.

Finally Steve asked him if he had any reservations.

No, none. Cooper was anxious to get started.

Tygo was drinking a cup of tea. He seemed calm and confident when Ali, Steve and Cooper entered the room. His morning fix, a hot meal and the relief of not being tailed by gangsters who could get rid of him at any moment had worked wonders.

Ali had hardly finished the formal introductions when Copper fired his first question, point blank and without any warning. "Tygo, you're an experienced chemist, aren't you?" he asked, looking him straight in the eye.

Ali and Steve were taken aback, but decided to let him carry on and see where it was leading.

"Yes, at least I think I am," Tygo replied, looking around with a friendly gaze for somewhere to escape."

"Then how could you fail to realise that Render's plan B was flawed from the outset?"

You've got a loose cannon here, Ali. Who knows where this is going to end up now? thought Steve, glancing at her out of the corner of his eye.

"Yes, I realised straight away, but I carried on playing the game. Render and I were in the same boat. Goran and Newton were breathing down our necks and threatening us. We needed more time...."

"I don't believe you, Tygo," Cooper replied. "Kurt would never have designed a drug that could harm the user. There was something else in the drugs that killed these young men that he didn't know about," he added, raising his right eyebrow and gazing at him without batting an eyelid.

Tygo gulped and picked up his glass of water, holding it in front of him in both hands. He needed something to hang onto.

For a few seconds he twisted it on its base with his fingertips. The water inside it made the grain of the wood on the table appear magnified.

Cooper was like a magnifying glass that held up to scrutiny the cracks in his story, and he seemed prepared to get inside them to find out the truth. Tygo wouldn't be able to keep anything back. He would have to tell them everything.

Hesitant and unsure of himself, he said, "Well yes, there was something else…it was my idea, but it's not my fault. You have to understand that we needed time, we were under a lot of pressure…."

"Get to the point, Tygo." Steve broke into this new attempt at justification that was starting to get boring.

"Please." Ali was conciliatory. "We must have specific details, Tygo, we know all the rest. We can talk about all that later. Right now we need to know what was and still is in those pills."

"OK, OK." Tygo sighed and wiped away beads of sweat that had started to gather on his brow. This time he wasn't going cold turkey but facing facts, the unvarnished truth about the drugs that he had manufactured. "Since the Virin formula that we were trying out was safe but only had a mildly stimulating effect, it was obvious that we needed to add something stronger to hook up the user. The sedative and stimulant effects of the new formula were modulating each other out, resulting in a very pleasant sensation, a sense of well-being and a very exaggerated self-confidence that only lasted for the time that the drugs remained in the blood stream. After six or seven hours, all this started to wear off, and the users were ready to pay any price for another dose. That's how it is…."

"OK, so the Virin formula you were using before was safe but weak. What stimulant did you add to it?" Cooper asked incisively, taking notes in a little book.

"A formula modified with mephedrone, Meow Meow."

"And did it work?" By this time, Cooper was motivated by a purely scientific interest.

"More or less. In some cases it worked very well, but in others...well, you've seen it for yourselves. The study needed widening to look at the adrenergic and cholinergic effects...."

A technical dialogue had started up, and that was exactly what Ali was looking for in order to better understand the compound Tygo had created.

"Did you not consider the fact that if the individual drinks a lot of alcohol, smokes cannabis and on top of that takes this mixture of Virin and mephedrone, the risk of a lethal overdose is very high? Cannabis inhibits the vomiting reflex and means that all this mixture remains in the body." Cooper was oblivious to the fact that he was surrounded by non-specialists.

"Yes, I know. But there was nothing wrong with the formula, it just need a bit more development..." answered Tygo, already feeling a bit insecure to engage in a discussion with someone who could understand him and consider him an equal.

Technically Cooper was still a prisoner, though his manner of speaking, his questions and observations were those of an expert advicer.

One look from Ali was enough to make Steve understand that he had to stay quiet and let the *technical experts* carry on with their dialogue. Everything was being recorded and would be discussed in detail later with other specialists.

Not for nothing was it called the *soften room.*

"Do you think it was this mixture that caused the deaths?" asked Cooper bluntly, with a strange look in his eyes revealing a scientific curiosity verging on either madness or naivety.

"Possibly. But it's also possible that it might have been the combination of those two drugs with alcohol. I'm not sure. All this had to be investigated, but...."

"Did Render know that you were testing that combination of drugs?"

"No, he didn't. I told them that Render was a genius and that we were getting close to the final product. I led them to think that it was his formula. I only wanted to keep Newton and Goran happy. Unfortunately, that was when Kurt went off to South America and crashed in the forest, and I was trapped. I didn't have any other choice than to follow the line I was working on. You know the rest."

"Did you ever see the notes that Render took?" Ali asked. "A notebook, exercise book or something like that?"

"I saw him taking notes once or twice in a light brown, leather-covered notebook. Render was very conscientious, almost obsessive, but he didn't trust anyone. He took notes all the time, but he never used a personal computer, because he was afraid that it could be hacked into. All his important notes were hand written in that notebook."

"Did he ever leave his notes in a safe?" enquired Steve.

"No, he never did that. He didn't trust anyone. He had a lot of scattered information; everything was very scattered and very confused, but I think all the answers were in that little book. All the experience he gained from the Virin project was contained in those notes, and they're lost forever in the forest."

"What a shame. An irreparable loss…" said Cooper, gazing into his coffee cup and turning it slowly.

"We went through everything he had after the accident, but we didn't find anything. When I told them I needed the book, they told me they'd been looking for it."

"What?" Ali looked at him attentively.

"Goran said he was going to send someone to England. That's all I know."

"When was this?"

"Around the end of the summer, I suppose. I would have liked to get access to that book. Perhaps we could have completed his work. It would have been an important scientific contribution."

Steve struggled to control a smile that Tygo and Cooper might have found offensive. "People don't need any more drugs, Tygo, there are enough of them as it is. They'll never solve drug problems with more drugs. That's not the idea, do you understand?" He tried to conceal his thoughts but he couldn't avoid falling into an ideological trap that he couldn't get out of so easily.

"No? So how do you explain the massive demand for alcohol and tobacco, when it's well known that either of them kills more people than heroin and cocaine put together?"

Showing unusual caution, Cooper decided to stay silent as he reflected that in the United Kingdom, tobacco is the principal cause of avoidable illness and premature death. Around 107,000 people died annually from illnesses related to tobacco and 33,000 related to alcohol. He could not help recognising that there was an element of truth in Tygo's words. More than one hundred people an hour were admitted to hospital for alcohol related problems, and every day forty people died from liver disease and road traffic accidents.

The argument grows even stronger if one considered that the number of people who died in accidents relating to heroin was 1500, just a small fraction of those caused by legal drugs.

Those facts didn't exonerate Tygo from blame, but they changed the background against which Cooper was judging him. Deaths caused by people like him were nothing compared with the deaths related to socially acceptable products.

"I'm a victim of the crap system that you represent," Tygo protested. "Experts like me become trapped between hypocritical laws, bureaucrats and gangsters. You put us here because you need to crucify someone to justify yourselves. You don't seem to realise that it's people like you that give Newton and Goran something to feed off when you make consumption illegal. It's the users and the scientists who end up in prison. I'm here, but where's Newton?"

"Soon we'll be arresting him too, Tygo," replied Steve with a frown.

"I doubt that very much." Tygo spoke with an expression of bitterness. "If they let me produce the drugs legally that they want on the street, just as they do with alcohol and tobacco, there would be enough funding to produce safer products. But no, your bourgeois laws have pushed me to the margins, to those wretched caravans that I ended up in."

"Very sad," was Steve's reply, delivered with bland irony, while Ali stayed silent as if enjoying a firework display.

"It's you who are putting people like Render and me into this position, Steve. I'm not proud of my work in the caravans, but you shouldn't be proud of yours."

"We're doing very different things for very different reasons, Tygo."

"Sure. You're upholding the law. The same law that allows your doctors to give methadone to millions of people who stay on the margins and don't cause any trouble. They have no choice, because you know what's good for them better than they do themselves."

"They're addicts, Tygo; they're sick," replied Steve.

"That's your point of view. Don't tell me how I have to live or what I have to do. It's my life! I didn't ask because I don't need your protection. What I need is the freedom to produce and take stuff that's safe, good quality. If you're going to ban and persecute, let's go back to prohibition and the temperance movement instead of facilitating the investigation and development of new, safe drugs."

"Your view of the world is very interesting, Tygo. You'd like to live in a world where everyone who isn't high is drunk."

"And if that's what they want, what's wrong with it?"

"Because we don't live in isolation. These same people drive cars in the streets that I cross and my neighbour's children use as they come back from school."

"Exactly, because your neighbour children's are the same people who will get drunk and stoned when they go to college. The main thing that your governments need to get on top of the accidents, crimes and mafias is a drug that is safer than tobacco, alcohol, heroin and cocaine. It's an obvious fact. If you carry on spitting in the wind, you'll only end up with anonymous biochemists introducing even more legal highs like mephedrone, Meow Meow, Cat M, K2, Black Mamba and Gogaine. In under a year they've introduced a hundred and forty-four new legal drugs. Your war against drugs and the people who produce them is a lost cause, but unfortunately some have to be jailed so you can save face."

Cooper was listening attentively as he reflected that madness always had a grain of truth in it.

"What do you think you're going to do with the new generation of unemployed, Steve? Poison them with more beer, spirits and junk food? Dull their brains with more television, video games, fantasies and let them think that they're getting an education or a stake in society?" Tygo went on challenging Steve.

Cooper knew that a group of British experts had recently concluded that forty per cent of cancers were related to life style. An ambiguous term used to avoid a direct confrontation with any of the industries that made the biggest contribution to the state coffers: tobacco companies, breweries and distilleries and junk food.

"Do you have any idea of the cost to the taxpayer? They have to pay twice. Once for what they buy and again for the health services that treat the problems they give rise to," he said, with a conviction that Steve didn't buy.

"Sure, Tygo. Your motives in getting involved with Goran were purely humanitarian," he replied.

Cooper was on the point of intervening, but once more he restrained himself.

"All right. I'm not trying to make excuses for myself. I just don't want you to rush to judgement. Human beings have been taking that mixture of poppy, cannabis and ephedrine they call *Soma* for three thousand years now. I'm following in that tradition."

"No, Tygo, you're following in the tradition of people who exploit human weaknesses. You're a dangerous cynic."

"That's where you're wrong. I'm a pragmatist, a realist with a vision that goes beyond the prejudices that your petty bourgeois mentality allows you to see. It's too easy for you to label me as *junkie,* a criminal or a madman."

"So Newton and the Mafia bosses behind the new drug are trying to save the world with the shit they're selling. I'm very sorry if I haven't understood you properly, but this is a very old argument. You and they just want a quick return and a lot of money, but there's a clear line that we all know about. If you cross that line you have to pay the price. You know it as well as I do. It's called the Law. That's all there is to it," said Steve with a conviction that sounded genuine.

Ali listened intently, then decided to break into the discussion. She had heard enough. Tygo had given away more than he realised; the rest was detail that would be picked over in further interview sessions. "We're not here to discuss the legalisation of drugs, nor are we here to change the world, but we can get you to a safer place in one of our establishments, courtesy of Her Majesty's Prisons Service."

"Thanks," Tygo replied, with an ironic bow.

"Don't mention it. Now we have to hand you over to our colleagues. They'll take care of you. Good-bye, Tygo," was Ali's last intervention, but this time there was nothing friendly in her voice.

"Tygo's no fool," said Cooper, addressing Steve for the first time. "And I would agree with some of his ideas, but I would never have adopted his methods, so to speak. Tygo is a highly qualified professional, but at the same time he's a very sick person. He oozes resentment."

Cooper made these reflections, feeling part of the team and conveniently forgetting the place he had to go back to in a few minutes.

"There are a lot of Tygos out there," he went on, "and getting more all the time. In my profession a tiny change in the chemical structure of a product can turn a poison into a remedy, and vice versa. It's like that with some people. There must be some good in Tygo, though I must admit that basically he's still pure poison."

"OK, Dr Cooper," said Mike as he rejoined the group. I think we had enough to be getting on with for today. Gareth and Edwin will take you to Helfen. You've made a positive contribution, and you'll be hearing from us soon."

"Thank you, Mr Atherton. Good night."

"Thank you, Dr Cooper," said Ali, while Steve, without meeting his eyes, gave an undecipherable grunt that could have been taken as a good-bye or a thank you.

Cooper left, escorted by the two young agents who would take him back to his cell, but the prisoner returning wasn't the same as the one who had set out. His expectations had been raised, and now he could see a light at the end of the tunnel.

"These people are really weird."

"We live in a weird world, Steve," Ali replied, helping herself to a cup of coffee.

"They're more dangerous than they look," Steve went on. "Behind their scientific knowledge and mathematical logic, they're hiding the same murderous instincts as any of the hundreds of people we've arrested."

"What makes you think there are differences between them?" said Mike, putting his mobile down on the table.

"They're not like the others. They aren't after financial rewards only, their final objective isn't just money, it's something else. I don't know – they're driven by a more personal motivation," Steve replied thoughtful.

"I think I know what you mean," said Mike. "It's much easier to deal with someone who's just out for money or power. Personal motives are always more difficult to unravel."

"I think crimes committed to get money are, how can I put it…easier to explain," Ali said, and smiled as she took another sip of her drink.

"That's true. Newton and Goran are easier to understand than Tygo or Cooper. I'd put Render midway between them," said Steve, moving his outstretched hand to the right, as if trying to draw a line between different invisible objects that were in front of him.

Ali smiled. "Because you're trying to see them in terms of black and white. We live in a world of many contrasts, and appearances are almost always deceptive. There are all sorts of dubious interests flourishing, even in the Mediterranean sunshine. Same as everywhere else," she added, while Steve watched the pale pink smear that her lips had left on the cup.

"I don't think this situation is too difficult to understand. Goran and Newton are in it for the money. Tygo has always been gripped by a deep resentment that finished up by ruining himself and everything around him. Render's case is more complicated. He was talking about social control that ultimately means power, and power always comes down to sex and money in the end. Anyway, all this is hardly relevant. It will just go towards explaining each of their motives when they come to trial," announced Mike.

It always took an effort for Steve to appreciate the subtleties. "As long as there is a demand for drugs, there will always be someone ready to satisfy it, if the price is right," said Steve as trying to define a complex problem.

"Yes, the invisible hand that always maintains the balance between supply and demand," replied Ali.

"Invisible hand?" asked Steve.

"It's the old invisible hand of a man called Smith. Oh, forget it!" said Ali.

"Is he a drug trafficker?" Steve asked curiously.

"No, Adam Smith died two hundred years ago. He didn't know anything about drugs, but he knew a lot about human nature." Ali was almost laughing as she spoke.

Steve gave Mike a piercing look and asked, "You think that Render and Cooper were mad. Is it possible that our governments could use these drugs or something similar to control unrest?"

Mike gave a hint of a smile and turned away so as not to meet his gaze. "How would I know, Steve? For the moment, questions like that don't arise. The day they do, it would probably be way outside my brief."

"I'll drink to that," Ali said, raising her glass.

Steve couldn't muster much enthusiasm. "Ali, I learnt a long time ago that sometimes it doesn't do to go into too much depth, because you can end up digging your own grave. I just do my job. No more, no less."

"Quite right, Steve." Mike replied, joining in the toast. "Here's to everyone who works hard and doesn't ask questions."

"But it's no good drinking a toast in coffee," Steve pointed out, helping himself to another whisky.

Glass still upraised, Ali glanced at her English colleagues and replied, "Coffee is the toast that our political correctness attitude deserves. The champagne is for those who know the answers to the questions we don't dare to ask. Cheers!"

XXIX

THE SUN WAS SINKING BELOW the horizon, throwing splashes of deep yellow colour onto the blue green sea, and adding a red tinge to the evening sky that turned pink as it caressed the clouds and deep blue as it heralded nightfall.

The spectacular display of colours was reflected on the facades of the houses that lined the sea front. The bright colours they had been painted made them share and reflect the daily display of natural beauty that, for a limited number of prosperous homeowners, was part of their daily routine.

Newton Crowe was one of them. He lived in an eight-bedroomed mansion with a sea view not far from his office in Long Beach. The main residence was surrounded by gardens filled with a wide variety of palms, Bishop pines, incense cedars and various other varieties native to California that had been tastefully spread around by the landscape artist who had designed it.

For many people it would have been a dream house, but for Newton it was more of an asset, with the added advantage that he could make use of it, although he never spent much time in it. His life was his work, and doing a job well meant getting more profits. His idea of a finely decorated environment was a VIP lounge in an airport, a room in a luxury hotel or the office in which he spent most of his time; basically, any environment that combined extravagance with functionality.

Newton had built that paradise on the sea-shore from very practical motives. First, to show off a status in society that would make him respectable. Second, to ease his entry into the social circles that meant business opportunities. Third, to keep his wife, Lynn, happy.

It was several years now since Lynn had ceased to be a social drinker of mature years and turned into an elderly alcoholic in a downward spiral. No drink, facelift or therapy had succeeded in making her feel better since her daughters had left home.

Her older daughter Sandy was always immersed in a social whirl and never had time to visit her mother. Terry, on the other hand, had distanced herself from her family and was working for an NGO that was dedicated to rescuing street children in Honduras. Lynn was convinced that Terry had decided to *throw away* her life on *that work*, just to spite her family.

Lynn, left alone with her emptiness, turned to drink. Under a thick layer of make-up, her mirror reflected a face full of wrinkles as much as frustration. The years seemed to have no mercy on flesh-and-blood, real live Barbies.

She had never understood, and she didn't want to know about, her husband's business or where the funds came from that she squandered so lavishly. Her job was to spend, not earn them. That was how she had been brought up, and that was what Newton and his friends expected of their wives.

Conversations with Lynn were as trivial as they were predictable, and her drunkenness was very contagious. Perhaps that was one of the reasons why she lived in splendid isolation, surrounded by expensive objects and alcohol.

Now his daughters had left home it wasn't so easy for Newton to keep out of her way, although he did everything possible to avoid her. Perhaps that was why Lynn began to see a different side to him that she had never noticed before.

During the last months, Newton was spending more time in the house, withdrawn and saying little. He seemed worried.

Lynn did not dare to raise the subject, because she knew very well that if she did, she would come up against an impenetrable wall of silence or an evasive answer. One night she caught him by surprise in his study, lost in thought. He was on his third glass of whisky. Lynn was no genius, but she knew all there was to know about whisky and isolation.

The momentary weakness that Newton was displaying drove her to invite him out. A quiet supper, just the two of them, at the golf club. He rose to his feet and kissed her forehead. "No, thanks," he replied, and for a few seconds his eyes met hers.

Lynn started to worry. *Oh God, this is worse than I thought.* Her anxiety reached new heights when, just as she was leaving, she noticed a pistol in a desk drawer that was half open.

Newton would only use a weapon to defend himself or to attack, never for suicide. Now she understood why his study had been converted into a fortress from which he emerged only to have a drink by the pool and stare into the sky, deep in thought.

Lynn thought her husband was seeking inspiration from the heavens to solve his problems, when in reality his concern was about helicopters and drones spying on his residence.

The information that Ali had been sending from Europe for several months now was all that was needed by the intelligence services investigating Crowe and his associates. When all the bits of the jigsaw puzzle were put into place, they would make their move. The evidence was sufficient for the district judge to put out warrants for his arrest and to search his home.

They now had the green light for action.

The order came through on a Tuesday at 3.37 p.m. Intelligence from the agents parked outside his mansion told them that Lynn had been out for most of the day, and Newton had been visited by two burly individuals with bronzed complexions and dark hair who emerged about twenty minutes later, around midday.

Their photos had been taken, and they were waiting for the results to identify them. At 3.52 pm, three black vans with darkened windows drew up, containing the group assigned to arrest Newton and search his home. Two men in suits and ties got out of one of them and made their way towards the main entrance, escorted by four uniformed agents carrying heavy weapons.

The official in charge lost his patience when, after several minutes, there was no answer to the third ring of the doorbell. He knew that Newton was in there, and resistance was futile.

He gave the order. "Break the door down, and take care as you go in."

The imposing, sturdy oak door gave way easily at the first push, and the armed team went in rapidly and fanned out.

"Police! Newton Crowe, we have a warrant for your arrest," shouted the sergeant in charge of the armed group.

Nothing. An eerie silence reigned in the large house, and there was no one to be seen.

They went in through the main hall to the first large reception room, which gave a view onto the gardens and the large pool. The large patio doors that led outside were open, and a gentle breeze pushed the curtains, shading them from the intensity of the brilliant light coming from the patio.

"Come here, quick!" yelled one of the agents, who had gone round to the back to make sure that no one would try and escape that way.

The body of a man with his limbs spread-eagled like St Andrew's cross was floating face downwards in the pool. He gave the grotesque impression of someone trying to reach out for something much bigger than his arms could embrace.

Forensics would later inform them that he had been strangled and then thrown into the water.

Newton knew too much for them to let him be arrested. They had silenced him. No doubt his powerful clients had been kept well informed and could access the necessary resources to make sure that their business remained confidential.

Once more, they were ahead of the game.

They were not only protected by a small army of dummy enterprises, international bank accounts, legal consultants and financial intermediaries, but also very well informed people in Washington, London and Zurich.

Investigating these ramifications wasn't part of the mission that Ali, Steve and Mike had to follow through to its conclusion. Their intervention in California had also met a dead end.

XXX

AT EIGHT O'CLOCK in the morning, two days after Tygo's interrogation had finished, Ali and Steve were making their way slowly up the M1 to Manchester International Airport. The brief sense of freedom that they had enjoyed on getting out of a ten-mile traffic jam was disappearing as they got stuck in the next one.

Steve had promised his friends to pick them up at the airport and take them home, and Ali wanted to meet them. At the end of the day, everything they had done had been for people like Johnny and Moira. To her, their faces were the faces of all those who had died, but also of those who had been saved by their intervention. Meeting face to face with Johnny, Moira and Chris would help her to keep her feet on the ground. They were the human face of her job.

Ali's mobile rang just as the traffic was starting to move and her favourite Blur tune was playing on the radio. With one hand on the wheel, Steve turned down the volume.

Her face changed as she took the call. Ali listened attentively and asked a few questions. "Thanks," she said and hung up. "That was my boss. Crowe's dead. They got to him just before he was going to be arrested."

Without taking his attention from the traffic that was now beginning to flow again, Steve bit his lip. "Bah, I'll have to knock him off my Christmas present list."

"I wanted you to know. This happens all the time."

Ali's professionalism never ceased to surprise him.

"Where do you think the blow came from?"

"It's difficult to know at the moment, Steve, but we'll get to the bottom of it."

"And how do you feel about it?" he asked.

"It's not a triumph, but it's not a disaster either. We did our job, but they had an advantage over us."

"They?"

"You know, whoever is behind Newton."

Steve looked at the traffic ahead of them, but his mind was elsewhere. "What does your chief say?"

"He's happy. We've done what we had to do. The rest is California's problem. They're the ones who lost him."

"You're right."

"We're in the clear. The Belgians and the Dutch have seized the labs and arrested about fifteen from the list we handed over to them. The media aren't talking about anything else, and the authorities are capitalising on the political gains from the operation."

"I hope that smooths things over in Amsterdam."

"Let's leave the politicians and diplomats to get on with their jobs. We've done ours," she said.

"Sure, Ali. Everything's working out fine, but I've got a feeling it's not all over yet."

"It'll never be over. There'll always be something else. That's how it is."

"I bow to your superior wisdom, Agent Riley."

"I know it's hard to accept, but it happens to be true. The reality is much tougher than we like to admit, and that's why politicians lie about it. If they say what they really think or make decisions based on evidence alone, no one would vote for them."

"That's true, they're not scientists or philosophers," Steve replied. "They're politicians, they have to win elections, and we work for them."

No one drives from London to Manchester for pleasure, and Steve was no exception, although Ali's company put it in a different light. The journey, although long and tedious, gave him the chance of trying a more personal approach, which, with a bit of luck, could turn into intimacy.

This was the last day they would spend together, and he wanted to make the most of it right up to the very last minute. After all, at the end of the day, what is life but a succession of moments, following one after the other?

Ali was in her thirties and still pursuing a career path in which she ran the risk of finding herself trapped. Steve was a little older, but he was well aware of her story because he had been there, and that had been his main reason for taking off and looking for new horizons in Marbella.

Johnny was the first to come through the double doors, followed by Moira, who was looking at him proudly, and Chris, who greeted him from afar with a smile, his hands full from pulling along two very heavy cases.

Steve went straight up to Johnny and hugged him.

"Welcome home, mate."

Moira was at his side, eyes shining, unable to suppress her happy smile. When her turn came to greet Steve, there were so many things she would have liked to say, but all she could manage was "Thank you."

What gratified her was not so much the feeling that she had taken revenge, though she was thankful enough for that, but the fact that they had been noticed. People had done something for her, risking their lives for her and Johnny. It made her feel like she and her son were valued and worthy of respect. That wasn't something they had experienced often in their lives.

Ali was moved by the scene and the natural way in which they could all express their feelings.

"Welcome home. We're very happy to see you back and looking so well," said Steve as he made the necessary introductions.

When he came up to his friend, Chris stopped and put down his luggage, holding out his hand. "Hello there, mate. Good to see you."

Relieved, Steve took his hand in a grip as strong as the friendship that united them. "Good to see you, too, Chris. But we can't stay here. Let's get them home. This odyssey is over now."

Ali couldn't help breaking into a friendly smile at not being able to find the right words. This was a very special time, one of the rare occasions when she saw close up the people that gave some meaning to her work, which up to now had been her life. But suddenly she felt a bittersweet taste in her mouth.

She found herself face to face with life itself, with all its fragility, uncertainty, complexity, conflict, freshness, spontaneity, naivety and unpredictability, and her career seemed an irrelevant formality. Hours of meetings, protocols, operations and strategic decisions seemed like secondary chords, which were just the accompaniment to the first violin playing the principal melody.

Johnny and Moira were the real leitmotif that pulled everything together and gave it meaning.

These profound and fleeting intuitions that suddenly come to us out of the blue set her apart for a moment from the meeting. No one noticed, but it was hard for her to relax her guard and find the spontaneity that, to her regret, she lacked. That was dangerous in her job, and her job was becoming her life. As her face softened, the mask was slipping away. A swift cloud of anxiety accompanied her uncertainty, a fleeting thought. Was it already too late?

She didn't welcome this thought, but she was still smiling as the others engaged in animated conversation on their way to the car park. She felt they could look at her face, but it was not the real face that she herself had forgotten long ago and perhaps wouldn't ever know again. In those brief moments, Ali became aware that she was trapped by the wall of secrecy that both protected and isolated her at the same time.

In a few hours, she would be heading for DC, and they would become just another memory that would soon be forgotten. Was that what she really wanted?

In reply, Ali only felt a vague sense of disquiet, the emotion of that meeting and what she secretly felt for Steve, although she couldn't put it into words. She knew she was going to miss him. He was a man whose uprightness could be mistaken for naivety or simplicity, a man she would have liked to get to know better....

Johnny never stopped talking throughout the fifty minutes it took for them to get home. He was no longer the pale, skinny, gawky boy that Chris had known when they met for the first time; he had put on several pounds during the last months. Now his mind was clear, and he had plans to go back to college and work as a peer mentor in a local community programme for deprived areas. He was grateful and wanted to give back something for what he had received. Helping others would also help him in his recovery.

Chris had pulled some strings here and there to secure the council job for him that had been recommended by his recovery centre. That could be the start of a promising career in social services and a leap forward out of the orbit that his family had moved in until then. The advantages he would enjoy as a local authority worker would be a guarantee of greater financial and emotional security at home.

Moira was a different person, too. Her son had recovered from a very serious illness, and this seemingly negative fact had filled her with new hopes. For many years she had been teetering on the brink of the abyss and on several occasions had been on the point of falling in, but finally she found herself on firm ground. Long hours of uncertainty and desperation had made her reflect and think about her own life, her suffering and the options open to her in the future. For the first time, she was ready and willing to leave behind the bad memories that always got her down, the ties that only led to destruction, drugs and alcohol. In some strange way, she felt that the burst of positive energy that she had channelled towards her son during his stay in the ICU had been a catharsis for her.

Day after day, week after week, Moira had never left Johnny's side. All her thoughts and feelings had been with her son, far removed from drugs, dealers and others whom she couldn't really trust but she used to call her friends. Little by little, and almost without realising it, a huge gap was widening between the world she was now living in and the lifestyle she had left behind.

But this mysterious transformation was nothing new to Chris, who had understood right away the road that Moira was travelling and the distance she still had to go. He knew that this great crisis had also become an opportunity for her. Chance, fate or providence had decreed that mother and son would embark on this journey together.

Hugs, kisses and promises were exchanged on their departure.

"I'll call you tomorrow," said Chris, just before he got into the car. "Good-bye."

"Good-bye Moira, good-bye Johnny," called Steve as the car pulled away.

"Good-bye, Mr Dariet," Moira answered, blowing a kiss to her friends. Ali joined in the chorus of farewells, waving her hand in a movement at the same time quick and delicate. "Look after yourselves, both of you."

"Good-bye, and thanks," said Johnny, still smiling and waving farewell to his friends as they drove away back to their own worlds.

XXXI

STEVE HAD HAD NO MORE THAN A pleasant chat with Ali on the way up, and bringing Chris back with them ruined whatever hope he had had of making any progress with her.

They hit the road before dark, in good spirits for facing a long journey back and unpredictable traffic jams.

The plan was to drop Ali off at her hotel and then go with Chris to the cheaper one they had booked. Steve wanted to say good-bye to Ali in the morning, and Chris had some business to see to in London before going back to the North.

By around 9.30 p.m., Steve was driving through Regent's Park towards Bloomsbury. Although he was tired, the journey hadn't been as difficult as he had expected.

After the meeting with the Hansons, he had noticed a subtle difference in Ali's attitude. Perhaps more responsive. Not only had she told him the name of the hotel she was staying at, but she had also made some more personal comments that allowed him to find out more about her tastes and preferences.

"I like red tulips."

Who would ever have guessed that behind those icy blue eyes there existed a liking for colours, and perhaps intense emotions? Not a big deal, but it was much further than he had managed to get in all the weeks they had spent together.

The Cromwell was a very elegant hotel near the British Museum, which Steve and Chris later estimated at no less than £400 a night. Testosterone-fuelled gossip.

"The Americans are more generous than our agencies when it comes to paying travel expenses," Steve complained. "The budget reductions have got to three stars. For now...."

A uniformed porter appeared out of nowhere to open the car door for Ali with one hand while welcoming her with a touch of his hat with the other. When he realised that no one would open his door, he got out and walked round the car to accompany her into the hotel foyer.

Without a word, Ali walked slowly to the lifts and then suddenly stopped and turned on her heels. Steve, who had been following close behind her, suddenly found himself unexpectedly face to face with Ali. Closer than expected, but not as close as he wanted. She looked into his eyes and asked him point blank if he would like to stay for a coffee or supper in her room.

Suddenly, the prospect of a meal with Chris in a three-star hotel was turning into a night that promised to be full of surprises. Steve felt as if he had been struck by lightning. In a fraction of a second, ideas and feelings flooded into his head, and he felt confused. Ali's lips seemed glossier and her eyes held more depth, radiating an enchantment that made her seem very sure of herself.

Why not?

Steve got rid of Chris, who wished him a good night with a broad wink.

Next morning at around ten o'clock, they ordered breakfast in their room.

When the service arrived, Steve opened the door, dispatched the waiter with a generous tip and after shutting the door with his foot, brought the tray to the bed. Steve drank his *macchiato* and remained staring at the fanciful shapes left by the coffee grounds at the bottom of the little cup. The same ones that some people used to tell the fortunes or misfortunes that the future holds for us.

He wasn't concerned so much with what might happen as with what had happened already.

His thoughts were all about Ali. The time they had spent together hadn't been long, but it had been intense. They were professionals in every sense of the word, but he was still sure that there was something more in the relationship that bound them together, which neither of them could put into words.

What does it matter? he thought. *We have to move on.*

Move on? What on earth did it mean to "move on"?

Did it mean forgetting the past? Moving on without stopping, but not knowing where you are going? That was what they had done for years, but where had it got them? They had progressed up the career ladder, but he wasn't sure that they had made any progress in life.

"Did you sleep well?"

"Yes, thanks, did you?" she replied, looking up at him and raising her eyebrows. It was a very sexy gesture that came naturally to her.

"Like a log. Everything ready for your return flight home?"

"Yep." Her eyes bored through him mercilessly.

Steve seemed to be avoiding her gaze. "New York?"

"DC. Duty before pleasure. That's the rule, not so? I've been following it for the last few weeks," said Ali smiling and letting her head fell back onto the pillow.

You never know with Ali. What's going on in her head right now? he wondered.

As if guessing his thoughts, Ali brought him down to earth. "What about you? What are you going to do next?"

"I'm going back to Marbella. I hope to carry on settling down there. I'm going to get a new car."

"I've never been to Marbella."

"It's a great place if you like sun and sea."

"I do like sea...and sun...and a warm climate and good food."

"Then you'd like it. Why don't you come with me?" he suggested.

"Why not? Maybe one day...if we stay in touch."

"I will, but I'm going to need your phone number."

"I'll call you, Steve, but I have to finish off this job first."

"Isn't it finished yet?"

"Well, there are still some bits and pieces I have to sort out... you know how it is."

"Sure, I can imagine."

Ali put her hand to his cheek and kissed him.

Steve pulled her towards him in a strong embrace and kissed her with the desperate passion of an imminent separation.

A few hours later, in the lobby, would come the formal good-byes and indiscreet murmurs.

"Good-bye, Agent Dariet. I'll call you when I get the chance. I don't think you'll have to wait too long."

Steve shook her hand and nodded, with a knowing smile. "So long," he murmured. A few feet away were the agents who would accompany her to the airport, and he still couldn't bring himself to let go the warm hand of his lover. "So long."

Ali recovered her composure, picked up her phone and started to give orders to her team.

They still had outstanding issues to resolve that Steve couldn't begin to imagine.

PART III

In search of a never-ending source of pleasure and social control

XXXII

MY NAME IS MARLOW, BUT SINCE I was a child everyone calls me Joe.

I've been a member of the Virin Project team for some years now, but I got involved for the first time in Wuppertal, a small industrial town in the north of Germany.

I had been invited to put myself forward for a project that I didn't know much about, but even the little I knew was enough to present an irresistible attraction. It was a unique opportunity to participate in the development of new pharmacological interventions along with other technologies that would have a huge social impact on the years to come. At that time, I would never have imagined that a few years later, I would end up involved in a series of research programmes, the outcome of which would affect my own personal safety and the social stability of the Western capitalist world that we call civilised.

I wasn't sure how I had been selected or who was behind this round of interviews. That's not unusual, especially when the project has great strategic importance. The principal sponsors always try to keep their anonymity, so as not to arouse their competitors' suspicions. There are times when one can do a lot of work without knowing too much about who or what it is for. A technician's job is not to ask questions outside his own sphere of work.

The general idea was to participate in small groups, discussing the effects of new drugs and innovative communication technologies that have the capacity to modify human behaviour and influence the conduct of particular groups.

My fellow candidates were a select group of neuropharmacologists, sociologists, social psychologists, linguists, social media experts, information systems engineers and hackers who came from all over the planet. In spite of the superficial differences, we all had something very important in common: our undivided commitment to our area of expertise.

All the participants had an IQ well above 140, which is very high in itself. There could have been one or two genius there, but I am certain no saints or idealists have been invited!

We think about things from very particular points of view. Our horizon is limitless, but our area of interest has narrow margins. That is the real world of scientists and technicians. The rest is politics and business.

Because of that, most of us are comfortably unaware of the political or religious consequences of our researches and projects. All of that lies outside what can be measured with relative precision. That's the very reason we have a special appeal for strategists and entrepreneurs with global interests.

Well, as you will see later on, we also attract the attention of other groups that operate at an international level. Without wishing to defend or justify myself, I would say that we are just well-paid technicians. Our job is to create new systems and technologies whose use can vary from time to time, according to the needs, fashions, tendencies and caprices of the markets. Many years ago someone made heroin into a cough medicine, which later came into use commercially as a painkiller and today is one of the addictive drugs that makes the most money on the black markets. The people who invented dynamite or discovered nuclear fission didn't do it in with the intention of devastating large cities or their inhabitants. If they had stopped to think of those consequences, their creative energy would have been stifled and their instinct for innovation paralysed. Someone else more decisive and less prejudiced would have stepped in to fill the vacuum they left behind.

Our entrepreneurial spirit is only interested in coming up with the best product and achieving the best result in the least possible time. That's the first rule of our game, more or less like the bankers, and like them, we live in a different world!

Most of us are usually advisors to the big decision makers. We prefer to stand back in the safety of the second or third lines of fire and not become too exposed to the limited understanding or unstable mood of the masses.

Somebody once said that our aversion to the limelight could only be compared to our ambition and greed. An unfair remark, but all the same it can't be denied that there is an element of truth in that statement.

We were warned that the job interviews would not follow a conventional structure. First there was a social reception and afterwards an introductory chat.

I had hardly entered the main reception room when I was confronted by an assiduous waiter armed with a tray which, as adroit as he was elegant, he balanced with his right hand.

"A glass of wine, sir?"

"Thank you."

"Red or white?" he asked in reply, this time with a hint of a smile.

"Is the Riesling well chilled?"

"Certainly, sir."

"A cool, sweet taste is good to start with, don't you think?"

"Most definitely, sir."

With a glass in my right hand and the refreshing taste of Moselle grapes in my mouth, I started to move towards the centre of a group of colleagues who looked interesting to me. There were some people there whom I knew from routine meetings at academic gatherings, or as associate members of teams working on multinational projects. The majority of those round me were the heads of important projects that, from time to time, they had made headlines on the nine o'clock news.

At first sight there were no scientific celebrities to be seen. Whoever had brought us together didn't need opinion leaders. The *professors* who would come later to give their blessing to our products and act as their guarantors were closer to the marketing or public relations departments than to the labs.

Allan Duffel was there, well known for his work on the use of MDMA (ecstasy) in the treatment of post-traumatic stress in veterans returning from Iraq and Afghanistan. Before working for the army, Allan had made a name in California treating victims of gender violence and sexual abuse in civilian life. His results were so promising that the American army offered him a grant to continue his investigation, this time including patients who did not respond to conventional treatments with psychopharmaceuticals or psychotherapy.

The British army was also embarking on a similar project, following in his footsteps. The main reason for their interest in this treatment was no longer the high rate of suicides among war veterans, but the outbursts of uncontrolled aggression that ended in the shootings and indiscriminate slaughter of innocent people, not just in Baghdad or Kandahar but also in Tucson, New York, Manchester and London. The general public feels inclined to support just wars that defend their country's interests, as long as the bullets and bodies only appear on television in exotic, faraway places.

I also recognised Clayton Revel, who had been working in America and Europe on a series of new stimulant drugs that could keep one awake for seventy-two hours, without feeling at all tired, without losing concentration and, most important of all, without becoming paranoid. Although Clayton never talked about his clients or his sources of finance, a lot of people suspected that he was working for agencies that deployed special forces, antiterrorist groups and spy networks. Some people joked that his research was flawed from the start, as the subjects on he was using to investigate the effects of his drugs were all mad. To that, Clayton replied very seriously that even if this was the case, his studies showed that the drugs didn't make them any worse. No one could decide if he was joking or serious.

Clayton was shy and reserved, which meant he was always surrounded with an aura of mystery, suspicion and the resulting gossip and fantasies that feed off each other. I never knew if this was due to the secretive nature of his sponsors or simply because he was the retiring type. Some years later, he was found dead from a shot in the head. His death was as discreet, silent and surrounded by mystery as his life had been. The coroner's investigation concluded Clayton committed suicide, and the case was closed, but nobody could ever explain why the entry wound came through the back of the skull. Perhaps because nobody dared ask.

After meeting Allan and Clayton, I wasn't surprised to see Sacha Ivanov, better known as the *Siberian Bear*. I knew him long before I could see him, as soon as I heard his laugh, as thunderous as it was unmistakable, from the other side of the room. When I turned round, he was just as he always was: exuberant, larger than life, overwhelming. In our small circle of experts, Sacha was a living legend for his way of life, for his great successes and his catastrophic failures. Everything about him was over the top. Sacha had been part of the team that developed a derivative of fentanyl, used by the Russian special forces to liberate 850 hostages captured by Chechen terrorists in the Bolshoi Theatre in Moscow in 2002. After two and a half days of negotiations, the Russian authorities put an end to the discussions and decided to take the theatre by surprise, kill all the terrorists and free the hostages. However, things did not turn out according to plan. The problem was that to eliminate

39 terrorists they used a special gas that also killed 129 of the hostages. The death rate was more than three hostages per terrorist. The Kremlin was heavily criticized for the excessively drastic way they had carried out the operation, but the response of the authorities was to shrug their shoulders and say they had no choice.

However, it didn't take the international media long to find out what had really happened, the true motive behind such slaughter. The doctors who attended the victims quickly diagnosed severe poisoning with some sort of sedative that affected the nervous system and brought on respiratory failure. Their antidotes didn't work, and people started to drop like flies, without their being able to do anything about it. The security forces had used a secret chemical weapon, and they weren't prepared to release the antidote.

The messages sent out by such an event were as clear as they were forceful, in the purest Russian style. Terrorist attacks would not be tolerated. On the contrary, they would be completely crushed, without any mediation or negotiation. In the ex-Red Army's order of priorities, their strategic weapons (drug and antidote) were worth 129 deaths.

In spite of this, as you might expect, not everyone in Moscow thinks along the same lines, now that even politicians in the Kremlin have to pay the price for their military decisions. A few weeks after the incident occurred, the bills started to arrive at the offices and headquarters of the operational commands. For Sacha, this meant he was reassigned to a special lab dedicated exclusively to the production of a modified and better version of the gas and the antidote used in the Bolshoi.

All this had happened several years earlier, and God alone knows what project Sacha was working on at that time and why he was standing there among the candidates.

Amidst the superficial conversations, artificial smiles and canapés of Beluga caviar, I kept glancing from side to side, looking for someone else I knew among the people around me while trying to keep up with the thread of the conversation. With a great effort, I tried to avoid being a victim of my curiosity and bourgeois formality. *C'est la vie!*

Some minutes and three glasses of Riesling later, I was able to recognise a few faces that seemed familiar to me. There were faces I had once seen at a distance, though I had never exchanged a word with them. Among them, someone stood out who, in our little world, was considered a sort of celebrity of the moment. This was an intelligent man with a sharp mind, shrewd and with interesting ideas, whom the present circumstances had catapulted to notoriety. There was Chakra Singh in person, Chak to his colleagues in Oxford and Harvard, equally well-known for his distinctive purple turban, thick black beard and unfailingly good-humoured smile.

Chak was a rare combination of IT genius and sociological expert in social media and networks. His insatiable liking for curries could only be compared with his aversion to eating lamb.

With a market of 14.8 billion users of social networks, Chak's studies and researches had not passed unnoticed by the companies that had recently financed his projects, seeking new algorithms to penetrate specific markets.

However, all that changed on Saturday, October 6, 2011, at 10.45 p.m. after the incidents flared up by the death of a 29-year-old black male from North East London was shot by the police when he, allegedly pulled a gun.

"Everyone from all sides of London meet up at the heart of London OXFORD CIRCUS. Bare shops are going to get smashed up so come get some free stuff! Fuck the feds we will send them back with OUR riot! Dead the ends and colour war for now so if you see a brother...SALUTE! But if you see the feds SHOOT... MUST RESEND TO ALL CONTACTS!"

Several hundred thousand similar messages traversed the reddened skies of London for three consecutive nights, demonstrating that the world was changing faster than the forces of law and order could keep up with it.

The rules of urban combat had been rewritten.

Use of social networks and mobile phone technology would from then on had to be included in training programmes for the security forces. Communications experts were urgently required. Chak's studies could have made a contribution, if not preventing, at least limiting damage.

The greater part of the looting, vandalism and burning had been provoked by groups of youngsters who communicated with each other using text messages.

After exhaustive interviews with hundreds of participants from the riots, the intelligence agencies reached the conclusion that that particular section of society preferred to communicate by Blackberry Messenger (BBM for short.) Most of the lootings, vandalism and arson had been coordinated by young people communicating through this system, which held various important advantages for them:

- it is free for users
- it enables sending a message to a lot of users at the same time
- it protects the anonymity of the original sender

Chak had carried out several studies in this sector of the population and knew of their preference for BBM, but he had never imagined the potential danger it held until that moment.

Though Facebook has more than 900 million users, it was not very popular within the social groups that participated in the riots. Due to their precarious consumer capacity, they had been left out of the marketing studies. But owing to their great capacity for social disruption, their communications habits had started to be monitored by the security agencies, not only in England but in other countries of Europe, America and Asia that displayed similar social tensions. Young people from the predominantly Afro-Caribbean estates of South London were not interested in smart phones. They preferred cheaper communications systems. Consumerism had not caught up with them yet, because they were still too poor to own a credit card and make online purchases.

When Chak was faced with this problem, he suggested an idea that was both simple and effective: *viral triviality* he called it.

"If they can't afford to consume real goods, let's give them virtual ones for free. We'll keep them busy and entertained. Triviality is the most consumed virtual stuff," said Chak stating his expertise in the matter.

The central concept of viral triviality is that a trivial message (one that neutralizes aggressive behaviours) can have wide distribution through the networks, infecting the targets with high degree of specificity. The result is sudden massive reaction of silly messages and replies of epidemic proportions, that reduce the disruptive behaviours leading to social tension.

His studies encouraged the development of algorithms to collect very specific information about users' tastes and preferences and in that way to generate personalised messages on social networks. Chak had analysed those groups, considering the particular sector and the geographic distribution of where the leaders of the demonstrations belonged. The limited value that this algorithm held for marketing enterprises was inversely proportional to the one the security agencies assigned to it.

"At the end of the day, viral triviality is another sophisticated online marketing strategy if you want, but instead of promoting consumerism, it induces apathy," Chak used to say proud of the ingenious technique he had created.

Innumerable marketing studies have demonstrated time and again that the vast majority of people browsing the web were still more interested in sporting events, celebrities, fairy tales, magicians, vampires, star wars and superheroes than in the harsh reality of everyday life. Constant massive bombardment with trivial messages could neutralise social conflicts, together with their worrying consequences, to create an artificial atmosphere that still had overtones of reality, based on the simple fact that everyone was talking about the same thing, interested in the same thing and most important disinterested in the same thing. A trivial fantasy would always be more attractive than a complex message that needed some thought.

Bread and circuses had caught up with the digital age.

Huxley's vision of a world at ease with itself had been imposed on Orwell's violence and tyranny nightmare. The masses would submit to Big Brother only if he provided them with products and services for their entertainment. Otherwise, they would burn everything down. Stability would consist of a state of constant flux, virtualising and trivialising daily life in such a way that, on the surface, everything would be new, mysterious and attractive, but underneath everything would stay the same.

Chak knew that the new generations had *bought into* the idea of doing away with an intimate private life and doing everything publicly. Their shared experience enshrined in the social networks was fun and a protection against loneliness, even at the cost of an element of risk that they were prepared to take. For several years he had worked at studying specific social networks, especially in South London. That social group shared many of the characteristics of similar groups in the outskirts of Paris, Rome, Washington, New Orleans and other important cities. During this time Chak was able to implement marketing strategies by introducing several ideas that modified the behaviour of its members. All their operations were precisely measured and analysed; nothing would be left to chance.

The results showed that the spread of ideas and trivial behaviour had nothing trivial about it. The results were mathematically perfect, and they could exercise absolute control by inducing selective or complete ignorance.

Most of what I knew about Chak and his theories (not many knew that they were being put into practice) was through scientific publications and specialist journals, but some close friends had filled me in on the rest of the story. The concept of viral triviality was very quickly accepted by social engineers to prevent, block, deactivate and control certain sectors of society. What he never imagined was that viral triviality and the new drugs that we were going to create would join forces to re-organize the known world and transform it into something safe and trivial. That was the price that would have to be paid for social harmony, and we would all contribute to it gladly to fulfil our own trivialities.

I should have known what this project was about, even before the welcoming speeches and the presentations began. The faces around me spoke for themselves.

But far from feeling disillusioned, I was excited by the prospects, because it's in these small and very exclusive events they recruit for major projects. I know, it's OK. You think I'm no saint, but who is? Are you?

I doubt it. But at the end of the day, what does it matter?

Every one of us in that heterogeneous group shared a philosophy that consisted of doing our job, hoping for the best, preparing for the worst and, as long as we could get something out of it, keeping on course.

The conference took place in a beautifully restored *art nouveau* mansion on the outskirts of a town that had seen better times many, many years earlier. During the eighteenth and nineteenth centuries, Wuppertal had been one of the great industrial capitals of the continent, and even today it is a big manufacturing centre for textiles, metalworking, chemicals, pharmaceuticals, electronics and other things. I wondered why a convening group with vast resources would have organised the conference here, but discretion was crucial, so I kept the question to myself.

On the first day, we were welcomed by a man who must have been a good sixty years old, wearing an elegant suit of blue alpaca with light stripes, and that unmistakable style that could only have come from Savile Row. He greeted us with a paternal expression and a pleasant smile, which could turn out to be either intriguing or ironic in this context.

"Welcome. My name is Dr Doe, Dr John Doe."

We all broke into genuine, conspiratorial smiles. With his first few words, he had us in the palm of his hand.

Dr Doe was no longer young, but his mind was quick and sharp as a razor. His way of talking, his style and gestures showed clearly that he was a man of refinement whose world vision went far beyond technical considerations.

His chat sounded like a cross between the academic and the snobbish entrepreneur, delivered in a measured tone. At the same time, he made delicate gestures with his hands to emphasise his words as he watched us with an eagle eye.

"Among the various notables born in Wuppertal, there are two who symbolise the acumen we shall be looking for during this recruitment process. Their legacy has exerted a decisive influence on the history of the twentieth century, and their concepts have moulded the way in which social and political engineers tackle the problems of our post-industrial society.

"The first was Felix Hoffman, who, as many of you will know, was a chemist who worked for Bayer in Wuppertal, a company that until that time was dedicated to dying textiles. Thanks to his technological advances, it developed until it became one of the largest pharmaceutical companies on the planet. In 1897, in just one week, Dr Hoffman synthesised two drugs that were to change the way we live forever: aspirin and heroin. The current demand for these products creates a market today of some one-point-two billion dollars for aspirin and a global *irregular* market estimated at fifty-five billion dollars for diamorphine, or heroin, as it is better known."

Up to now he had told us nothing new, but at least he had answered my first question: why Wuppertal?

"The second notable, was Frederick Engels."

My brain struggled to find a link between this notorious capitalist and the legendary revolutionary of bourgeois origins. "Born in eighteen-twenty, he was always an agitator, until he got involved in politics, and after that he became a revolutionary. For that reason his father, a wealthy textiles manufacturer, decided to send him to England to work in the Ermen and Engels Victoria Mill factory that the family owned in Salford, Manchester. Engels had been living in his new country for two years when he wrote *The Condition of the Working Classes in England*, published in German in eighteen-forty-five but translated into English forty-seven years later."

The digression was going on a bit, and I began to wonder if I had come to the wrong room.

"His original ideas, together with their unintended consequences, brought both relief and misery to millions of people during the next hundred years. Engels and Hoffmann, together with many others, are symbolic of the genius and the vision of the thinkers and creators at the heart of the industrial revolution in nineteenth-century Europe. Technology, science, social engineering and political vision, brought about by ambition and creativity and not just by greed, would transform our societies forever."

Wait a minute! What's all this leading up to? I thought, feeling both intrigued and confused at the same time. I thought I'd been invited to a friendly competition with colleagues to take part in a project that would let me get away from the daily routine for a few days, but this was turning into something very different.

I realised I wasn't the only one who was perplexed when my eyes met with those of a Japanese man two seats away on my right. He looked puzzled and was trying to find someone else feeling the same way. For a few brief moments, our eyes met, and not a word was spoken, but the look said it all; and we took comfort in the knowledge that we weren't the only rare birds. We turned back to Doe and continued to listen quietly.

The reference to Engels was particularly interesting, given that no one in the room seemed to be a communist or hold socialist ideas. On the contrary, they were all highly qualified professionals coming from the upper middle classes of their home countries, very well aware of the commercial aspect of their discoveries and technological innovations.

But, on second thought, Frederick Engels would have been at home in that group. His lifestyle in England was typically bourgeois, and he was funded by the sweat of the German workers from his family's factories in Wuppertal. Engels never let go of his dream on that account and rarely thought about the contradiction between his ideas and his lifestyle. Since then, that has become a tradition among socialist elites; it is the first lesson that communist leaders learn, and they apply it extremely rigorously, to always exempt themselves from the laws that they pass. The communist ideology got rid of the idea of God, only to turn their leaders into high priests of a new abstraction that they called *the Masses*.

"They were men with an arrogant bourgeois compassion and revolutionary tendencies," Doe continued, as if reading my mind. "They studied the harsh conditions people were living in on the edge of the abyss of the new social structures that were emerging, thanks to the Industrial Revolution. The waters of the River Wupper and Salford Junction Canal still flow on impassively. Technologies, industrial processes and the resulting social problems that used to provide fertile soil for these ideas have developed to unprecedented levels, with consequences unimaginable in those days. But one hundred fifty years later, these flourishing industrial centres have crumbled away or moved to the Far East. Today, Salford and Wuppertal are only shadows of what they once were. Hundreds of red brick Victorian factories lie abandoned in ruins in suburbs, where you can still find descendants of the workers Engels talked about. Day by day, the third or fourth generation of unemployed families live around the former industrial centres in northern and central England and Germany. Their population is wilting away, and they are becoming ghost towns. Our governments have created massive structures of social protection to contain the flood from these sectors, to which is now added the arrival of immigrants from Africa, the Caribbean and recently Eastern European countries. The international financial crisis, together with interracial and ethnic conflicts, are creating favourable conditions for social explosion in these areas, where there is overcrowding and unemployment. Other cities in Europe, Asia and America face the same problems.

"These facts have led economists and sociologists to conclude that the prophecy of proletarian revolution, foretold by Marx, could come about if we don't take adequate measures very soon. Marx said that *religion is the opiate of the people,*' but for many today, the world is an unforgiving place, with no family or god to look after them; and the only moment of consolation, relief and pleasure they can look forward to is when they take drugs or alcohol.

You have been given a special invitation to this event to discuss how your knowledge of pharmacology, psychology, informatics, communications and social media could contribute to reducing tensions and defuse social explosions, or prevent general disturbances in what we can still call the *civilised world.*"

In spite of the dramatic content and the pompous style, it was clear that Doe was doing what he could to keep his audience interested by playing on their fears. He then concluded by explaining some operational details of how group and individual interviews would take place and reminded us that the Chatham House rules applied. This meant that, during our time there, everyone was completely at liberty to express his or her opinions, but whatever was said there should remain confidential. How Doe and his team would know if anyone talked out of turn, or what the consequences might be, was something no one in that room wanted to find out.

By the end of that first session, I began to get a glimpse of what they expected from me and worked out the logical syllogism. If religion, communism and permanent employment were dead, according to Marx's famous phrase, all we have left is morphine, alcohol and the new media. That's it!

The Romans have given them bread and circus, the church, communion wafer and wine; we would give them drugs and media triviality.

It was then that, as an expert on opiates and legal highs, I got ready to make my contribution to the new arsenal of weapons of mass banalisation that we were clearly about to start on.

Oh, Brave New World, you have finally arrived!

XXXIII

AT 2.20 P.M. EASTERN TIME, A SMALL aircraft winged through the pale skies of the North Atlantic at eleven thousand metres over Greenland. It was almost impossible to identify the plane from the ground; one could only guess it was there from the vapour trail that it left behind. It was a white Learjet 85 with double stripes of dark blue and gold around the fuselage, just below the level of the wings.

A year earlier, whoever would have thought I would find myself on board!

Six months after the Wuppertal conference, when I was already consigning my memories of all those interesting presentations and heated technical discussions to oblivion, two men wearing impeccable black suits came to visit me at my work.

When my boss called me to tell me about the visits, I felt embarrassed. I hadn't told anybody I was looking around for something else. I began fishing for an excuse, but he cut me short with a smile that was completely unexpected, especially coming from him. "Don't worry; have a quiet talk with them, absolutely everything is taken care of."

"*The hell it's taken care of, if even I don't really know what's going on,*" I screamed at the top of my voice, without making a sound. To complete my surprise and discomfiture, he left us in his office while he went to drink a coffee until our conversation was over.

The conversation was short, to the point, and finished with an offer that I couldn't refuse. They told me I had been selected to become member of a scientific team developing a new molecule, which they weren't authorised to give me any more information about. When I asked about the rest of the team, the place of work and the pay, they replied that there would be no problem, that everything would be in order and I would have nothing to complain about. I was disconcerted, and now that the events of Wuppertal were coming back to mind, it seemed that I was the one who was in the dark.

"Fine, but you'll understand I must discuss this proposal with my wife, and she'll want to know more about it. What am I going to tell her?" I asked.

Without turning a hair, the other man answered, "That'll be a problem the day you get married. You live alone and you rent an apartment on the outskirts of Slough. I can tell you the address and other details, if you want me to. We'll take care of your landlord, just like we did your boss. Your few friends won't ask any questions, and they'll soon forget all about you."

"And just what did you say to my boss?" I asked without conviction.

"We told him that today is your last day in the office, and that from tomorrow you'll be going to work for a government agency. We showed him the relevant paperwork. One of our superiors phoned to confirm our story and advised him not to ask any more questions than strictly necessary."

No doubt my boss, though intrigued, would have played by the rules of this strange game at once. First, because he always did as he was told, and second but not least, because here was a golden opportunity to get rid of me, the only likely rival for his post.

"And if I say no?" I asked sounding like a rebel child.

With the same bland neutrality that only comes out when someone is certain of wielding absolute control over another person, they answered that of course I could refuse, but if I did, there would be no more work for me here – and they would make it their business to see that I wouldn't be able to get a job anywhere else.

The truth is that I was dying to accept this new challenge, but I also realised that going to Wuppertal had put me in a situation I couldn't escape from, at least for the moment.

The next morning the same men came to pick me up at my flat and drove me to an American airbase near Oxford. After showing my credentials and exchanging some words with the officers at the entry checkpoint, a sergeant lifted up the first barrier and let us through.

At the second checkpoint, there were more questions; they needed fresh papers, and a guard with an unfriendly face examined the interior of the Range Rover and fixed his eyes firmly on me. "This man a civilian?" he asked.

"It's all here in the papers. We need to hurry, they're waiting for us," my guards answered firmly and convincingly. I tried to remain impassive and act as if I was used to these procedures, but the truth was that I had more questions than any of those security guards.

The guard's attitude seemed to relax after they examined the documents. "Mmm, yes. One moment, please." He made a call on an internal phone. Everything seemed to be in order, because his face relaxed as he spoke, and he nodded.

"Do you know where to go or do you need any help?" he asked my companions.

"Thanks, sergeant, we've been here before; we know where to go."

"Good. You can go through."

One of the men accompanying me raised his right hand to his head and made a gesture that seemed to be an acknowledgement, a farewell or a military salute. That was the only time I saw a hint of what looked like a smile from the men in black. No doubt they were at home here.

We got out beside a small private jet that I calculated couldn't have held more than twenty seats. "Wait here," they instructed me, in a tone that was friendly but firm. *Where could I go to?* I asked myself, as I did as I was told.

One of them moved towards the plane and, with his foot on the gangway, exchanged a few words with a blond thirty-something woman, who seemed to be directing the whole operation. After a brief conversation, which, from a distance seemed to be a short report, she looked in my direction and started to walk coolly towards me, making it clear to the security men who was in charge. When she was less than ten feet away I was able to recognise her. I had seen her fleetingly at Wuppertal. I'm not very good with names, but I never forget a formula or a face, especially that of a pretty woman.

The man in black moved back to the Range Rover and opened the rear door where I was sitting.

"Good evening, Joe. We were expecting you. My name is Alison, Agent Alison Riley, but everyone calls me Ali."

Ali was coming back home, but she wasn't coming alone.

When I got into the plane, she introduced me to two special agents of her crew, and another colleague joining the expert team, Dr Mel Cooper.

From the beginning, high ranking officials in Washington and London, have been negotiating Cooper's release in exchange for operational support to get to the bottom of the deaths in Europe and the capture of the perpetrators, wherever they might be. Finally, they had agreed on a special pardon for Cooper, granted by the Prime Minister for his extraordinary contribution to solving the crimes and preventing more deaths among innocent citizens. The secret deal also included a special permit to leave the country in the care of the American authorities, who would take responsibility for him. Cooper would travel to America as part of a joint research project that no one knew much about. Diplomats and politicians have no hesitation in coming to an agreement when it is beneficial for all concerned.

The British had, at the same time, got rid of an awkward customer like Cooper, cleared up the crimes and captured the perpetrators. The repatriation of two Britons held in America for computer hacking crimes was an unexpected bonus, because it had been thrown into the negotiations at the last minute. Cooper was a small price to pay for two news items that would lift the government's opinion poll ratings for several weeks. Once more the Anglo-American understanding of mutual political, military and economic support, forged in blood during the Second World War, had borne fruit.

It was the end of October when, from the comfort of her high-altitude seat, Ali was enjoying the extraordinary autumn colours in New England. Woods filled with spruce firs, oaks and pines displayed that intense range of yellows, greens and burgundy reds above the purple depths of the fallen leaves. For many, that is the best season of the year, and Ali thought so too, as she had been born and bred in Massachusetts. En route for Washington, DC, lost in the view and her thoughts, Ali remembered her parents. *They must be somewhere down there.* She couldn't help realising that this was the closest she had been to them and the rest of her family for the last ten months.

The elegance of the falling leaves of autumn heralded the arrival of winter. *The time's moving on,* she thought, picturing Steve walking beneath the warm blue Andalusian sky. Time was passing for her, too, and the distance from her loved ones was an omen of a cold future. She gave a pensive sigh. No one on board would have imagined of what was going through her mind.

During the flight, I tried to stay quiet and pay attention, because I knew that things would soon be made clear, and it made no sense to let my anxiety show through. Pleasant as always, Ali kept herself to herself, asleep in her seat – or pretending to be, so that no one would bother her with unwelcome questions or awkward comments. Everything had gone well up to now, and I tried to live in the moment, allowing myself to be swept along by events that were conducted according to the agenda of people whom I would possibly never get to know.

That wasn't the case with Cooper, who couldn't hide his excitement and anxiety. He shifted constantly in his seat and pestered the stewardess, asking for drinks and food, which he left half-finished to move on to one or other of the limited number of activities that are available in the small space. He stood up to go to the toilet, sat down again, then turned to look for something in his briefcase, went to the toilet again, came back to his seat, turned round to go through his briefcase again, as if he was searching for something, wrote a few lines on a piece of paper, looked out of the window, sat up, sat down again, turned to look in his case, took notes which he then crossed out, then crumpled up the piece of paper he had written on into a ball and threw it into a small waste bin, asked for some more water…. The anxiety he had communicated to me was changed into annoyance when he started to tell me his life story. Then I understood.

Cooper had negotiated his freedom during his first meetings with Ali, and now he felt like someone taking a breath of fresh air after being trapped underground. But it wasn't just the physical sensation that mattered to him; in some way he felt fully vindicated by his newfound freedom. We all knew that that wasn't so, but it made no sense to spoil his illusion.

Cooper could never return to practising medicine in England, and the Americans, pragmatic as ever, had made a deal with him because they needed him for a project. What would happen afterwards was a question that no one had bothered to answer.

"Ali, now that we're almost there, and before we land, I'd like to thank you for everything you've done for me," he suddenly announced, in a high-pitched, monotonous voice.

Ali's eyes were still half-closed, but she wasn't asleep. Cooper hadn't realised, or perhaps didn't care; anyway, his infantile selfishness meant he lacked the courtesy to leave her alone until we landed. The contrast between his childish attitude and his advancing years made him seem more naive than he actually was. Getting him out of gaol and taking him to America had been done neither as a favour to him nor in recognition of his services; it was a strategic need.

Ali opened her eyes and gave him a sidelong look, apparently forcing herself to come back to reality. Her delicate lips moved, revealing gleaming white teeth at the centre of a perfect smile, carefully practised to get the attention of her interlocuter and keep control of the dialogue. Time and again, she could switch off her mind from her body language in order to achieve her objective, however small. Feminine beauty combined with intelligence, working hand in glove, can exercise tremendous power, an art that Ali had mastered to perfection – and to which she had also fallen victim herself. It took an effort for her to peel the mask from her face.

"Thanks, Dr Cooper," she answered, breaking a silence that threatened to become awkward. "Welcome to America, but let me remind you that it is an invitation, and you will have to work hard to win the right to remain here. You understand?"

"Sure, Ali, I know, and I feel it's a privilege," Cooper returned, with a gracious bow. "This will help," he added, tapping the manila envelope that he was clinging to like a shipwrecked sailor, holding onto a plank.

Then he opened it and took out a thick book, bound in a dark brown leather cover. He took the book in both hands like a sacred object, put it on his lap and gazed at it affectionately, like an old friend.

It was Render's manuscript. The very one they had all been searching for.

Three months before the airplane crash in the Colombian jungle, Render had entrusted his small treasure to him during one of his visits to the prison.

"I don't think there's a safer place to look after it than in here," joked Render, as he handed it over. "Look after it, it could be very useful to you one day," he added with a wink.

During this period, because of his age, education and good behaviour, Cooper had been assigned to work in the prison library. There, it had been very easy for him to hide the manuscript on a remote high shelf, among a lot of old books that no one ever read. The precious document had been there all the time, under government protection. Render and Cooper were fully conscious of its worth; their lives depended on it.

The old friends needed an escape route from the situations that they had got themselves into. On one hand it would play a vital role in continuing the Virin project in a sensible way, without repeating the mistakes of the past. On the other, Cooper would use it appropriately at the right moment to buy his freedom. The moment had arrived.

One way or another, Cooper would have been brought to America, but Ali needed the manuscript, and she was sure he knew where it was. Once again, she had been proved right.

Everyone had got what they were looking for, and everyone had held onto their small secrets and enjoyed their small victories. Each thought they had put one over on the other, but they had all been manipulated in their turn.

XXXIV

WE HAD HARDLY DISEMBARKED from the plane when they transferred us to a black van with one-directional darkened windows and covered with aerials. From the front seat, Ali told us we were heading for a destination northwest of Washington, DC, near Langley, Virginia. During the trip, which couldn't have lasted more than ten miles, Ali spent the whole time making and receiving phone calls.

Cooper was sitting next to me and never stopped talking. He used me to give vent to his anxieties, whilst I tried to get a bit more information. During the twenty minutes it took for us to get there, he told me the rest of his story to pass the time, so I came to know his most intimate details. Rather to my surprise, or perhaps due to excitement and curiosity, the result was that it woke me up and gave me the necessary energy to stay lucid for the rest of a day that held even more surprises in store for us.

When we stopped at the first security perimeter and passed through the barriers, I could make out a building that was only two storeys high and completely covered with glass, surrounded by a flourishing, leafy plantation of pine, beech, oak and cherry trees. The mirror windows were just to highlight the beauty of their surroundings and disguise their existence. Later, I was to learn that it looked like a two-storey complex but had seven basement levels, containing installations for special projects split between various agencies, working for organizations responsible for national security. Nobody outside the facility, from a distance on the motorway or from the air, would have any idea of the technology that was housed in this building.

After passing through the final checkpoint, we made our way to a sector where a big automatic gate opened up for us, giving access to a wide, empty garage with a large metal rectangle in the middle.

Ali gave precise directions to the driver, and the vehicle came to a halt. A penetrating, loud buzzing sound, and a vibration told me that it was a vehicle elevator.

We went down to level 3 NVP. I wondered what the acronym meant, but I didn't have much time for guessing, because the door opened at once, and we were invited to step out.

Two tall men were waiting for our arrival to take us to the main reception at the level we had come down to. We followed obediently behind them, up to an imposing door of shining metal. When we arrived the guard in front placed his right hand over a tiny blue crystal screen that was set into another metal pillar. Everything gave the impression of being sparkling clean, clinical, solid and impenetrable. The door swung open on its own, like a post-industrial version of Ali Baba's "Sesame."

"Go ahead, they're expecting you. We'll wait for you here."

At this we followed Ali, who seemed to feel more at home in all this. A jolly assistant, older than she looked, came to meet us.

"Welcome; let me take you to the director general's office. He's been expecting you," she said with a broad smile.

Cooper was looking all round, unable to suppress a nervous smile. He was as surprised and excited as I was, although not as apprehensive. His eyes looked as if they were going to pop out of his head any minute now. His crossed his arms and clasped the manila envelope tightly to his chest, as if he was clinging to a talisman to protect him in this new world we were entering into.

When we reached the director general's door, Ali stepped forward and thanked the receptionist. From then on, she was in charge. She opened the door, saying, "Come in, gentlemen;

they're expecting you. Come along, there's nothing to worry about."

Inside, the vast office held a sophisticated mixture of classic and modern furniture that only a very refined taste could have put together to create an atmosphere that was unique and special. Only a brilliant personality could have arranged the objects in such a personal way, judging appearances and preferences over the fine line that separates the elegant from the vulgar. There, waiting for us in the middle of the room, was Doe, the very same Dr John Doe whom I had met at Wuppertal.

"Welcome, Mel and Joe; we've been expecting you for a long time," he said with a smile, coming towards us with outstretched arms.

"What the devil! Yes, it is you. You're alive! I knew it, I knew it," cried Cooper, as he was enfolded in an exuberant embrace with Doe.

"Does Dr Cooper know Doe?" I asked Ali blankly, as we watched their reunion like outsiders witnessing the meeting.

"Evidently yes; they've been friends for many years," she replied enjoying the scene. "It's time you knew that his name is doctor Kurt Render," she added, without looking at me.

Back from the dead, full of life and elegance, smiling and glamorous, once more Render had surprised all of us. Except one.

"Yes, I'm alive, and I hope to remain so for a good few years to come," Render answered, with a ready smile and confident expression, giving the impression of being completely in command of the situation.

"But how did you...I mean I thought you had died in the accident...but when Ali appeared, I began to wonder...the manuscript, my ticket, the right moment." Cooper carried on, talking almost to himself, trying to come to grips with everything that was going on. He scratched his head and eyed his old friend with surprise and some suspicion. "I knew deep inside that you'd planned it all, and you'd send someone to get me out. From what I can see, you're not doing badly in this *afterlife.*"

"I can't complain. I'm safe here, and the situation is very settled. There are a few minor limitations that we'll share while we're here, but you soon get used to that. Nothing's perfect, not even in Paradise," he joked ironically, without once losing his sense of humour, a sure sign of his insight and intelligence. Ali and I remained silent two steps behind, like unintended witnesses to a memorable event.

"How did you get here, Kurt?"

"It was part of my Plan C, Mel. Remember, Plan A was to produce Virin, but in case anything went wrong, there was Plan B that consisted of tricking Newton to gain time and produce a safe, effective drug. Things changed a lot, and everything got very dangerous. In the end I had to apply Plan C, with Ali's help."

"Plan C was to fake a plane crash," Ali interjected, "in the Colombian jungle, where you and Ed still have good friends. They took him in for a week or so, until everything cooled down, and we were able to bring him back with a reasonable safety margin."

"Reasonable?" Cooper asked.

"Newton Crowe's associates financed the whole project, and his people know that part of the world. If they had suspected anything, Kurt wouldn't be here today."

"Ali arranged my exit and yours, Mel," Render added. "Nobody knows where we are or what we're doing. Paradoxically, now that I'm officially dead, I'm enjoying more freedom than ever."

"I can see that. You hatched this all up from the beginning."

"A neat and logical plan, although full of unforeseen circumstances. Like the Virin project. This is where we'll be staying until we've finished working on it. We need to create the proper Virin. Ali must have explained everything to you, or nearly everything...."

"Yes, she did...nearly everything," Cooper replied, turning towards Ali with a conspiratorial look.

Ali shrugged her shoulders, smiling like a little girl who has just been caught out in a little secret or a fib. How, for example, the whole operation would be funded with money that Render, officially dead, couldn't touch but that had been accessed by hackers from Langley. That was a price that Render had decided to pay, in case it was necessary. Knowledge and funds for security and technical resources to achieve a mutually beneficial objective: Virin.

"This time we'll do it right, Mel. I've even managed to recruit some talented youngsters that we've never been able to rely on before. Like Joe, for example," he said, holding out his fleshy hand to me.

"All working for who?"

Render answered Cooper, but it was directed at Ali. "Well, I think we're all going to be working for Uncle Sam." Ali nodded without speaking.

"Now all we have to do is to concentrate on our research and nothing else," he went on. "Ali and her colleagues will worry about the rest. Isn't that so, Ali?"

"That's how it is, Doctor," came her laconic reply.

"You're right, Kurt; as always, you're right about everything. But let me give you something special I've brought for you. Something belonging to you," said Cooper, opening the manila envelope. "Here it is – my ticket to American liberty. Your manuscript."

Render held out his hand and took the dark brown leather-bound book, battered by the ups and downs of its fortunes and criss-crossed with fine lines brought by the ravages of time. "Thanks a lot, my old mate. It's a very special present on a very special day, and we should celebrate accordingly," he replied, putting the small treasure into a drawer in his desk.

"Like the old days?"

"Sure, just like the old days," Render replied, uncorking a bottle of champagne on ice that his assistant had brought in on a tray with four crystal glasses. "Armand de Brignac. It's always been my weakness."

Cooper smiled and held up his sparkling glass. "One of them, Kurt. Only one of them..."

"To the Virin project!"

"Why not!" I answered, joining in the toast and letting myself be drawn into a future as interesting as it was uncertain.

THE END

Acknowledgements

FIRST AND FOREMOST, those whose commitment and dedication to helping people to come out of their misery have been a source of inspiration and learning to me. The members of Pathways to Recovery first clinical team in Warrington: Damian Grainer, Peter Sheath, Sue Shaw, Carl Roberts, Bronagh Williams, Claire James, Alan Walker, Antoinette Stapleton and Wendy Cunnington. They have helped many hundreds to recover their health and dignity. Some parts of this book were inspired by life stories of people from Stoke-on-Trent, Sefton, Burnley and Accrington in Lancashire, but also by many inmates in several prisons across England and Wales. Rosie Graves is the one who ensured the recovery of the real life Johnny in Stoke. Now he is married with a child. I extend my gratitude to those working hard to improve the life conditions of people in need in the North of England, Mark Moodie, Stacey Smith, Prun Bijral, Peter Furlong, Stuart Fisher, Diane Rapley and many, many others always ready to walk the extra mile. None of this would have happened without the vision, the inspiration and the committed leadership of David Royce and David Biddle.

For his generous support in developing an academic and research structure that help to make evidence based decisions in recovering lives ruined by alcohol and drugs, I would like to express my appreciation to Tim Millar, senior researcher, and our colleagues from the University of Manchester.

I also want to thank Mark Gilman, Strategic Recovery Lead at National Treatment Agency for Substance Misuse, for his support and expertise in developing Asset Based Communities in the North of England.

My sincere appreciation for Dr Robert Lefever, whom I met for the first time in the Middle East and we ended up working together in London a few decades later. From the very beginning, we shared the same views on addiction and recovery models. Robert, the founder of Promis UK, is still a living example of what recovery is about.

I also want to acknowledge Peter Kagman and Jeroen Fisser for the rich discussions about addiction problems and addiction treatment projects we had in Amsterdam and Marbella.

I want to acknowledge the pharmaceutical companies manufacturing safe medications like methadone, buprenorphine and others that have saved millions of lives all over the world. They play a major role in helping people to get their lives back, not just by their products but also by the educational and research programmes they support.

I am very grateful to Liz Wright and the great job she did editing the original manuscript. I also want to extend my gratitude to John Stewart, Oscar Yebra and my wife Susan for their help and support reviewing and editing the final versions of manuscript.

Last but not least, I also acknowledge the courage and commitment of those working in police forces, security and intelligence agencies. I have learned a lot from them, the environment they operate in and things they do to protect our communities.

About the Author

OSCAR D'AGNONE is an expert in addictions with many years of experience as a clinician, academic and adviser for governmental agencies and international companies operating in Europe, America and the Middle East. He has written two books on cocaine and drug addiction prevention. In this novel he shows a broader picture of the social, economic and political context surrounding addictions.

Oscar lives in Buckingham, England.

Made in the USA
Charleston, SC
30 May 2013